Praise for *The Ghost at the Table*

"[A] compelling tale about the struggles families go through to understand each other."   —MSNBC.com

"A witty, moving and psychologically astute story about siblings and the disparate ways they remember common experiences from childhood. . . . Wholly engaging, the perfect spark for launching a rich conversation around your own table once the dishes have been cleared."   — *The Washington Post Book World*

"*The Ghost at the Table* will haunt you long after you have read the final page. . . . Berne is masterful."   — *Chicago Tribune*

"Berne's novel is perfect reading. . . . Perfect if you like compelling characters, acerbic insights and a gimlet-eyed look at the intense bonds between siblings. Berne explores how memory shapes family members in very different ways."   — *USA Today*

"Delicious. . . . Berne turns a witty tale of holiday dysfunction into a transfixing borderline gothic, her appealing heroine into an unreliable narrator seething with decades-old resentment. . . . A."
                                                      — *Entertainment Weekly*

"From its emotionally intricate first paragraph, Suzanne Berne's *The Ghost at the Table* is a crash course in sibling rivalry, with its cutthroat dueling for dominance and parental love. . . . The intersection of memory and morality is where this compelling novel makes its home."   — *O: The Oprah Magazine*

"In Berne's complex emotional minuet, no one is blameless. . . . Fixing on Cynthia and Frances with ferocious focus and narrative drive, Berne lets that gate swing wide open." —*Elle*

"Intellectually and emotionally stimulating. . . . Berne, winner of the Orange Prize, has a flair for domestic drama, recalling the work of Joyce Carol Oates or of Anne Tyler. . . . Berne creates striking characters and brisk scenes. . . . Fresh and intriguing."
—*San Francisco Chronicle*

"Ominous crimes, family squabbles, implosions. In Berne's universe, 'dysfunctional family' is a redundancy. . . . In *The Ghost at the Table*, Suzanne Berne continues to apply dark colors to her expanding universe of the American family. But evident, too—at the edges, even at the center—are streaks of light, images of hope."
—*The Cleveland Plain Dealer*

"Even more than the satisfyingly delivered family revelations, it's the barbed, spot-on evocation of these sisters' relationship that makes this book a must-read." —*More* magazine

"As the turkey is carved and the pies get passed, Orange Prize winner Berne shows how family members can live through the same events and yet end up with radically different impressions. . . . A disquieting novel that avoids pat answers."
—*The Christian Science Monitor*

"Suzanne Berne has a gift for creating unreliable narrators. . . . In *The Ghost at the Table*, Berne masterfully explores the parallel realities that can endure after a great sadness." —*The Boston Globe*

"The writing is lovely. The descriptions of Concord are so effective that you can almost smell the late fall and approaching winter. . . . The ghost at the table is neither constant nor defined. It can be a long dead mother, a still living father who no longer functions very well, a childhood friend or simply a memory that has rearranged itself into an invisible presence. To all of these: set a place, light some candles. Perhaps even Mark Twain will show up."

— *Chicago Sun-Times*

"Suzanne Berne solidifies her claim in the land of the literary domestic drama. . . . Berne's writing is sure-footed. She captures the New England gloom and quiet bitterness of the characters in deft strokes." — *The Charlotte Observer*

"A psychologically sophisticated, gimlet-eyed look at a family triangle. It's also a three-cornered story, with eerie echoes at every turn. . . . Berne is an elegant writer." — *The Kansas City Star*

"A brooding, emotionally potent novel about the myths and misunderstandings that form crucial chapters of our family histories. Suzanne Berne is an immensely talented writer." —Tom Perrotta

"Suzanne Berne has written a novel as nuanced and illuminating as it is gripping." —Elizabeth Graver

The Ghost at the Table

Also by SUZANNE BERNE

A Crime in the Neighborhood, a novel

A Perfect Arrangement, a novel

The
Ghost
at the
Table

a novel by

Suzanne Berne

A Shannon Ravenel Book

Algonquin Books of Chapel Hill

2007

ℝ

A Shannon Ravenel Book

Published by

ALGONQUIN BOOKS OF CHAPEL HILL

Post Office Box 2225

Chapel Hill, North Carolina 27515-2225

a division of

WORKMAN PUBLISHING

225 Varick Street

New York, New York 10014

© 2006 by Suzanne Berne. All rights reserved.

First paperback edition, Algonquin Books of Chapel Hill,
November 2007. Originally published by Algonquin Books
of Chapel Hill in 2006.
Printed in the United States of America.
Published simultaneously in Canada by Thomas Allen & Son
Limited.
Design by Anne Winslow.

This is a work of fiction. While, as in all fiction, the literary perceptions
and insights are based on experience, all names, characters, places,
and incidents either are products of the author's imagination or are
used fictitiously.

Library of Congress Cataloging-in-Publication Data
Berne, Suzanne.
    The ghost at the table : a novel / by Suzanne Berne.—1st ed.
      p. cm.
    "A Shannon Ravenel book."
    ISBN-13: 978-1-56512-334-2 (HC)
      1. Sisters—Fiction. 2. Family—Fiction. 3. Thanksgiving
Day—Fiction. 4. Domestic fiction. I. Title.
    PS3552.E73114L37 2006
    813'.54—dc22   2006040073

    ISBN-13: 978-1-56512-579-7 (PB)

10 9 8 7 6 5 4 3 2 1
First Paperback Edition

FOR MY DARLING DAUGHTERS,
Avery and Louisa

The truth is, a person's memory has no more sense than his conscience and no appreciation whatever of values and proportions.

MARK TWAIN
from *The Autobiography of Mark Twain*

Going home for Thanksgiving wasn't something I had planned on—or I should say, I hadn't planned on going to Frances's house in Concord, which over the years I've sometimes referred to as "home," simply because it's back east. But perhaps Frances heard me differently when I said "home," perhaps she heard more than I meant to suggest. She is my older sister, after all, and there is that responsibility, often mixed with impatience, that older sisters feel toward their younger sisters, especially if those younger sisters have been, in one way or another, less fortunate than themselves. In any case, every year Frances asked me to come for Thanksgiving and Christmas, but every year for one reason or another, I said no. My visits to her usually happened in summer, when we were more likely to leave the house. Though of all the people in the world I probably love Frances best, after a day or so at home with her I found myself becoming lethargic and moody, leaving dishes in the sink, taking long naps in the afternoon. Meanwhile Frances's normal good nature soon gave way to exasperation and apology. We both understood the effect we had on each other, only made worse by the holidays. Still Frances felt she needed to invite me, just as I needed to refuse. In this way, we absolved each other.

Or that's how it worked until one October day, over a year ago now, when Frances called to say that our father would be spending Thanksgiving with her, for the first time in a quarter of a century, and she literally begged me to fly to Boston.

"Please, Cynnie," she said on the phone. "It's the first time in forever that we could all be together."

All? I almost said. Our mother has been dead since I was thirteen. Soon after I was born she was diagnosed with Parkinson's disease, which was later complicated by a heart ailment. Our older sister, Helen, died three years ago of lymphoma. Her funeral in Bennington had been the last time I'd seen my father, or Frances herself, for that matter. My father and his wife, Ilse, drove up to Vermont from the Cape, arriving just as the service began. The church was full of Helen's patients and friends, several of whom spoke movingly of Helen, of her generosity and intelligence. Dad and Ilse stood at the back of the church wearing khakis and boat shoes, their hands in the pockets of their windbreakers. They refused to sit in the front pew with Frances and me, insisting that their legs felt stiff after the drive; then they skipped the burial and the gathering at Helen's house afterward.

But in June my father had had a stroke, and now he was also getting divorced, at eighty-two, from Ilse, who was only in her fifties, but claimed that she couldn't take care of him any longer. Frances had been making arrangements for him to enter a nursing home in a town near Concord. This was why he would be with her for Thanksgiving.

"Please come." Frances lowered her voice. "It would really mean a lot to him."

"Oh, I don't think so," I said.

"Please. Come for my sake, Cynnie. I don't want any regrets and I'm sure you don't, either."

"I don't have any regrets, at least not about him."

But Frances wasn't one to give up easily, especially when it came to finding a way to disguise some awkward angle or unsightly corner, which was perhaps why she'd succeeded so well as an interior decorator.

"Frankly," she said, switching tactics, "I could use the moral support."

"Moral support?"

"It might not be very easy with Dad, you know. A nursing home is a big change."

When I didn't say anything, she went on quietly, "And it's a holiday. And Sarah will be coming home, her first time home since September, and I want it to be nice for her. So that's a lot to manage, with Dad here, too."

Sarah was Frances's older daughter, a college freshman, who in the last couple years had become political. Sarah's most recent cause, besides campaigning against the current administration, was "Doing Without." People had too much stuff. Too much stuff was causing all the world's problems. (Pollution. Nuclear proliferation. Sprawl.) I could tell Frances was afraid that if she didn't make Sarah's first homecoming a happy family occasion, Sarah might hold it against her somehow. She might believe that home itself was another thing that she could Do Without.

"But it's only Thanksgiving Day that Dad will be at your house," I pointed out to Frances. "Pick him up right before dinner and take him back right after. I'm sure the girls will help you. They're old enough now. And Walter will."

I could hear a distant ringing, like a call coming in on another line. Finally I had to say, "Won't he?"

"Walter and I have been going through a rough time lately."

"What kind of a rough time?"

"I can't explain it on the phone."

This was crafty. If there's one universal covenant between sisters, it's a primal interest in each other's relationships. Frances and I had spent countless hours discussing the shortcomings of various men in my life, few of whom she'd ever met; yet she understood them perfectly and found complexities in their faults, which made those faults seem pardonable, or at least interesting, though she would always assure me that I was "better off" whenever one of them disappeared.

"Are you all right?" I demanded.

"No, I'm fine. I'll tell you about it when you get here. Will you come, Cynnie? Please?"

"Well," I said at last, "I *have* been meaning to visit Hartford."

"For your book?" she asked, too enthusiastically. "Is it done? I can't wait to read it. We can drive down together while you're here. To see Twain's house, you mean?"

"But I was going to come east in July, after I've finished a draft."

"Oh, not *July*," Frances almost wailed. "It can't wait that long."

"What can't wait?"

"*I* can't wait," she said. "To see you."

THAT NIGHT I CALLED my friend Carita for advice: Should I go home, to Frances's, for Thanksgiving, knowing that it might be a depressing visit, especially since my father would be there? Also, I wasn't feeling my best right then. I'd recently broken up with a man I had been seeing for almost a year. He owned a bookstore, which was where I'd met him, and he was married, which I had known from the beginning, just as I'd known I was going to be unhappy with him even before we'd started sleeping together.

"Don't go," advised Carita. "Families are toxic."

"But Frances says she needs me to be there."

"Frances can cope." Carita was washing dishes while she talked to me. I listened for a moment to the homely sound of clinking silverware and water splashing in the sink. Carita's family lived in

Arizona, where her father built shopping malls; a portion of his income went to support an evangelical church that looked like a shopping mall. Carita herself was dark and wiry and flippant about almost everything. I pictured her warm untidy little kitchen, the string of red light-up chili peppers over the sink; the open spice jars; the refrigerator covered with magnets of dogs wearing kimonos, holding up photos of Carita and her girlfriend, Paula, on their trip to Hawaii and of their old, bad-tempered Yorkie, Prince Charles.

"I *could* visit Hartford while I'm there," I said, "for the book."

"Aren't you originally from Hartford?"

"West Hartford."

"Just say no," she urged again. "Come over here for Thanksgiving. Paulie and I are cooking dinner."

But by then I'd made up my mind to go to Concord and had only called Carita for the comfort of having someone try to argue me out of it.

"I wish I could," I sighed, "but I guess blood is blood."

"Blood," observed Carita, "is bloody."

CARITA AND I BOTH WORK for a small company in Oakland that publishes a series of books for girls called Sisters of History, fictionalized accounts of famous women "as told" by one of their sisters. We focus on the childhoods, how one sister was marked from the start as unusual, special in some way, while the other was remarkable, too, but not *so* remarkable. Yet devoted. Always devoted. The books are meant to be cheerfully earnest feminist stories, emphasizing "the strong bonds between sisters" and illustrating the message that the most important things in life are human relationships.

Four of us do the research and writing. We find journals, memoirs, letters, contemporary accounts that mention our subject's sister and help create a persona for her. Then we make up what we can't find or make up something to conceal what we do find, if it contradicts those "strong bonds." On the company Web site we are described as "academic specialists in historical fiction," though none of us majored in history in college; in fact, we were all English majors, like our editor, Don Morey, and he came up with Sisters of History in business school, after attending a lecture on marketing responsibly to children.

I cover literary women, which I consider the best category. Carita writes about famous women athletes. She refers to our books as "hysterical fiction for girls" and the "Lesser Lights Series," mostly to needle Don when he starts talking about the social contribution we are making by producing books for girls that aren't about teenage movie stars and diet fads. In interviews, he calls us the "Sisters Behind the Sisters of History." Carita says he should call us the "Slaves of History," but we're paid pretty well, actually. Before Don hired me, I was teaching freshman composition courses at San Francisco State and proofreading for a magazine on exotic birds.

So far I had written books on Louisa May Alcott, Emily Dickinson, and Helen Keller, each from a sister's perspective. Patriotically, we were beginning with American women. During one of my summer visits to Frances I toured Orchard House, the Alcott place, which is right in Concord, not far from Frances's house. On another visit I borrowed her van and drove out to see the Dickinson home in Amherst. I never got to Tuscumbia, Alabama, to see the Keller homestead for *Witness to a Miracle*, the book I'd just finished. I felt the story suffered as a result. Context is everything when it comes to understanding a subject, and I like to include a blend of quoted detail and my own firsthand observations. "Here in the parlor on Lexington Street," I wrote in the preface to *The Little Alcotts*, "with 'furniture very plain' and 'a good picture or two hung on the walls,' it's easy to imagine the March daughters darning socks and staring into the fire. But it is the Alcott girls we are with today, and Louisa and her youngest sister, May, are having an argument in a corner by the Chickering piano."

May Alcott, Lavinia Dickinson, and Mildred Keller all turned out to be colorful (i.e., secretly resentful) reporters on their sisters' lives, and I had a file drawer full of letters from little girls saying how much they'd loved my books, that it was as if I'd written about them and their own sisters. Don had slated me to write about Harriet Beecher Stowe and her sister Catharine for my next book. In her later years Stowe had lived next door to the family of Samuel Clemens, Mark Twain; I used to pass by both places whenever we took Farmington Avenue to and from the highway in Hartford. Ever since I was a girl, I'd always felt a modest connection to Mark Twain's daughters. They'd grown up about a mile from my house, and there were three girls in their family, as there had been in mine. And throughout my childhood one corner of our living room had been occupied by a hideous old Estey player organ, inherited from my grandmother, which my father claimed had originally belonged to Mark Twain himself. Which is why when I turned in the Keller book I decided to ask Don if I could write about Mark Twain's daughters instead of Harriet Beecher Stowe.

This conversation took place about six months before Frances's phone call. To celebrate my new book, Don had taken me to lunch near the office at a little Mexican restaurant with a yellow tiled floor and sticky wooden tables decorated with hammered brass studs.

"Sounds pretty Freudian to me," he said, picking apart a crab-meat salad. "Mark Twain's organ. I don't know."

"Well, that part was made up," I admitted. "Mark Twain did have a player organ, but it was a different brand. My father was never one to let facts stand in the way of a good story."

"How parental."

Don was in a bad mood; he and his partner had been fighting again, this time over renovations to their house in the Berkeley Hills. But these lunches were a rare-enough occasion that I felt I needed to take my chances. Mark Twain's daughters had had a "unique" historical viewpoint, I argued (they'd met both Ulysses S. Grant and Uncle Remus, for example), which shouldn't be overlooked.

"Well, they can't all have the same viewpoint." Don put down his fork and looked around for our waiter.

"I'll choose one of them," I said, wishing I had Carita's easy, sarcastic way with him. "She can tell the story. There's always one person in a family who's got everyone else's number."

I didn't mention that I'd already chosen the youngest girl, Jean Clemens, to be my narrator, probably because Don would have objected as soon as I explained more about her. Little Jean. The "difficult" one. Twain's least favorite. Little Jean suffered from epilepsy and was given to violent rages. Photographs showed a stolid, suspicious-faced child, with a bulky forehead and an exacting gaze. As a young woman she once tried to kill the family housekeeper, although naturally I couldn't put information like that in my book. (Helen Keller also tried to kill the infant Mildred, by tossing her out of her cradle and knocking her head against the floor.) But I liked to collect unsavory facts about my subjects; I related better to them that way, especially as their journals and letters often insisted on one thing ("Had a gay luncheon today with the family, everyone home at last!") but hinted at another ("I felt rather tired afterward and went for a walk by myself"). Usually it was loneliness that was hinted at, and of course loneliness is where a person is most easily understood.

Don folded his hands and gazed into his ruined salad. His heavy-lidded eyes and long oval face often gave the impression that he was languid and inattentive; in the last year he'd shaved his head, increasing his look of impassivity, which he sometimes used to his advantage, like an alligator that only appears to be asleep in the sun. I'd frequently wondered what he noticed about me while seeming not to notice anything.

"Were they *fond* of dear daddy?" he asked finally, opening his eyes a fraction. "Those charming little daughters?"

I said I was sure they were. He was Mark Twain, after all. "They also lived next door to Harriet Beecher Stowe," I pointed out, "so some of my research on them could apply to a next book about her—"

Don frowned at me absently.

"And people *love* Mark Twain," I continued, twisting my napkin. "Think of that documentary on public television. Father of American literature. Mark Twain daily calendars. Mark Twain T-shirts. Mark Twain dolls."

For several years Don had been trying to get a toy company interested in manufacturing and marketing Sisters of History dolls, so far without luck. But a *trio* of sister dolls, I suggested now, Mark Twain's daughters, in delightful Gilded Age dress, packaged with an equally delightful book about them, might finally prove irresistible. And wasn't I his most dependable writer, conscientious about correct spelling, punctuation, and grammar, as well as my historical details? By the time the check arrived, he'd agreed to let me do what I wanted.

"Just don't get distracted by Daddy." He signed the check, then looked up and raised one eyebrow at me, smiling his alligator smile. "He's gotten enough attention."

"So are you coming?" Frances asked when she called again the next day.

It was one of those damp gray October afternoons when I had nothing planned for the evening. Fog pressed against the dusty windows of my apartment; the sour, flannelly smell of cooking beans had floated up through the heating vents from my landlady's kitchen below. As I listened to Frances's voice on the phone, I imagined her standing by her kitchen window, arranging apples in a bowl and looking out at the crispness of a New England fall. Sharp blue skies, geese flying overhead, the breeze filled with the scent of pine needles and woodsmoke. If the sun had been shining in San Francisco that afternoon, who knows whether I might have answered differently.

"All right," I said. "But on one condition."

"Anything. What?"

"That we don't get into a lot of old stuff."

"Of course not," said Frances, and I'll never forget how elated she sounded. "This is a holiday. I want it to be nice for everybody."

One

I had forgotten that airline passengers could no longer be met at the gate, so I was briefly disheartened when I looked for Frances as I got off the plane at Logan and didn't see her. But riding the escalator down to baggage claim, I spotted Walter's thick gray hair and big, important-looking head near the luggage carousels. He was wearing a pair of rectangular, dark-framed glasses, a much trendier style than I'd have expected on him. Otherwise he looked tired and pale in his wrinkled Burberry trench coat and impatient at being somewhere other than the hospital in the middle of the day. When our eyes met, he seemed relieved to see me.

"Frances asked me to pick you up," he said, as I stepped off the escalator. He stooped to give me a kiss on the cheek.

"How nice of you," I said, trying to hide my disappointment.

As soon as he'd grabbed my bags, Walter plunged off toward the parking garage, while I trotted self-consciously behind, hurrying to keep up with him. Once we were heading out of the airport in his car, he noted that he was glad I could make it and that my visit would cheer Frances up. She had been feeling very low lately. Morose. Apprehensive. Sometimes she had trouble getting out of bed in the morning; he'd come home at night to find her still in her bathrobe. Couldn't get errands done or manage to make dinner. Canceled appointments with clients for no reason, except that she was tired, or thought she might be getting the flu, or she forgot a date she'd made with friends, then was afraid to call to apologize in case they weren't speaking to her. Sometimes she spent the whole day in her bedroom.

"Maybe it's Sarah being gone," he said testily. "That empty-nest thing."

"But Jane's still at home," I said.

"Frances and Jane aren't getting along." Walter stared out at the road as a sleety rain began spattering the windshield. "Especially this week. Frances has been all jazzed up."

"Jazzed up?" I was having trouble figuring out my role in this conversation. In the twenty-some years they've been married, Walter had never spoken to me about Frances.

He gave me a meaningful look under his thick eyebrows. "Acting like Thanksgiving is some kind of official state ceremony."

"Well." I relaxed slightly. "You know how Frances loves an occasion."

Walter grunted. "Prepare yourself."

"Thank God no one has a birthday this weekend," I added, daringly, and we both laughed. I settled back in my seat, feeling comfortably dazed from the flight. Walter had put on a CD as we left the airport; now a meditative piano took over from a melancholy sax.

"Ever since your father's stroke," he began to say, "actually ever since Helen—" But then his beeper went off and he fumbled to unclip it from his belt.

I had forgotten about my father. It occurred to me that he might even now be at Frances's house, on a furlough from the nursing home, and that in a few minutes I would have to greet him.

Walter glanced at his beeper, then pushed it back onto his belt, muttering, "She can wait." When I looked at him inquiringly, he said, "A crazy patient."

"Really crazy?"

"Crazy enough."

I nodded sympathetically, though I wanted to ask, "Crazy enough to do what?" Instead I said, "So how's the home, by the way?"

"I'm sorry?"

"Dad's nursing home. How's it working out?"

"He's not there yet."

"What?"

"Frances didn't tell you?" Walter glanced sideways at me. "You and she are driving down to the Cape tomorrow to get him."

"Driving to the Cape?" I stared at him. "To his *house*?"

"The nursing home was supposed to have an opening before now, but I guess whoever was supposed to die didn't." Walter gave a glum little laugh. "Anyway, the plan is for you two to take him."

"But Frances didn't say anything to me—"

"Frances has been forgetting everything lately. She probably thinks she told you all about it."

"But she didn't."

"I can see that."

We stopped talking for several minutes as I gazed out at the trees alongside the highway. Maples and oaks, the trees of New

England. I always miss them when I'm in California, but whenever I come east the sight of them makes me feel claustrophobic, especially when they're gray and skeletal, as they were that afternoon. New England trees grow too closely together, and there's too much underbrush. Every Sunday when I was a child, my father used to herd us off on long damp hikes through the woods and old overgrown orchards of West Hartford, insisting on leaving the trail, crossing streams on slippery stepping-stones, bushwhacking through briars and blackberry bushes. Joking about Hansel and Gretel, asking if we had our bread crumbs handy.

I took a deep breath and turned back to Walter. "I'm sorry, but I can't drive to the Cape." My voice was calm, reasonable, the voice of a businesswoman with a full schedule who's promised to spend time with her demanding relatives but must be firm about limits. "I've made plans to go to Hartford tomorrow, to do some research. I came out here early especially to do that."

"Can't you go another day?"

"I'll rent a car to go to Hartford. Frances can drive down to get him."

"Frances has almost stopped driving." Walter kept his eyes on me. "She's afraid of getting into a car accident. She says she's having problems with her inner ear, that her balance is off, and she has dizzy spells and needs to get her thyroid tested, but it's all bullshit. She's depressed and she won't admit it."

Walter rarely used profanity. The air inside the car suddenly became charged and tense, but he continued talking, his voice growing hoarse. "It's been worst for Jane. Every time the poor kid walks in the door, Frances finds some reason to leave the room. She says it's because Jane blames her for everything and she can't stand it."

"But isn't that sort of normal?" I was trying to attend to what he was saying about Jane while also trying to understand how Frances could have neglected to tell me that I was going to spend two hours in the car with my father, driving him to a nursing home.

Walter gave a consenting groan. "It's been pretty much hell at home. Lucky for Sarah she's at college."

Although this was another worry, because Sarah was in New York. In October, Frances had read a magazine article about a potential terrorist plot to derail the presidential election by bombing major East Coast universities. From then on, she'd called Sarah two, three, four times a day, just to make sure she was all right, until Sarah stopped answering her cell phone.

"And you can imagine what *that* did to Frances." Walter jutted his chin at the road. Sarah hadn't been home once all fall, he told me, and had only agreed to come for Thanksgiving if she could bring a friend. "For protection," he added.

I sat up in my seat. Walter had always sided with Frances when she and the girls had differences, at least publicly. They'd had their problems over the years, of course, but in the way that mature, successful married people were supposed to have problems: as something to "work through" so that they could be even more satisfied with their lives than before, at least until their next set of problems. But the problems Walter was describing didn't sound like regular problems. With something like panic, I thought of my quiet apartment on Dolores Street with its pale blue walls and narrow view of the East Bay, and of the cheerful Thanksgiving I would be missing at Carita's apartment, mariachi music on the stereo, those chili lights glowing, her little dog barking as people came in and out.

Tomorrow I would go to Hartford, as planned. Walter could drive Frances to Cape Cod to pick up our father.

We passed a humped, sandy landfill, then a sign for Walden

Pond. Rain was falling harder now, streaking my window. Walter's beeper sounded again; this time he turned it off without checking the message. Somewhere the woman who had paged Walter was waiting for his call, perhaps sitting anxiously beside the phone, clutching a slip of paper in her hand. A horn section came on the CD.

"She also thinks I want to have an affair," he said abruptly.

I tried not to look shocked. Frances had warned me they were going through a rough time, but I'd never expected Walter to confide something so personal to me, just as I'd never expected him to complain about Frances, or that their rough time could involve an affair.

"Well, *do* you?" I turned in my seat to face him.

Walter flinched. "No. But Frances won't listen to me."

When I asked why Frances thought he wanted to have an affair, he sighed, finally loosening his grip on the wheel as we stopped at a traffic light. "Because she's afraid I'll have an affair. And these days she goes right from being afraid that something will happen to believing it's already happening."

"Could she *want* you to have an affair?"

But this thought was too capricious for Walter and he glared at the road, once more gripping the wheel. When the light changed, I asked more carefully, "Why is she *afraid* that you'll have an affair?"

He shrugged and said he didn't know.

"There must be some reason."

At the same time, I was thinking how amazing it was to be asking Walter such intimate questions. He was twelve years my senior and had always seemed like a remote person. Well meaning, decent, willing to be friendly and even solicitous toward me, but usually absent somehow when I visited, ducking out of conversations, excusing himself after dinner, content to go up to his study and leave me and Frances to our "girl talk." I found this male detachment a little oppressive—and a little judgmental—especially compared with most of the men I knew in San Francisco, who'd acquired a fizzy urbanity and liked "girl talk," even if they were straight. At the same time I'd always been conscious of being attracted to Walter's broad shoulders and brusque-looking five o'clock shadow, his shrewd, tolerant, ponderous masculinity that struck me as out-dated but also, in a way that was almost embarrassing to think about, chivalric. He was chief of radiology at Cambridge City Hospital, and whenever he spoke it was with a natural authority and confidence, which at the hospital must have sounded ordinary enough but outside translated into an intimidating complacency, amplified by the fold of belly over his belt and the quiet assurance of his medical experience, all that vital, appalling knowledge about the human body that most of us don't have, and don't want to have, either. But we want someone else to have it.

"So who does she think you want to have an affair with?" I asked, when Walter shrugged again.

"This woman she's hired as her assistant." He reached around with one hand to massage the back of his neck, then frowned for a moment in irritable concentration. "Mary Ellen . . . Mary Ellen . . . I can't even remember her last name. It's crazy. I've met her maybe half a dozen times. She comes to the house to do Frances's books and keep track of accounts, check on furniture or-ders. Nice person. Kind of an old maid," he added thoughtlessly.

"Why doesn't Frances just fire her then? Get her out of the way?"

"Good question," said Walter. "She's invited her to Thanksgiving dinner."

"To Thanksgiving?"

"You know how Frances loves an occasion," he said grimly.

We passed the town green in Concord Center, then the big white Colonial Inn with its long porches; a moment later we were going by the entrance to the Old North Bridge. Four or five school buses idled in the parking lot as we drove by, and despite the rain a troop of children in bright yellow and blue raincoats were vanishing toward the river.

"So, have you *ever* had an affair?" I felt emboldened by the unusual rapport that had sprung up between us in the car.

His face stiffened. Then he frowned and pushed his glasses back onto the bridge of his nose. Walter had a large fleshy handsome nose, broken in high school, though not by playing football, as you might expect; he fell off his bicycle when he ran into a fire hydrant. He said carefully: "What I think all this is about is that Frances is worried about your father."

"Well," I said with a little laugh, because Walter hadn't answered my question. "I'm not surprised she's worried. She's hardly seen him in decades and now suddenly he wants to be part of the family again."

Walter made a noncommittal noise.

"You know the old story, don't you?" I asked.

"What story?" he said warily.

"I'm sure Frances has told you." I leaned back in my seat, finally enjoying the clandestine feeling of talking about Frances with Walter. "That everyone used to think he killed our mother?"

Walter glanced at me sharply, his small grayish eyes alert with disapproval. "To be honest, Cynthia, that's just the kind of thing I'd like you to avoid raising with Frances this weekend, if you don't mind. We've got enough going on."

I stared out my window at a gray stockade fence, then at a dark stand of pine trees. No need to warn *me* to behave myself. I was no wallower in the past—the present had more than enough swamps, thank you very much. And I hadn't asked to fly out here, either; we could damn well turn around and drive straight back to the airport if that's how it was going to be.

But the conversation was over anyway, because we were pulling into the gravel driveway of Frances's house. I just had time to ask, "So why didn't Frances tell me that she was having such a hard time?" and for Walter to answer, "Because she was afraid you wouldn't come," when there was Frances herself, standing under the vines in the doorway, smiling and waving to us.

"An airy, barnlike Colonial" was my description of the Alcott house. "Perfect for neighborhood gatherings and amateur theatricals but snug enough for quiet evenings by the fire." For Dickinson's home in *Emily's Room,* I wrote: "Cloistered behind a row of hemlocks waits a neat Federal-style redbrick house, hardly remarkable from the road, yet look closely, and you'll see it's lit from within by a bright unwavering spirit." (*Compliments of General Electric?* scribbled Carita in the margin of this passage, knowing quite well that Don favored this sort of sentimental curlicue, my specialty.)

If I had to describe Frances's house, I might begin by noting the old fieldstone walls, shaggy with English ivy, and the faded-looking forest green trim on the windows, also the wide-timbered double carriage doors set into a wing of the house that Frances had remodeled to look like an old stable, now the office for her interior design business. Perched atop the slate roof was a slatted dovecote crowned by an oxidized copper goose. Even this late in November, the lawn was dappled with yellow maple leaves.

A spray of bittersweet hung on the front door. The rain had thinned to a mist and as I got out of the car the sun came out for an instant or two, which made everything seem luminous, the yellow leaves, the bittersweet, the old stone walls, and also slightly artificial, like a hand-tinted photograph.

"You're here," cried Frances, hurrying down the steps into the driveway, opening a big red umbrella over her head. "I can't believe you're here. And for Thanksgiving! *Incroyable!*"

"I can't believe it, either." I smiled idiotically as Frances dropped the umbrella onto the gravel and seized my hands. She held out my arms and gave them a joyful little crisscross swing, then surveyed me in my ratty sheepskin coat.

"Don't leave that umbrella lying there open like that, Frances," growled Walter, slamming the car doors. "It'll get wet."

He shouldered past us with my bags, giving us both a bear-like stare over the shoulder of his trench coat. I wondered if he was already regretting that I'd come. I always took up a lot of Frances's attention during my visits, which I knew he sometimes minded. And Frances looked well enough. I'd been prepared for a gray-faced wreck, but she looked the same as always: tall, angular, comely. Elegant even in an old wool fisherman's sweater, worn corduroy pants and scuffed leather boots, her auburn hair twisted in a casual knot, those light green eyes radiant with restrained but eager sympathy.

"Oh Walter," she called after him. "It's an umbrella, for godssake!" She drew me closer, whispering conspiratorially, "He's getting *cantankerous.*"

Then she pulled me up the front steps and into the house,

clucking over how tired I must be, how hungry after my long flight now that the airlines had stopped serving food, not that airline food had ever been edible. Inside, the house hadn't changed much since my last visit. Exquisitely unfussy, arranged with Frances's "finds": the mahogany coat rack with its tarnished brass hooks, gently faded Turkish rugs, the huge ornate old cloudy French mirror, slightly canted on the wall, so that whoever stepped into the hall saw themselves softened and framed, caught in a genteel tableau. The mirror was set over a handsome old walnut mourner's bench that Frances had rescued from one of the fire sales or flea markets or estate auctions she was always attending. ("What are you looking for?" I asked her once, when she insisted that we had to drive all the way to Brimfield to an antiques fair. "Oh, everything," she replied, smiling faintly.) The house even smelled as if it belonged to another era, a staid, ample, more enduring time when people baked every day, with real butter, and made their own soup stock, and used pie safes and enamel-lined ice boxes, both of which Frances had installed in her pantry, though she owned a modern refrigerator, of course, too. It was all completely familiar, more familiar somehow even than my own apartment, and yet as Frances took my coat I realized something was different.

It was the light, the house was too dark. Though it wasn't yet four o'clock, Frances had turned on a lamp made from an old wooden sextant in the front hall, and also a lamp in what I could see of the living room—she didn't believe in overhead lighting—and pulled the heavy moss-colored velvet drapes. There was also a sharp musty odor that struck me as strange. Frances was usually a scrupulous housekeeper, especially as the house doubled as an informal showroom for her clients.

"It's so damp today," she explained, when she saw me notice the curtains. And for the first time I did think she seemed altered somehow, a little furtive. But the next instant she was her old self, smiling comfortingly. "Now what can I make you? Do you want a cup of tea? I have really nice Scottish tea.

"But we have to stay out of the dining room," she went on, leading the way to the kitchen, usually the brightest, warmest room in the house, with a sanded wood floor and tall windows with folded-back shutters and Frances's enormous old white Glenwood stove. Today the window shutters were closed and the kitchen felt as damp as the hall; only a small lamp above the stove had been switched on.

"Jane's with her math tutor."

Through the dining room door I could hear murmurings and what sounded like pages being turned. Frances listened tensely for a moment, then rolled her eyes. "Algebra. They've just started on variables."

"Variables." I sat down gingerly at the round oak table by the windows. "Is Jane having a lot of trouble with math?"

"Jane's having a lot of trouble period." Frances was filling the electric kettle. "Though nothing serious, of course." She turned to face me. "I mean, she's in high school. Do you remember high school?"

"Mostly I've tried to forget it."

"Well, she's in the middle of it and so she forgets everything else. Which, frankly, has made me a little scatter-brained myself lately." Frances opened a glass-fronted cabinet. "Now, I had a tin of shortbread cookies in here. We have to have shortbread cookies if we're going to have Scottish tea. I hope Walter and Jane didn't eat them all."

"So, Frances," I said, figuring it would be best to get this over with. "Why didn't you tell me that Dad wasn't in the nursing home yet?"

Frances continued to riffle through her cabinets for a moment longer. Then she sighed and turned around, brushing a long wisp of hair out of her eyes.

"Look, I'm really sorry, Cynnie," she said. "I meant to tell you, but I kept thinking I'd have it all worked out before you got here. The woman who runs the home told me it was just going to be a few more days, then that turned into a few more days. I didn't want to worry you, and right up until yesterday I thought it was all going to be taken care of. They were going to send a van down for him in the morning, but now that's been messed up, too. Something to do with the holidays." She sighed again and tucked another loose strand behind her ear. "I'm starting to wonder about this place, to be honest, though I don't know what other choice we have at this point."

I'd watched her closely during this speech, but she remained composed and regretful, gazing back at me.

"Can't he stay on the Cape until after Thanksgiving?"

"I'm afraid not. Ilse is going off traveling somewhere."

"Bird-watching?" Ilse was a biologist at the Oceanographic Institute in Woods Hole. Her specialty was shore birds.

"Something like that. But she says she's let him stay longer than she agreed to as it is. I'm really sorry about this, Cynnie."

It was on the tip of my tongue to say, Well, I'm going to Hartford, so you'll have to deal with Dad on your own. But Frances looked so chastened, and so concerned about distressing me, that I stopped myself. How often on previous visits had I lain on one of her sofas with a headache, letting her bring me cups of tea and plates of sandwiches, listening to her repeat that she was sorry I wasn't feeling well? I'd promised myself on the plane that this time I would not become pathetic around Frances.

"I *was* going to go to Hartford tomorrow," I said instead.

"I know it's a big imposition. You don't have to come if you don't want to."

"No, it's all right."

"Really, it won't take that long, I promise. We'll drive to get him, drive to the nursing home, then be home in time for dinner. We could go to Hartford the day after tomorrow. Or right after Thanksgiving. Whatever you want."

"I'm sure it'll be fine," I said, magnanimously.

The kettle had boiled. As she made our tea—the real way, warming the teapot first and using leaf tea, not tea bags—Frances talked about how nice it would be to see the Cape again, get a glimpse of the ocean, at least see Buzzards Bay. She'd opened a package of chocolate wafers, having given up on the shortbread cookies, and was arranging them on a Delft-blue china plate when the door to the dining room swung open behind me and I heard Jane come into the kitchen.

"Aunt Cynnie!"

"Well, if it isn't the wee colleen," I said, as Jane leaned over the back of my chair to give me a hug.

I'd called Jane the "wee colleen" from the day she'd been born with bright red hair. But now she pulled away as if insulted, and when I turned around I realized my mistake. Jane had never been a pretty child—not in the robust, effortless way Sarah was pretty—but she'd been sassy and lithe and humorous, with her freckles and that curly red hair, elbows sticking out like coat hangers as she put her hands on her hips to announce that she was not tired enough to go to bed or that she would *not* eat putrid green beans at dinner, they were an *excrescence*. But in the two years since I'd seen her she'd lost the dignity of childhood and had begun to assume the absurdity and pathos that goes with having an adult body. She was suddenly, shockingly, fat, with a pronounced bust that she was trying to hide underneath a baggy black shirt, worn over a pair of black cargo pants stuffed into black lace-up commando boots. Her hair had grown bushy; she was wearing it in two stiff braids. Acne studded her chin and forehead. On the side of her neck was a small tattoo, which I hoped was temporary, of a heart with a knife through it.

I smiled in confusion and made a doddering comment about how much older she looked, caught up suddenly in remembering myself at Jane's age when my father used to call me "Pork Chop" or sometimes the "Porcellian princess."

Behind her stood a slender young Chinese man. Frances waved at him with a little flourish and introduced him as Wen-Yi Cheng. "Our math savior."

"We call him Wen-Two-Three," scowled Jane.

Taking no notice of either or them, Wen-Yi nodded in my direction, then declined Frances's offer of tea, saying that he needed to get home, though his eyes strayed to the plate of chocolate wafers.

"Wen-Yi lives in Arlington," Frances told me. "He's a doctoral student in applied mathematics at Tufts."

Wen-Yi nodded again as if these facts explained him entirely. He was a good-looking young man, no more than twenty-three or -four, a little bony and stoop-shouldered in his blue nylon cardigan, but with thick shiny black hair he kept tossing out of his eyes and a narrow face that had a lazy brooding sensuality about it, which suddenly sharpened into an expression of concentrated enthusiasm when he turned toward Frances.

"I see you Wednesday afternoon?"

"That would be fine, Wen-Yi." She smiled as she opened the back door for him. "And don't forget you're coming to dinner on Thursday."

"I don't forget." He gazed at her with something of the same interest he'd displayed in the plate of chocolate wafers. "See you then. Bye for now."

"*He's* coming?" Jane's mouth fell open in exaggerated affront when Frances had closed the door behind him.

Frances turned toward me. "He wanted to know if he could bring a pumpkin pie for Thanksgiving. He calls it 'pump-king' pie. Isn't that sweet?"

"Why didn't you *tell* me Won Ton was coming?"

"Stop it." Frances frowned at Jane. "He'll hear you."

"*Mom.* He's already in his *car.*"

"No, he's not."

"Won Ton," repeated Jane loudly.

Through a gap in the window shutters I could see Wen-Yi, a lit cigarette in his mouth, climbing into a rusty mud-colored Datsun, parked out back by the potting shed. Hungrily pinching the cigarette between a thumb and forefinger, he took a deep drag, then leaned back in his seat to blow a luxuriant cloud of blue smoke at the windshield before starting the car and driving away. When I glanced up, I saw that both Frances and Jane had been watching, too.

"I've asked him not to smoke in the house." Frances was moving back toward the stove. "Anyway, I said pumpkin would be fine. Although I don't really like store-bought pie. But someone else is baking a couple pies, anyway."

"Who?" demanded Jane.

Frances picked up a dishrag and began wiping down the stove's surface. "Your father has just informed me that he's invited a new resident and his wife for dinner. They're Egyptian."

Negative remarks about the Middle East had recently been made in the doctors' lounge, Frances went on to explain, remarks overheard by the young resident. Walter wanted to smooth things over.

"Great." Jane gave her a dark look. "Thanksgiving at the UN."

"At least we know Wen-Yi eats turkey," Frances said, ignoring Jane. "And of course pump-king pie."

"*He's* the Pump-King." Jane began fiddling with a wooden pepper mill, scattering pepper across the tabletop.

"He's lonely," corrected Frances.

"Or maybe he's a summer squash. Little and yellow and—"

"I said stop it." Frances reached out and seized the pepper mill. For a moment she and Jane glared at each other.

"You get pissed at me for everything." Jane was the first to look away.

"Watch your language," snapped Frances.

"Well, you *do*."

"Look. This is a nice young man who drives all the way out here—"

"Oh right. Like he's not getting *paid*."

I stood up, saying that I needed to use the bathroom, and went out into the hall. From the time Jane was small, it had been like this: Frances pruning Jane, Jane bristling back. Say please, say thank you. Don't do that, that's not nice. Pick, pick. Frances had always been restrictive with Jane, right down to the plainness of her name, while Jane treated each of Frances's comments as a minor but incapacitating outrage. Yet I was never more envious of Frances than at moments like these, or maybe I was envious of Jane. I can't recall ever arguing with my mother, who spent most of her time in bed with the bedroom door closed and the shades pulled down. Though from what I'd just glimpsed in the kitchen, the current squabble between Frances and Jane was complicated by some jealousy as well, created by a shared interest in Wen-Yi, who was taken with Frances, which Jane had figured out.

The argument was still going on. In the bathroom, I splashed water on my face, then combed my hair with a tortoiseshell comb I found in the wooden medicine chest over the sink. Afterward I sat on the toilet lid for a few minutes, imagining myself back in my Dolores Street apartment, looking out my front window at the park across the street, where on sunny afternoons couples ate sandwiches under squat palm trees that looked like big pineapples. Deciding whether to make myself a salad for lunch that could serve as dinner as well. Deciding not to call the bookstore owner, then calling him at his store and hanging up when his wife, who worked with him, answered the phone. Recently, I'd been told, they'd gotten caller ID, at her insistence. I wondered if he had left a message on my answering machine, which would join others left on my answering machine, messages that I didn't erase, but kept skipping over, delaying the moment when I would have to listen to them.

The kitchen was quiet when I returned. Frances was sitting alone at the oak table, drinking tea.

"Not a very welcoming scene," she said ruefully. "Sorry about that."

I let her pour me a cup of tea. Frances used teacups and saucers for tea, never mugs. China creamers, sugar bowls, real silver teaspoons. Tea, for Frances, was an occasion. I always began my visits by enjoying her ceremoniousness: the lighting of candles at dinner, the use of cloth napkins and napkin rings, the sprigs of lavender placed between folded sheets in the linen closet. There was something almost religious about Frances's attention to detail. But then the rigidity of these domestic rituals, their exhausting thoughtfulness, plus the unspoken demand for appreciation, started to curdle my enjoyment of them and finally made me feel put upon, until I couldn't wait to get home to my own slipshod habits. Which always became more slipshod after one of my visits to Frances's house.

While I was stirring milk and sugar into my tea, Frances said, "You probably think I'm too critical of her."

"I don't think anything. I just got here."

"She's into the Goth look, as you may have noticed." Frances blew on her tea to cool it. "There's been some teasing at school."

"That's too bad."

"And she's gained a little weight."

I nodded, recognizing that something was being asked of me.

"Walter thinks she should see a therapist."

"He does?" I said cautiously.

"She came downstairs one morning with a couple scratches on her arm."

"Scratches?"

"They were probably just scratches. Walter wasn't sure. But my feeling is, you have to be careful about these things. Pay attention but not *too much* attention. Because then they'll just do it to get more attention. And Jane's always been after attention."

"But it seems like you *have* to pay attention—"

Frances wasn't listening. "Piercings, tattoos. You saw her neck. Henna," she added quickly. "But who knows what's next. I wish she wouldn't wear so much black. If she would just try to *look* like someone in a decent mood she'd have an easier time."

I cast around for something helpful to say, but my head felt cottony and congested, as if I'd caught a cold on the airplane. Also, I was waiting for Frances to bring up the "rough time" with Walter she'd alluded to on the phone.

Frances made a face. "Oh, it's just the age. I know I'm too critical. But she's so *hard* sometimes. She thinks everything is my fault. Though I don't know what she's so angry about, frankly. She's had a perfectly nice childhood."

She gave me another rueful smile. "Then again I suppose everything *is* my fault. It has to be someone's fault, so it might as well be mine."

I understood now that I was being asked to enlist on her side, ranged against unreasonable adolescence, so I nodded again. But my true sympathies lay with Jane and her bullheaded tantrums. I'd had terrible rages myself as a child, often directed at Frances. I remembered exactly that feeling of falling down a dark hole of rage, then being stuck at the dank bottom, with a mouthful of dirt. But mostly it was Jane's refusal to act in her own best interests, her inability even to see what those best interests might be, that I recognized so well.

"What time do we need to leave for the Cape tomorrow?"

Frances stopped smiling and gazed into the teacup in her hands. Instead of answering she put down her cup and turned it around a few times in its saucer, making a hard chalky little noise. "Come into the living room for a minute," she said at last, standing up. "I have something to show you."

I don't know what I expected to see, one of Frances's latest "finds" I suppose. Certainly I never dreamed it would be what greeted me from the far end of the living room, at first almost invisible in the rainy afternoon light filtering around the edges of those heavy drapes. Set into an alcove by the fireplace, in a spot previously occupied by a green velvet love seat, and illuminated by a single standing wrought-iron lamp, sat my grandmother's player organ, which I had not seen since I was thirteen and had not imagined ever seeing again.

"Where did you get that?" For a moment longer I held on to the hope that it was not our old organ, just one like it.

Frances explained that when Ilse had called to say that she was divorcing our father, she'd offered the organ to Frances, perhaps as a sort of bribe in exchange for Frances making all the arrangements for him, or perhaps because Ilse had remembered that the organ was sitting in a climate-controlled storage facility in Hyannis and thought someone might come after her for the fees.

"Can you believe it?" said Frances. "The one thing he held on to."

Upstairs Walter and Jane were walking around, their footsteps making the old floorboards creak. A window opened then shut. The rain had started up again.

Frances's face had a flushed, exultant look, though again an apologetic note had come into her voice. "He probably figured it would be worth something someday."

I was away at boarding school when my father sold our house in West Hartford. My mother had died six months before and he was anxious to get rid of the house and everything in it. One April morning he'd held a yard sale of all our furnishings, selling also my mother's books and her china and silver, and even our family photographs, which I guess people bought for their fancy brass frames. Only because he called Helen at the last minute, and she borrowed a friend's car and drove to Hartford from Boston, were we able to salvage a few knickknacks, mostly things from our own rooms. People are shocked whenever I tell this story, which is probably why I've told it so often—I'm not immune to the glamour of the dysfunctional childhood—yet at the time my father's desire to be free of his past life, so encumbered by illness, made a miserable sort of sense. Of course Helen couldn't have loaded the organ into a borrowed car, even if she'd wanted to. But I did recall her mentioning that the organ wasn't out on the lawn that day, with all the chairs and tables and rolled-up rugs, the gray stitching on their undersides wet with dew, and half a dozen embarrassed-looking neighbors brushing past the rhododendrons and azalea bushes, picking through damp cardboard boxes of old clothes and record albums.

Frances had been watching me; now she gave a penitent little moan. "I *know.* It's lousy. I shouldn't have sprung this on you, too.

I was going to say no when Ilse asked if I wanted to take it, but then I thought we should at least have *something* to keep in the family."

Clearly she'd hoped that I would be pleased that the organ had been rediscovered and was now regretting her decision to surprise me. Even so, I could feel her struggling to suppress her excitement.

"You know, an heirloom," she persisted. "Some kind of legacy. Something to hand down to the girls."

It was even uglier than I remembered. Plangent, with those carved garlands flowering along the upper cabinet, a morbid-looking urn on either end of the stop knobs, the two columnar legs ending in clawed animal feet. It was also more battered than I remembered, scarred from years of being abused by my sisters and me, and probably by children before us, who had banged at the keys, pretending to play "Pilgrims' Chorus" from *Tannhäuser*, or a Bach minuet, while the organ's internal machinery turned the old music rolls. When I examined the mahogany case, I saw that the varnish had coarsened, gone rucked and bumpy like an old hide.

Frances was still watching me anxiously, waiting for some response. Not sure what my intentions were, I crossed the room and sat down on the organ's bench. Self-consciously, I touched a few of the keys. No sound at all, except the tap of my fingernails against the celluloid. I'd forgotten that you had to pump the footboards first and get the internal bellows going. The whole thing smelled deeply, richly, almost intoxicatingly of mildew—the smell that had greeted me when I first came into the house. So much for climate-controlled storage.

"Isn't it gorgeous?" Frances had come up behind me. "There's a whole box of music rolls, too. And look at this."

She reached behind the hinged music rack into a little hidden cupboard I'd never known about and pulled out a brown-spotted pamphlet titled "Instructions for the Care and Working of Your Estey Player Reed Organ," which opened with a list of its bass and treble stops. "The world's most miraculous instrument!" read an encomium on the front of the pamphlet. "A mechanical apparatus endowed with human capabilities!"

"They're pretty rare now," Frances was saying as I handed back the pamphlet. "I looked them up online. And this one's in perfect condition. I just need to get it cleaned and tuned."

Rain slashed at the window panes. "Oh Cynnie," she whispered, resting one hand on my shoulder. "I just thought you'd be glad that there was something left, you know, after all this time—

"Of course," she said, withdrawing her hand, "you can have it if you want."

This was offered insincerely. Frances was a generous person, who gave to charities and volunteered for school committees and fed stray cats like Wen-Yi and listened for hours to her friends' marriage problems and their worries about wayward children. But she had a streak of real greed when it came to heirlooms. One of the few things Helen had saved for me from that yard sale was an old porcelain Wedgwood bowl with a raised pattern of blue grape leaves. The bowl used to sit on the front hall table, holding Christmas cards during the holidays, and during the rest of the year extra house keys, pennies, receipts, ticket stubs, bits of junk. Frances always minded that I had it. When I told her that the bowl had cracked—a man I was dating had mistakenly poured boiling water into it one night while we were draining spaghetti noodles—a look of actual pain crossed her face. Though later she'd agreed that things like bowls were meant to be used.

The organ seemed to be gathering gloom as the afternoon ticked away and the room grew darker. Such rot, I thought, sliding my hands off the keys. Heirlooms. Legacies. Such fraud.

"I mean, you're the historian," Frances added, looking at me searchingly. "And there was that story Dad used to tell about Mark Twain—"

"It's fine," I said, standing up. "I don't want it."

My father's story was that Mark Twain had given the organ to my grandmother when she was a little girl, after he caught sight of her red hair in the Vanderbilt Hotel in New York. She was having iced cakes in the lobby with her father while some other child stumbled through "Fur Elise" on the hotel piano, and Twain heard her say that the only bad thing about pianos was having to play them.

Pure fiction. Iced cakes. The Vanderbilt Hotel. "Fur Elise." All except for my grandmother's red hair and perhaps that innate unwillingness to apply herself, a stubborn incapacity that from all accounts may have been her defining feature.

"But," objected Frances, determined to be selfless now that she'd secured what she wanted, "it's yours if—"

"I don't have room for something like that. Anyway, it's fine."

And it was fine. In a few days I would be back on the plane to San Francisco, returning to my apartment and my desk made from a door laid across a pair of dented aluminum file cabinets. Fog would drift past the windows, my landlady would simmer her beans, and Frances and my father would return to being things I didn't need to think about very often. Tomorrow we'd drive him to his nursing home. Sarah was arriving from New York the next day. Frances would make chestnut stuffing for the turkey. It would be splendid. There was nothing wrong with her. Walter was just getting cantankerous.

Frances gave a caught little laugh. As if she'd read my thoughts, she said, "You're such a good sport. To come out here, when you didn't want to. And then to put up with all my—" She shook her head helplessly at herself.

Then she pointed to the slim gold watch on her wrist. "Hey look, it's after five. Time for a glass of wine."

"How about a whole bottle," I said feelingly.

She laughed again and began walking around the living room, turning on the rest of the lamps. "Two bottles!" Her hands were shaking, with relief, probably, at having successfully staked her claim to the organ. I watched her fiddle with the silk lampshades, making sure they weren't crooked; suddenly I couldn't bear to see her face and what I imagined must be her expression of post-poned gloating. Instead I looked around the living room at the framed antique botanical prints and the bookcases full of china figurines and handsomely bound books. Frances had recovered her two Knole sofas in a subtle floral pattern of carmine and cream, one sofa with the colors reversed, both of which went perfectly with the old Persian carpet on the floor. In this bower of sense and order the organ looked like a toadstool, lurking in its unlit corner. But Frances seemed not to notice. She was telling me that she and Walter had recently bought a case of wine on eBay, which was stored in the basement ("our version of a fall-out shelter") along with a stationary bike and a freezer full of Lean Cuisine fro-zen dinners, and fifteen cans of lobster and sherry bisque, which Walter had won in a raffle.

"Good to know that you're planning ahead for the Apocalypse," I said. "But somehow I can't picture Walter buying raffle tickets."

Frances corrected the position of a celadon bowl filled with beach stones. "Oh, my assistant's always selling tickets for one good cause or another. She's not here today, but you'll meet her at

Thanksgiving. Mary Ellen. Such a sweetheart, and she's been a lot of help to me, but kind of a kook. Walter feels sorry for her."

"He mentioned Mary Ellen," I said. "In the car."

"Oh, he did?"

She turned to smile at me. Frances had one of those rare, encouraging smiles that made you feel not only important in ways you'd never felt with anyone else but that also made you want to confess all your sins and petty crimes to her, convinced that she'd continue to believe the best of you and overlook your failings.

"He didn't say anything about raffle tickets, though," I went on. "Or about feeling sorry for her."

"No, he wouldn't." Frances turned away again. "Walter likes to think he doesn't get emotionally involved with people. He can't afford to, as a doctor. Now, what should we have for dinner? Lobster bisque, since I mentioned it? While we get smashed?" Then she added soberly, "Too bad we have to drive to the Cape in the morning."

"Well, all the more reason to get drunk tonight."

"Yes," she said. "All the more reason."

As we were heading back to the kitchen, she glanced back at me over her shoulder. "By the way, do you mind driving tomorrow? I've finally given in to bifocals, but my new glasses give me vertigo if I wear them for too long."

Before dinner I asked Frances if I could lie down for half an hour. Almost since my arrival, I'd felt as if I could not catch my breath, and a glass of red wine had made me dizzy. Frances led me upstairs to Walter's study, a long, pleasant, low-ceilinged room on the second floor at the top of the stairs, with three windows at the far end, overlooking the driveway and part of the front lawn. Walter himself had gone for a run, leaving Frances and me to pull out the sofa bed, which we made up together. When we were done, Frances covered the bed with one of her crazy quilts, randomly pieced from old dresses and skirts she found at thrift stores and rummage sales or from old clothes of her own that she couldn't bear to throw out. Quilting was one of her hobbies, along with cooking, gardening, restoring furniture. She had that knack, almost extinct these days, for making what she needed out of whatever was available or remaking something so that it served a new and better purpose. She would spend any amount of time on these projects, especially if they were intended as gifts. Sarah and Jane each had a quilt Frances had created for them from scraps of their baby clothes, and she made one for Helen a few months before Helen died. I saw it after the funeral, hanging on the wall of Helen's living room: fabric squares silk-screened with poems and good wishes and photographs of smiling people, mailed to Frances at her request by Helen's friends.

The quilt on my bed was done in subdued, faded colors, from what looked to be scraps of dish towels. It was actually very pretty. When I praised it, she bent down to smooth out a corner. "You can have it if you want." Then quickly, because she never liked to be thanked, she said, "What I like about quilts is, you know, the months it took you to make one, that's where they went."

We stood for a moment longer, contemplating Frances's crazy quilt; then she went to Walter's rolltop desk to close his laptop computer and tidy a few things away, among them a pair of balled black socks, which she dropped into a drawer. On the back of the door hung several men's dress shirts on wooden hangers.

Frances saw me looking at the shirts. "I've had a cough. Walter sleeps in here sometimes so I won't keep him up all night."

"I'm happy to sleep downstairs on the sofa," I offered, though I did not want to sleep downstairs on the sofa and felt cold despair even at the prospect.

Frances held her forefinger to her mouth. "Don't be silly." She smiled quickly at me, then backed out of the door, lifting Walter's shirts on their hangers as she went. "Come down whenever you're ready."

The girls' rooms were also on the second floor. Next door, on the other side of the wall, Jane was rattling at her computer keyboard. I lay down on the bed and closed my eyes, listening to Jane typing and to the comfortable sounds of Frances moving around in the kitchen below, the scrape of pots being set on the stove and footsteps as she walked back and forth. Briefly I pictured the lean, bearded face of the bookstore owner, then with surprising ease put him out of my mind. The phone rang. Jane clumped down the stairs. Bits of conversation floated up to me, including a short emphatic argument that had to do with homework.

As I lay there listening, I found myself thinking about my mother, lying in her dim cluttered bedroom day after day while the rest of the household went on without her. Hearing the voices, laughter, complaints, feet on the staircase, doors slamming, the occasional clogged sound of angry weeping. I wondered what had passed through her mind on those long afternoons. It wasn't that we'd forgotten about her. We'd simply learned not to require her, at least not in the most basic way that mothers are required by children: to be present without causing concern, or pity. In nearly all my memories of my mother, she is in bed, propped against the cushioned green vinyl headboard, surrounded by stacks of books, framed photographs behind dusty glass, squads of medicine bottles, boxes of tissues, all swimming in a kind of yellow murk created by mustard-colored cretonne drapes pulled across the windows. She looks up from a book, gazing fretfully around, looking for Helen or perhaps wondering if Mrs. Jordan, our housekeeper, is coming up with her tray, or when Frances and my father will be back from their evening walk. "Oh Cynthia," she says, smiling vaguely at me in the doorway, "it's you."

I must have fallen asleep still thinking about my mother because though I was in Frances's house, it was also the house in West Hartford, and Mrs. Jordan was there. She was ironing bedsheets and telling me that an old man had once lived in Frances's house. His family was gone; he'd lived alone. No one had bothered to check on him and he was found days after he died, sitting in a chair in the living room.

"But your sister doesn't mind him." Mrs. Jordan wagged her tall black wig. "Not the way some persons would."

"Who?" I asked. My voice sounded like a child's voice, though in my dream I was a grown woman.

"*You* know," said Mrs. Jordan, in her old impenetrable way of answering questions by not answering them. Then she went back to ironing, muttering and shaking her head. As I watched her brown arm move back and forth with the iron, I saw that the bedsheet was one of Frances's crazy quilts but like the one she'd made for Helen, with writing and good wishes and smiling photographs on it.

When I woke the room was dark and my mouth was dry. I was afraid that everyone had gone ahead and eaten dinner without me. But I'd only been asleep for twenty minutes, according to my watch, though as sometimes happens with unrestful naps, it had felt like so much longer.

The next morning was gray and colder, edged with that stealthy New England chill that turns your fingernails purple even inside your gloves. Frances was worried about snow as we headed south in her big white Plymouth Voyager. She sat huddled in the passenger seat, looking ashen and aristocratic in a long high-collared black cashmere coat buttoned to the neck, turning on the radio every few minutes, hunting for a weather forecast. The rest of the time she looked out her window.

I was glad to be driving, something I've always been good at and enjoy, although I don't own a car myself. But once in a while I borrow Carita's old Dodge and spend the day driving along Route 1 through Marin, a perilously scenic road that curves and snakes first along cliffs above the valley, then above the ocean. I find it soothing, negotiating switchbacks and hairpin turns, then at last bursting out onto those lion-colored headlands. The wide view of the Pacific you get from up there is sometimes blue, sometimes silver or gray, and like all views of the ocean, always exhilarating, but also strangely upsetting, like a place remembered from childhood but forgotten until it's right in front of you again.

During dinner the night before, Frances had tried to tell me what to expect when I saw my father. She and Walter had visited him at Cape Cod Hospital after his stroke. The stroke had left him partly aphasic and paralyzed on his right side. He was having trouble feeding himself and needed to use a wheelchair most of the time, although he could walk short distances with a cane. "He's a shadow of his former self," Frances told me, her voice quavering. She'd had quite a lot to drink by then, and I saw Walter unobtrusively take the wine bottle and put it on the floor by his chair.

Now in the car she began to hum to herself, tapping her fingers together. Several times she began to say something, then stopped. Her hands were trembling again. I didn't know how to feel about the prospect of confronting my father in his helpless condition and I resented the sight of Frances's trembling hands and the easy access she seemed to have to sadness, or regret, or whatever it was that was gripping her just then.

Other than at Helen's funeral, the last time I'd seen my father was five or six years before over lunch at a seafood restaurant in Barnstable. I'd come east on one of my summer visits and Frances and I were spending two weeks in a rented house in Wellfleet with Sarah and Jane, while Walter stayed in Boston and came down on the weekends. It was Frances's idea to call our father. We'd just found out about Helen's diagnosis and Frances was frantic. Helen had gone all the way through medical school, had passed her board exams and completed her residency, only to set herself up in Bennington as a homeopathic practitioner. Now she was intending to treat herself with homeopathic remedies. Frances wanted us to hold a family conference to talk Helen out of this plan, which Frances insisted to me was suicidal. She tried to persuade Helen to come down to the Cape for a weekend—the excuse was my visit—and at first Helen agreed. But at the last minute there was some crisis, an outbreak of whooping cough among her patients, or German measles, some disease that shouldn't be around anymore, and Helen begged off. She must have known what Frances was up to. By then Frances had arranged lunch with our father, and it seemed too late to back out. So she made the girls pull T-shirts over their shorts and bathing suits and one afternoon we drove to one of those dowdy little seafood places that serve beer in waxed paper cups and steamed clams in a plastic bucket.

Our father met us inside, wearing a coat and tie; he'd shaved off the trim little moustache he'd always worn and without it his face looked naked. I found it embarrassing to look at him. "How's Seattle?" he asked me, then apologized when I reminded him that I was living in San Francisco. "Hard to keep it all straight at my age," he said, giving me a cagey smile.

Ilse had come along, too, tanned and ready-looking in a belted khaki pants suit. She had always tanned impressively, especially with her light blue eyes and her white-blonde hair, which she still liked to wear in a topknot. Ilse didn't say much at lunch until the bread came and Frances declined to take a roll from the basket, mentioning that she was cutting back on starch. With a heavy sigh, Ilse began to criticize diets that advised people to avoid starches and carbohydrates. In Switzerland, she noted, in Lausanne, where she had grown up, no one worried about starches and carbohydrates. She grew almost animated as she listed the reasons for consuming starches and carbohydrates, chief among them being the importance of "eating sensibly," followed by an anecdote about refusing a bowl of boiled oats one morning in childhood and then going to school hungry. "I never did that again," she told us with satisfaction. After that she stopped talking, but as if to prove her point, she ate her lunch steadily and thoroughly, a fine mist of perspiration gathering above her short upper lip, strands of hair sticking to her temples.

Dad talked mostly to Sarah and Jane, though he kept looking at Frances. He asked them polite questions about how they were enjoying the beach, then insisted on paying the check before we were done eating. Frances did not bring up the subject of Helen; instead she played with the piece of broiled fish on her plate and watched him talk to the girls, a tense, abstracted look on her face.

In the van, she reached once more for the radio, then changed her mind and folded her hands in her lap.

"It'll be all right," I told her. "If you're worried about Dad, I'm sure he's resigned himself by now. It won't be that big a deal."

Frances cleared her throat.

"Listen," I said. "He's probably relieved to be shut of Ilse at last. No more boiled oats for breakfast. Or muesli. Isn't that what they call it in Switzerland? *Muesli.* She probably made him eat *muesli* every morning. Think of that."

"You're right," she said. "I'll think of that."

"So how can she do this to him, do you think?" I asked after a few minutes had gone by with neither of us saying anything. "It's pretty extreme. I mean, she's never been *that* awful, and she knew he was older when she married him. His getting sick can't be unexpected."

Frances stared at the windshield. "She doesn't want to care for him anymore."

"Well, of course not. No one *wants* to take care of someone, but they *do.* People are always doing it. What I don't understand is why now she won't do it."

Frances looked stony. "It got too hard for her."

We drove on. Frances consulted the sky every few minutes to see if it was starting to snow. Bands of oak trees flickered by, a few coppery leaves clinging to the branches. Open marshes appeared ringed by pale yellow cattails and sumac stalks, then disappeared again. Here and there we passed the wooded backyards of small plain houses. When we went by a service island, Frances asked if I thought we should check the air pressure in the tires; they had looked low to her when we got in the car. Every time I accelerated to pass another car, she clutched the door handle.

"Why don't you tell me about the nursing home where Dad's going," I suggested, the second time she mentioned checking the tires. "What's it called again?"

"Greenswood Manor. And it's an assisted-living facility."

"Like a climate-controlled storage facility?"

She gave me a repressive look. "Did you read that brochure I sent you?"

I had read the brochure. Whirlpools, physical therapy, adjustable meal plans. "Organized Activities" included arts and crafts, sing-alongs, and ice-cream socials. Private rooms on every floor, some with kitchenettes, each with a small balcony overlooking "spacious grounds," until you got to the fourth floor, which was the "full care" wing. No kitchenettes. No balconies. No more spacious grounds. "Shared accommodations" were provided.

"A secure environment," I quoted from the brochure, "for those entering a transitional phase of life."

"I visited six or seven places," Frances said defensively, "and this was the best one. At least for what he can afford."

"I'm not criticizing. Who wouldn't like a secure environment these days?"

"He won't like it if you start making jokes."

"Frances." I kept my eyes on the oil truck ahead of us. "He's not going to like any of this. He's not supposed to. So let's both stop pretending there's some way to make it nice."

"Well, it *could* be nice," she said with a strangled little laugh. "It just depends on your attitude."

"*My* attitude?"

"A person's attitude. In general."

SEVERAL TIMES DURING the drive to the Cape I tried to ask Frances about herself and Walter, but she brushed off my questions as if she had no idea why I would be asking them. Then she asked if I was interested in anyone, so I told her about the man I'd been seeing, that he was tall and funny, French Canadian, and that he owned a bookstore in Berkeley, which was not doing well. I omitted that he was married, falsely implying that it had been my decision to end things when the truth was that he'd cooled off almost as soon as I'd said I was in love with him. We were standing inside an Oakland coffee shop we often went to, waiting for a table, looking out the plate glass window at the sidewalk as it started to rain. As I watched the pavement darken, he told me that he and his wife had decided to "give it another chance." "How many chances do you get?" I recall asking him, genuinely curious, but I must have sounded bitter because he only shook his head and said he was sorry.

"It wasn't going anywhere," I said to Frances, trying to seem weary of the whole idea of relationships with men.

"That's too bad," said Frances, looking slightly bored herself. Usually she would have demanded all sorts of particulars.

For a time we listened to the radio and talked about the wealthy women who were Frances's clients, several of whom were cheating on their husbands and ignoring their children.

"Everyone's out there looking for something else," said Frances reproachfully, "when they probably already have it right at home."

In my experience, home was what usually sent people out looking for something else, but I refrained from saying so. Frances went on to deplore the new trend in interior decorating, favored by these same clients, which was called "Simple Living." Sleek, spare, stern-looking rooms. Slate-topped coffee tables, taut leather chairs, recessed lighting. Nothing extraneous, nothing old. A place you could leave in a minute and it would look as if nobody had ever been there. The opposite of Frances's own curatorial style, which I privately referred to as "Ancestral Manse."

"Mary Ellen's into it, too. She's been pushing me to get into feng shui." Frances was gazing out the window at a gray cement industrial office complex with medieval-looking black slits for windows. "Mary Ellen's into curative atmospheres. You know, healing sounds. Fragrances."

I imagined a small olive-skinned woman. Frizzy black hair, large expressive eyes. Expensively textured clothes, heavy silk pajama pants, big soft sweaters of merino wool, bought out of some fretful need for consolation.

"Well, are you?" I asked.

"Am I what?"

"Letting her push you into it."

Frances sighed. "People like a house to feel like a home. I know that sounds obvious, but it's true." She pressed her lips tightly together for a moment. Then with a peculiar vehemence, she went on, "No matter what kind of house it is, or who the people are, I can make it look like they've always lived there. Not how they would have *actually* lived in the house but how they *wish* they'd lived there." She gave an agitated little shrug.

"Well," I said, "home is where the heart is."

"That's right," said Frances, though I had been joking.

We drove for a while longer in silence, the wooded areas getting scrubbier and sandier, denser, with more pitch pines, which meant we were getting closer to the Cape.

"How's the book coming?" Frances asked, when we again had been quiet for too long. I told her that my research was coming along well, then without thinking added that I'd brought along the outline in my shoulder bag.

As soon as I'd spoken, Frances said, "Can I see it?"

It was just an outline, and I'm usually reluctant about showing unfinished work to anyone; but a distraction seemed like a good way to stop Frances from worrying about snowstorms or whether we were going to have a flat tire. She opened my bag and fished out the manila envelope with my summary inside, maybe six or seven pages in all, then took out her brand-new bifocals and settled back in her seat.

She read quietly and absorbedly, slipping each page neatly behind the last one after she finished it. I tried not to watch her read, though I noticed she kept smiling; once or twice she murmured something I didn't catch.

When she was done she looked up. Her face was flushed, almost damp.

"Oh Cynnie," she said. "It's so *good*."

"How can it be good?" I said, pleased but trying to sound off-hand. "It's not even written yet."

"But everything you have here is so wonderful. Those three little girls and that big house. The people who came to visit. All their pets." She gazed down at the pages in her hands, scanning different paragraphs. "'A cat named Satan and a kitten named Sin.' I *love* that. And the plays they put on in their schoolroom, pretending to be English queens in their mother's gowns. And Christmas, with Twain dressed up as Santa, writing them letters beforehand about what presents they wanted. How he gave the oldest one a wooden ark, with two hundred carved wooden animals, 'such as only a human being could create, and only God call by name without referring to the passenger list.'" Frances's eyes were shining. "That's so perfect."

"He acted like God, all right," I said, flattered.

"And how there were three girls, like us. I can't wait to read the whole thing when you're done."

"Well, my deadline's in about six months."

Frances was hardly listening. "Their mother sounds lovely, too. The way Twain called her 'his gravity,' and she called him 'Youth.' And the removable wooden cherubs on their bedposts that she let the girls take off and wash in the sink and dress up in doll clothes." She glanced up again. "But what was she sick with?"

"Various ailments. Heart problems eventually. She was always sick. They were all hypochondriacs. The whole family. Always trying out new fads, water cures, different diets. They really got into this thing called the 'mind cure.'"

"What?" said Frances absently.

"The basic theory was you could cure yourself of anything just by deciding you felt better."

Frances shook her head over the page in her hand.

"The oldest girl, Susy, was neurotic," I offered, as she went back to reading, "and probably anorexic, although she died young so no one really knew how she would have turned out. Clara, the middle one, was pretty screwed up as well. She had a nervous breakdown when their mother died. Then with Little Jean, the youngest one—"

But Frances was once again immersed in the outline. "I love

what you've got here about Clara, how accident prone she was, but no matter how many accidents she had, she was always fine."

I glanced at her sideways. "Of course, those accidents weren't always *her* doing."

As is probably clear, my favorite part of writing historical fiction is divulging material about my subjects that I can't include in my books. I love the amused interest in people's eyes as they listen to an off-color anecdote about the Alcotts—the nudist who'd lived with them for six months, for instance—or Helen Keller, who in middle age tried to elope with a much-younger suitor by climbing out of a window (an attempt foiled, by the way, by Mildred). I love their guilty pleasure in debunkings. Everyone enjoys hearing about the indignities and blunders and terrible losses suffered by other people, especially if those other people were admired or special in some way. Unfortunately, or fortunately, if you're a novelist, it's human nature.

"That family was *full* of accidents." I shifted more comfortably in my seat. "Three fires. All in the nursery or the schoolroom. Near drownings. Collisions. Like the time Twain let go of the handle of Clara's baby buggy on a hill to light his cigar, and she bounced out and landed on her head. Or the time Jean was run over by—"

"But kids are like that," Frances interrupted. "They're survivors. It's amazing what they can go through and come out without a scratch."

I gave her a sharp look, but she was perfectly serious. She leafed to the last page, smiling happily. "This is great what you have here about the parents. How they sent notes back and forth by the daughters when the mother was sick and couldn't see the father, and the daughters read the notes and sometimes changed them if they thought his language was too strong, or if he got 'carried away' in describing something that made him mad. He must have had quite a temper," she said admiringly.

"He had a terrible temper. His children were afraid of him."

Frances looked startled. "But he sounds so funny and charming. Those stories he made up for the girls, about the bric-a-brac on the mantelpiece. How they would boss him around and make him tell the stories a certain way. They adored him." She rustled the papers. "You've captured that so well."

"Frances, I'm writing a book for fourth graders."

"Well, they're lucky," she said, reaching up to twist a button on her cashmere coat. "I wish I'd had something like this to read when I was that age."

For some reason I felt rebuked, even though once again she'd been complimenting me. We passed a cranberry bog, watery and secretive-looking this time of year, hedged by tall yellow grasses and gray bracken.

After a minute Frances sighed. "Dad used to love Mark Twain."

It was part of family lore that *The Adventures of Huckleberry Finn* was the sole book my father claimed to have read from start to finish. Even with the newspaper, he only read the first parts of articles on the front page; he rarely bothered to find the continuation of a story to see what else had happened. I have no idea how he got through the insurance claims he'd had to review at his office.

"Remember Dad's Twainisms?" Frances asked dreamily some time later, taking off her glasses as the high gray arch of the Bourne Bridge appeared in front of us. "Those sayings he used to quote? Did you know he got them off a daily calendar I gave him one Christmas?" She looked proud at this recollection.

Then she said, "Remember the notes he used to send up on her tray?"

She was talking about the tray Mrs. Jordan used to carry back and forth between my mother's room and the kitchen, once my mother stopped coming downstairs for meals. Often my father would scribble a note to her before he left for work in the morning and leave it to be carried up on her breakfast tray.

"Did you know," said Frances, "that he sometimes used to put sayings on the notes, to cheer her up?"

"I remember," I said, merging with the traffic onto the bridge, "that she didn't like Mark Twain."

"She didn't?" Frances turned to me in surprise.

Irritably, because I felt I'd been more familiar with these notes than Frances had, I said, "She thought Twain was a big blowhard. Especially compared with the writers she liked."

"Who did she like?" Frances looked honestly puzzled.

"Jane Austen. The Brontës. Willa Cather. Didn't you ever go in and read to her?"

I asked this question knowing full well that Frances had never read to our mother. Especially toward the end Frances had avoided her whenever possible, almost insolently, pretending not to under-stand when she spoke, pretending not to hear when Mrs. Jordan said, "Save my legs," and asked her to carry something upstairs to our mother's room.

"I don't remember," said Frances, shaking her head. She stacked my pages and slipped them back into their envelope.

Steel pylons flicked past as we crossed the bridge. Below gaped the gray canal, scattered here and there with white sails, like torn bits of paper.

"Are you okay?" Frances asked, once we were over the bridge.

"It's a little hot in here," I said. "Do you mind if I open the window?"

"It doesn't feel hot to me. Are you getting carsick? Remember how you used to get carsick on the way to school?"

"No," I snapped. "I'm just *hot*."

"Well, by all means," said Frances, a little crossly. "Open the window then."

We reached the town of Pocasset just before noon. My father had bought a small shingled cottage here when I was in college, so that Ilse could be close to Woods Hole, where she was conducting some sort of postgraduate work, and he could have a view of the sea, which he insisted was the only view embraced by human beings that never changed, since it was always changing. But for years he and Ilse traveled so much that they rarely had a reliable address. The cottage was rented out except for the summers. But when my father turned seventy-five, they decided to live there year-round, and that's when Ilse went to work at the institute. What my father did with himself after that, I never knew.

The clouds were clearing as we drove through the little town and it seemed as if the Cape had been having milder weather than up north. Most of the scrub oaks along the back roads still had their leaves, and when we turned down a sandy dirt driveway where FISKE was painted in faded letters on a splintered gray oar nailed to a pine tree, and drove out onto the spur of land my father owned above the bay, we discovered an exquisite little Japanese maple, defiantly scarlet, planted by itself, like a flag, on the grass in front of my father's cottage. A row of neat hydrangeas edged the walkway, a few pale blue petals showing here and there among the faded brown flowers. The breeze was fresh after the drive, and full of salt, and as we got out of the van we stopped for a moment to appreciate the calm silvery gleam of the bay.

Ilse opened the door before we had a chance to ring the bell. She was wearing a white blouse that was slightly too small for her, white sweatpants, and white leather moccasins. Even though it was November, her face was darkly tanned.

"Come in." Ilse's accent sounded more clipped than I remembered. "He has been waiting for an hour."

"I'm sorry, but the weather held us up." Frances was trying to remain polite, but the wings of her nostrils flared. "We thought it was going to snow. And there was traffic coming over the bridge."

Ilse stared at her moodily, then stepped aside so we could enter the foyer, which opened into the living room and the kitchen. I had only visited the cottage a few times before and my impression had been of airy rooms full of watery light from the bay. But the cottage seemed to have grown smaller, what I could see of it from the foyer, and more crowded. Even the view had shrunk. Framed by the living room's picture window, the bay looked flat and metallic, as if it were hanging on the wall.

"Hello, Dad," called Frances, as Ilse shut the front door.

Ilse did not offer to take our coats, and with relief I understood that this visit was meant to be short. The cottage was very warm. The smell of bleach rose from the foyer's tiled floor, mixing with an almost tidal reek of bathroom odors and fried meat and stale heated air, queasily cut with a floral air freshener.

"Dad? We're here."

No answer.

Ilse had packed him two suitcases. They were crowded into the foyer along with six or seven large cardboard boxes, each labeled with black marker in Ilse's blocky scientific print: SUMMER CLOTHES, WINTER CLOTHES, BOOKS, PAPERS. One box was marked: ROBERT FISKE/PERSONAL EFFECTS. I just had time to reflect, not very coherently, or originally, on the sad irony of how much went into the making of a life, yet how quickly it was packed away, before I realized that there were too many boxes for my father's "shared accommodations" at Greenswood Manor.

"Frances," I murmured, "he knows where he's going, doesn't he?"

"Of course he does."

She turned to Ilse, who was now standing by the suitcases with her hands on her hips, surveying us as if she were deciding whether we might fit into a box as well. *Robert Fiske/Estranged Daughters.* Ilse's eyes seemed to be watering, but that could have been her contact lenses. When I first knew her she'd worn heavy black-framed glasses—the type once favored by Aristotle Onassis—which had made her wide Scandinavian face look not just severe but slightly insensible. The glasses were gone, but she still had the same white-blonde hair gathered into a topknot, perhaps a little scantier now, still the same impersonal blue gaze. Still the same pale swollen voluptuous mouth, startling in such an otherwise dispassionate face. *Liver Lips,* Frances and I had called her, when Ilse first appeared at our house. She'd never changed her name, either. Ilse Arnholm.

Though when I looked more carefully I saw that what I'd taken for a tan was taupe-colored makeup, thickly applied, extending from her hairline to just below her jaw, as if Ilse couldn't be bothered with her neck, figuring no one would look that far.

Frances said quietly, "Ilse? You told him about the arrangements, didn't you?"

Ilse squinted back at her with pursed lips. "Arrangements?"

"He knows where he's going, right?"

"He is going with you."

"She means," I cut in, "where we're taking him."

"He is going with you." Ilse was peering closely at Frances. "He
thinks he is going to you."

I felt my face go white. "But I'm sure Frances made it very
clear—"

"He wants to be with you."

"But you made it clear," I insisted, turning to Frances. Frances
stared back at me, eyes wide above the black collar of her coat. I
waited for her to say something, to remind Ilse of their arrangement, agreed upon weeks ago, but she seemed too shocked to
speak. It was worse for her, I remember thinking. She still had
some unresolved feelings for our father—whatever had led her to
visit five or six nursing homes and worry about jokes made at his
expense—while I had none. I did not care what became of him.
It was fury on Frances's behalf that led me to round on Ilse in that
close odorous little foyer.

"Listen," I said. "Frances agreed to find a good place for him.
Which she did. And as I understand it, you promised—"

"I did not promise anything." For the first time since our arrival, Ilse looked directly at me, with surprise.

We'd been keeping our voices pitched low, but now suddenly
from the living room came the sound of my father shouting unin-
telligibly in a harsh, glottal voice. When I took a step backward, I
could just see the toes of his shiny black wingtips, resting on the
metal footrests of a wheelchair.

"You can't do this," I said to Ilse.

"Do what?"

"Leave us with him like this."

"I am not leaving you," she pointed out, returning her gaze to Frances. A cautious, calculating look had replaced her surprised expression. "You are taking him."

"Making *us* tell him," I said.

Pale hair wisped around her face, a few strands catching in the corners of her mouth. "He is your father."

"He's *your* husand," I shot back. "You married him."

"I was very young." She twisted her mouth. "I did not know anything then."

"He had plenty of money, you knew that."

I expected some retort at this accusation, which was not entirely fair—Ilse had never been interested in money; on the contrary, she'd always insisted on a rather frugal lifestyle with my father—but as I was speaking a surprised expression had once more come over her face. She glanced at Frances and then returned her gaze to me, shaking her head in disbelief. "You really do not know?"

"Know what? How you used him?"

"Used *him*?" Ilse gave a barking laugh.

Else, Frances and I used to call her, pretending to misunderstand her name. As in: Or Else. Ilse was Norwegian, though she'd grown up in Switzerland. *The Swiss Miss. The Goatherd.* We'd spent hours mimicking her accent up in our rooms: *Vell, vat do you sink of cuckoo clocks und chocolate? Vee ver neutral during zee war, had to stay home to protect zee cuckoo clocks und zee chocolate.* Stuffing ourselves with potato chips filched from the pantry, our mouths greasy with spite and despair. *Heidi marries her grandfather. She keeps his wallet in her dirndl.* In return, Ilse had never looked upon us with anything more than a quiet, enduring, annihilating disregard.

Yet now, a quarter of a century later, when Frances and I should be impossible to disregard, when we were grown women, with a husband and children, in Frances's case, with lives at least as adult and significant as Ilse's own, it seemed that she had once more outmaneuvered us. Ilse didn't want to deal with her old husband's wrath at being stuck in a nursing home—let his daughters be the ones to tell him. Then she could go back to measuring the wing span of storm petrels, or researching the nesting habits of pelagic birds, or whatever it was she did, while we hauled his molting old seagull carcass away.

Or that's how it seemed to me at the time, though even then I had the feeling that I was missing something, some confusing undercurrent running just below the surface of this encounter. Ilse was not a wicked person, only phlegmatic and self-absorbed. Her tone was most likely not as clipped as I heard it, her reddened eyes not impersonal but full of guilt and worry and exhaustion and panic. But during those few minutes in that narrow foyer, I was overcome by the feeling that nothing had changed, that once more I was a frightened, furious teenager, and that if I stayed in that house another half hour, I'd be calling her Else and making snide comments about cuckoo clocks.

"You old bitch," said Frances, breaking her silence.

I don't think I'd heard Frances insult anyone since she was seventeen, when she'd decided almost overnight to adopt a Victorian code of conduct that excluded saying anything overtly unpleasant—the same code that now required her to use teacups instead of mugs, and forgo overhead lighting, and insist that Jane would feel better if she stopped wearing so much black.

"I want a list," Frances began sputtering now, her voice high and breathy, almost childlike. "I want a list of every dime he's spent on you and I want it back."

"There is no money," said Ilse, a small humiliating smile playing about her lips, "if that is what you came for."

"Liar."

"Frances." I reached to take her arm. Frances continued to glare at Ilse, while Ilse gazed back at her. She looked more interested, than anything else, in what Frances would say next. I might have even caught a quiver of pity in the attentive way she examined Frances's face.

"Is that what you think I have had with him?" she asked finally. "Some life of leisure?"

Frances was almost panting. "Oh, go to hell," she said, ridiculously.

Ilse gave another little smile, as if she weren't seeing Frances at all but only someone pretending to be Frances. "I was very young then," she repeated. "But I am not young anymore." Then she sighed and pushed at her pale hair.

At that moment I found myself actually feeling sorry for Ilse, for her skeletal years of tending an old man and satisfying her appetites only at meals, watching the sunset every evening from a picture window. No children of her own for company, his never visiting. She had indeed been young when she married my father. By my reckoning, Ilse couldn't be more than a few years past fifty now.

"Well, take care of him," she told Frances. "You have waited long enough."

An eloquent look of dislike passed between them, though once again there seemed to be something else as well, a kind of concurrence that I did not understand, as if something had been finally agreed upon that had previously been in doubt.

But perhaps even then I'd begun to get an inkling, because the next moment I heard myself say to Ilse, "Just out of curiosity, suppose we decide to leave right now without him. What about that?"

"Then he goes to a motel." Ilse's lips drew back, exposing both rows of her square white teeth.

I pictured my father sitting alone in his wheelchair beside an empty swimming pool, a fluorescent pink VACANCY sign winking behind him, one letter burnt out.

"You wouldn't do it," I said.

Ilse shrugged. "People are always doing things no one thought they would do." Then, raising her eyebrows, she gave Frances the strangest look, almost a warning look, as if the two of them were speaking over my head, the way adults do around children.

"I don't know what you're talking about," I said.

"No?" Ilse held my gaze for another moment, then gave a final shrug and led the way into the living room, where my father was waiting for us.

FRANCES MUST HAVE prepared me better than I thought, or maybe I'd prepared myself over the past weeks of reading brochures about whirlpools and physical therapy, because the sight of him was not a shock but rather confirmatory. He sat bonelessly in his wheelchair, his mouth sagging to one side, his skin the color of damp paper towels. Eyes dull, nose tumid, neck a tidepool of wattles. A mollusk in a blue blazer.

Worse to remember what he had been: Slim, very upright and fastidious—sprightly, if that word didn't imply girlishness. A head of thick auburn hair and that glossy little red moustache, which he used to stroke between his thumb and forefinger. His face long, fine, triangular. The same shape, in fact, as Frances's.

He was always moving in those days, fiddling with his tie or a button on his jacket, snapping his fingers, glancing around, growling demands or complaints or funny, disparaging comments. Impatience seemed to galvanize him, like electricity. Even in the coldest weather he went without a hat or scarf, leaving his coat open, a man of barely contained internal combustion. My mother, on the other hand, had had poor circulation and was often cold. She aged very quickly, as chronically ill people do, while he continued to transmit itchy vigor and a youthful sure-footedness, springing up on the balls of his feet as he walked, climbing stairs two at a time. Now he was bloated and shriveled, with a fat abdomen and spindly arms. A straggle of thin gray whiskers hung from his cheeks.

Heidi's goat, I thought, before I could stop myself.

Litter surrounded his wheelchair: Styrofoam cups and paper plates, dirty napkins, piles of old newspapers, some gone yellow. The rest of the cottage was, at least as far as I could tell, as neat as it had been the last time I saw it, except for this one corner of the living room, which Ilse had ceded to my father. Wisps of steam trailed over his head, issuing from a round plastic vaporizer that whispered behind him. The bad smell I'd noticed earlier was stronger here. For a moment I was afraid I might be sick.

"Well, we made it," Frances announced at my elbow. "Just like the postman. Through snow and sleet." Gratefully, I realized she was trying to sound unflappable, which must have cost her something after that ugly skirmish with Ilse. She stepped over an open box of doughnuts. "Hi, Dad."

He snarled something that sounded like "Get out."

Frances blinked. "I'm sorry, Dad? What was that?" She turned to me with an apprehensive look. "What did he say?"

Ilse had come up behind us, carrying what looked like a black leather bowling bag. MEDICATIONS was written on a strip of masking tape on one side. She smiled curtly. "You will understand him better when you spend more time with him." Then she busied herself with rotating his wheelchair so that it faced the foyer. With an effort she managed to roll the wheelchair right over a drift of newspapers.

Stepping back, she gestured for me to take the handles as if she were a pilot handing over the controls. "It is not going to snow here," she said, as I began pushing the wheelchair toward the door. "It has not snowed once all fall. We do not usually get snow until Christmas."

With Ilse's help, I navigated my father's wheelchair out of the cottage and down the walkway, where I parked him next to the minivan. He sat barking out furious vocables. "Ha!" he cried, his face turning blotchy and purplish. "Hey!"

"Don't worry, Dad," said Frances firmly, but looking scared. "Everything's going to be all right."

Then he stopped saying anything, his hands lying open on his knees like an empty pair of gloves. Frances went back into the cottage with Ilse to get his suitcases and boxes, leaving me to keep watch on him. I turned my face toward the bay, inhaling the fresh briny air.

"Well, Dad," I began. I was waiting for him to shout at me, as he had done so often when I was younger, pointing and snapping his fingers, growling at me to be quiet so he could hear the weather report on the radio, or the baseball score, or a commercial for razor blades. I even expected him to hit me with one of those limp-looking hands, and half hoped he would, so that I could feel justified for not caring what happened to him. But he never looked in my direction.

Together Frances and Ilse made several trips from the house to the car, loading suitcases and boxes in the back of the van. "I guess that's it," said Frances. We helped my father into the backseat and belted him in. Again I expected him to protest and thrash around, but he was compliant enough, motionless once we'd got him settled in his seat. Ilse handed in his overcoat and an old dented gray fedora. Then she demonstrated how to fold and unfold the wheelchair, which was stowed last. Frances climbed into the passenger seat once more and sat looking down at her lap. Ilse had gone to stand near the Japanese maple, one hand shading her eyes, though the day was still overcast. The back of her white blouse luffed in the breeze.

"Good-bye," I said. Then I surprised myself by adding, "I'm sure he'll miss you."

"He never cared so much for me," said Ilse.

She stepped over to the curb and stooped to peer in at the old man inside the van. He refused to look at her but sat staring out at a lantern-shaped bird feeder set on an aluminum pole near the driveway.

"Be well, Robert Fiske," she said. When I looked again she was up the stone-flagged path, shutting the door to their cottage.

To postpone the moment when I would have to be alone with my father and Frances, I walked over and picked two or three of the brown hydrangea flowers. There wasn't anything more to do—no further ceremony marking the end of this part of my father's life and ushering him and his boxes into what was left—so with a final look at the bay, I got into the van and laid the flowers on the dashboard. Maybe during the drive to Boston I'd ask my father why he'd held on to that organ all these years, when he'd got rid of everything else. But probably Ilse hadn't told him about that, either, that she'd forged his name and signed the thing over to Frances.

Donated his organ.

I shocked myself by laughing out loud.

"What?" Frances looked whitely over at me.

"*Stop*," she hissed, leaning over the emergency brake. "Stop laughing."

I found a tissue in my coat pocket and blew my nose, then took several deep breaths before starting the car.

"So, Dad," said Frances, as we pulled away from the curb, her voice as cheerful as if we were taking him out to the movies. "Off we go."

When he gave no response from the backseat, Frances turned to smile at him, then quickly turned back around.

"Shouldn't we tell him?" I murmured. "Where we're heading?"

"No," said Frances, her smile still fixed. "Not now."

But as Buzzards Bay disappeared behind us, followed by the cottage with its green lawn, the Japanese maple and the tidy hydrangeas, I glanced into the rearview mirror at my father's pale slack face and saw that of course he knew where he was headed, even if no one was going to tell him.

The affair between Dad and Ilse began the summer before Frances was a high-school junior and I was a freshman. My mother had been sick all that summer, so sick that we couldn't go to the house in Wellfleet we usually rented for the month of August. Instead Helen ferried Frances and me back and forth from the West Hartford Country Club pool in a little orange VW Beetle that my father bought secondhand from a neighbor. The plan had been that Frances would take over this job after Helen went to college, but Frances kept failing her driving test. When Helen left for Wellesley at the end of August, Ilse was hired as an informal chauffeur and given use of the VW Beetle in exchange for driving Frances and me to the pool in the afternoons. She drove us to the dentist and to doctors' appointments, and once to buy school clothes downtown. In September, when school began, she was hired to coach Frances in math and science two afternoons a week, because Frances's grades were poor and my father was afraid she wouldn't get into a good college. Ilse was a graduate student in biology at UConn. A friend of my mother's whose husband was the department chair had recommended her.

A bit of company for the girls, the friend probably said. *A little distraction.*

But soon enough, people must have seen what was going on, that the wrong company had been distracted. Someone must have tried to interfere, especially in the first weeks after my mother died, when it became clear that Ilse had moved into our house. I like to imagine that one of the neighborhood mothers met Ilse in the supermarket, firmly blocking the aisle with her grocery cart.

I'm sorry, but would you mind telling me what's going on here? Those girls have just lost their mother.

Then again, Ilse was not easy to talk to. Back then her English was imperfect, for one thing, which often made her sound coldly formal even during casual exchanges ("May I compose for you an egg?" she asked me once at breakfast). This unsociable impression was underlined by those severe eyeglasses and her habit of calling my father by his full name. But to be fair, there had always been a shyness about Ilse and, in the case of Frances and me, a reluctance to address our confusion and resentments straightforwardly, perhaps because she didn't understand what to do for us and was afraid that we would fall upon her, like wolves, at the first sign of uncertainty. She had indeed been young, only in her midtwenties.

It was hardest on Frances when Ilse moved in. She refused even to speak to Ilse and, if she absolutely had to request something from her, would go to elaborate lengths to request it through me. With our father she adopted a shrill, wisecracking tone, calling him "Oldster" and "Grandpa" at every opportunity. Whenever he put on a raincoat she called him the Ancient Mariner. Frances had always been our father's favorite. Willing to go for walks with him in the evening when he got home from work; play games of Scrabble; laugh at his jokes. She did not deplore him, like Helen, or sulk at him, like me. I suppose after enjoying so many years of preference, Frances could not understand how he could suddenly prefer Ilse.

We were not invited to attend the ceremony when our father and Ilse got married that spring under the Tuscan columns inside Hartford's City Hall, but neither was anyone else, except my father's lawyer. Frances and I were both in boarding school in New Hampshire by then, hastily enrolled after Christmas. For their honeymoon, my father and Ilse planned to take a cruise to the Arctic Circle. His indemnity company was sold to Aetna at around the same time, and it seemed prudent to retire. The business had been losing money for years.

And people in the neighborhood were talking. A cousin of my mother's had written to the office of the Connecticut Medical Examiner, asking about an inquest, though nothing came of it but the rumors that followed. It was the neighbors who'd told our cousin about Ilse, how she'd moved in two weeks after my mother died. *Going in and out the front door like she owns the place. He's old enough to be her father.* They hinted to the cousin that my mother might have been given something. Slipped an overdose of one of her medications. It was clear who could have done such a thing: a man who buried his wife and took up with a foreign blonde girl practically the next day.

Meanwhile Ilse did her calisthenics in our living room every morning, in tights and leotards, by the French doors, in full view of the men on the street driving by on their way to work. She made her own yogurt in squat plastic containers. My father bought her a little dog, a dachshund; in the evenings she walked it through the neighborhood, her topknot bobbing. By April, when Ilse and my father got married, the whispering was loud enough that even Ilse, with her imperfect English, was disturbed. And so off they went. No house. No furniture. No children. They sold the VW Beetle. They even gave away the dog. It wasn't as hard as you might think. Get rid of one thing, then another; it becomes quite easy. Simple Living, they probably thought of it. Doing Without.

I was recalling this history of my father and Ilse as we stopped at a McDonald's for lunch, because I still could not fathom why Ilse had turned him out of their house. Nothing that had taken place in their cottage this morning explained it. He had been old for a long time. She'd been in the habit of looking after him for years. Even given my father's stroke and the additional care he required, I could not figure it out.

Ilse never would have allowed my father to eat at a McDonald's, for instance, but when I suggested it, he did not object. I ordered for all of us from the car window into a speakerphone set into a gigantic lit-up menu, though my father didn't answer when I asked him what he wanted. So I ordered him a hamburger and a Coke and the same for myself. Frances only wanted a cup of tea, which they didn't have.

After we got our order, I pulled into the parking lot, where it took us several minutes to arrange my father's meal for him in the cardboard tray that had been provided. I saw him watch Frances's hands shake as she spread a paper napkin on his lap. He ignored his Coke and did not touch his hamburger. When I was done with my lunch I handed his tray to Frances and took mine; together we walked over to a yellow trash barrel beside the restaurant doors.

I tried to speak matter-of-factly. "Listen, Frances. We can't just arrive at this place without him knowing what's going to happen."

"I don't know what to say." Frances was once again looking frightened.

"Just say, I'm sorry, Dad. I don't know what Ilse let you think, but you can't live with me. I've got too much to take care of as it is."

Frances gazed at me helplessly.

"There's your work," I prompted. "And Walter's schedule."

My father said nothing when we got into the van, but I could see in the rearview mirror that he was clutching his knees. Knobby-looking knees, jutting uncomfortably under the woolen fabric of his dark blue trousers.

Once we were back on the highway, I waited for Frances to begin. She sat with her hands tightly folded, gazing out her window at the scrub pines and the occasional rocky outcropping, laced with snow.

"Frances?" I said. "Isn't there something you wanted to say?"

She turned toward me with a stricken expression.

"Something you wanted to tell Dad?"

She grimaced, then shook her head.

"Thanks a lot," I muttered.

"Dad?" I said loudly, keeping my eyes on the road. "Frances and I want you to know that we've found a nice place for you to live, not far from her house. A really good place, where you'll get the appropriate sort of care."

Appropriate. A cold finical word that I'd always disliked. But I went on to describe the physical therapy program at Greenswood Manor, the adjustable meal plan and the spacious grounds, mentioning that Frances had visited a number of residences over the past few weeks and had chosen this one as the best. "Very sanitary," I added, thinking that maybe this, at least, might appeal to him, after that moat of dirty plates and doughnut boxes.

He said nothing. I couldn't tell if he was surprised, or relieved, or whether he'd even been listening. He pretended to be asleep for the rest of the drive.

The sun came out near Brockton. Frances tapped her trembling fingers together and hummed. Every now and then she would start to say something, then change her mind and go back to humming.

"What's with your hands?" I asked around Braintree. We'd reached the outskirts of Boston, the gray harbor in the distance, and the wharves and warehouses, the rickety triple-decker houses by the highway where even in winter people hang sheets and underwear on the lines between back porches.

"Just cold," she said, almost inaudibly.

"They were shaking yesterday, too."

"I'm *cold*," repeated Frances, tucking her hands inside her coat sleeves.

Soon we were on the Mass Pike and a few minutes later taking the Watertown exit. Frances directed me through a residential area full of modest capes and duplexes, American flags fluttering over the doorways. Light was draining steadily out of the afternoon, sinking into the trees and darkening the streets to a slate-colored blue.

The entrance to the nursing home was just off a main thoroughfare, set back from the street by a parking lot and a sloping lawn. Feathery white pines shielded the view of a neighboring service station and a supermarket, apparently the extent of the spacious grounds. Greenswood Manor itself was a long L-shaped, two-story building, constructed of that staring yellow brick so often used for municipal courthouses and Greek Orthodox churches. In the parking lot I found a space in front of the cement walkway, which led to a set of automatic glass front doors.

"Here we are," I announced.

Still he said nothing. Getting him out of the car proved harder than getting him into it. He refused to give us any assistance; in fact, his door was locked when we went around to his side, and I wondered if he'd locked it while Frances and I were opening the trunk and wrestling with his wheelchair (the keys, fortunately, were in my coat pocket). Once we had his wheelchair unfolded and set up by his door, he held on to the armrest of his seat, refusing to move. But just when I thought we'd have to drag him out, he allowed us to swing his feet onto the van's running board, then help him step down and ease him into the chair. After that I was able to push him up the walkway and into the building without any trouble.

A young Haitian nurse was sitting behind the reception desk. She took my father's and Frances's names, then smiled shyly and pointed to a waiting area around the corner, promising to let the director know we'd arrived. We rolled my father into an atrium-like common room, which had a curved wall of long glass windows that appeared not to have been washed in several years, the whitish film of accumulated dirt cutting down, however, on the glare from the lowering sun. A wide-screen TV was bolted onto another wall, faced by rectangular sofas and square chairs upholstered in shades of toast. Several elderly men were sitting on the chairs, one staring at the floor, two reading newspapers.

We sat down by windows overlooking a cluster of leafless syringa bushes. My gaze kept sliding down to my father's black wingtip shoes, which Ilse must have polished for him. They had the oily sheen of anthracite. Television babble floated toward us from a corridor, accompanied by the humid, rather comforting smell of starchy unspiced food being prepared in large quantities in an invisible kitchen. Frances stared at the squares on the linoleum floor. My father closed his eyes.

We waited ten or fifteen minutes. The two old men rustled their newspapers. A few nurses in pale green scrubs walked by. At last a heavy, copper-skinned woman came threading her way toward us through the chairs, calling out, "Mrs. Rosenfeld?"

Her voice had a pleasant islandy lilt to it. West Indian, maybe. Frances and I stood up. With an empty smile, Frances asked the woman to please call her Frances, then she introduced me as Cynthia. The woman nodded but introduced herself as "Ms. Watson" and reminded Frances that they had spoken several times on the phone. She looked to be about my age, with a short afro of apricot-colored hair. She wore a peacock blue dress and red patent-leather toeless high-heeled sandals, an outfit chosen, it seemed to me, to enliven her surroundings as much as possible. Around her neck hung a plastic beaded necklace, which might have been strung by a resident during Organized Activities.

"Hello, Mr. Fiske," she said, bending down to smile into his face. She took one of his hands between hers. "Nice to meet you."

Then she straightened up and in the next breath declared that she was very surprised to see us.

"Surprised?" I echoed.

Ms. Watson continued to address herself to Frances, who still wore that empty little smile. "I thought I had made it very clear the last time we spoke, Mrs. Rosenfeld. We do not yet have the opening we anticipated."

"What? I'm sorry, what did you say? I'm his other daughter," I explained, when Ms. Watson glanced questioningly at me.

"We anticipate there will an opening for Mr. Fiske." Her broad face remained polite, though now more guarded. "But at present we do not have one."

"I don't understand," said Frances tentatively.

"You don't have an opening?" I said.

Ms. Watson gazed down at my father. "I am sorry, Mr. Fiske, for your inconvenience."

"There's no room for him tonight?" I repeated foolishly.

"I am very sorry," she told me, the lilt to her voice becoming more pronounced. "But I believe I made myself very clear on this, you know, to Mrs. Rosenfeld here, when we spoke last week."

"Frances?" I said, feeling like a latecomer to a long, complicated conversation. "What's this about?"

Frances's smile had vanished. "Of course there's an opening," she said. "They're just trying to get us to pay for a more expensive room. I hear about this kind of thing all the time."

"I assure you"—Ms. Watson gave her an austere look—"there is no room available."

"No room at the inn," said my father suddenly. His voice was low and slurry, as if he were speaking through a mouthful of ice cubes.

"What, Dad?" said Frances. "Did you need something?"

"He needs a room," I told her, my face growing hot. "And it doesn't look like he's going to get one here. At least not today."

"Nonsense." Frances was still gazing at my father. "This is some kind of a mistake. Or someone's trying to take advantage of us."

"No one is taking advantage of you, Mrs. Rosenfeld."

Ms. Watson frowned at Frances, while behind her the long dirty windows glowed with vanishing afternoon light. How pushy Frances must seem to her. How entitled, with her "nonsense," her fussy worries about being taken advantage of. But Frances was always clumsy with people she was trying to get to do something for her. It was one of her few flaws.

I beckoned to Ms. Watson and the two of us moved several steps away from my father's wheelchair.

"If you don't mind, could we go over this again?" I lowered my voice. "Just so I understand. My sister called you a month or so ago and asked about putting my father on your waiting list. And you told her that you expected to have an opening."

"Your sister and I have had several conversations about an opening for your father," interrupted Ms. Watson. "We have a great deal of demand at present. Especially for acute care."

"But she said she's been calling to check on the waiting list, and you spoke to her last week—"

"I told her there wasn't an opening."

Frances had joined us by then. She glanced uncertainly at me. "I remember her saying that a space *would* be available. That's what I heard her say."

I kept my eyes on Ms. Watson. "Did you say *when* you expected an opening?"

"I said I would let her know when we had one."

"And a van. Did you say you had a van that might be able to go get him?"

"We do have a van, yes." Ms. Watson sounded puzzled. "I probably mentioned that. We do sometimes provide transportation for new residents."

Frances gave me a level look. "Cynnie. There's been a mix-up. That's all."

I ignored her. "But you don't have an opening today?" When Ms. Watson shook her head, I said, "Is there any way that—"

That she hurry along the resident who was lingering so inconveniently? Fix up a bed in the supply closet? Whatever it was that had prompted the beginning of my question, it did not reach my mind as a full-blown idea and I stopped abruptly, too rattled by

Frances's inexplicable misunderstanding to chase down whatever possibility had slipped past me.

A buzzer sounded. From a distance came the sound of voices, one of them raised in a nearby room. "I didn't *say* that," said the voice, reedy with frustration. "I didn't *say* I wanted my dinner tray put *there*. What I *said* was—"

"We're not leaving," said Frances, "until you find him a room."

Ms. Watson laced her hands together. "I am very sorry," she told me, turning decisively away from Frances. "When we have an opening, I will be sure to telephone you."

"Oh *please*," cried Frances, her voice grating in that quiet room full of dusty windows. "We've just driven two hours from the Cape. What are we supposed to do?"

Ms. Watson suggested that we might have to drive back again, adding once more that she was very sorry but that she had nothing to offer us.

Frances unfolded her arms and pointed dramatically at my father. In her long black cashmere coat, she looked queenly and bleak, the opposite in every way from Ms. Watson in her crayon-bright clothes; yet Frances had also, it seemed to me, dressed to set a certain tone. And for the second time that day I found myself wondering what I might be missing, what stabilizing piece of information lay just beyond my reach.

"His wife won't let him back in the house. *Look* at him," she demanded, in a voice that must have carried all the way to the automatic front doors and out to the bare syringa bushes. "Look at him," she cried. "He's old and sick. He has nowhere to live. He can't take care of himself. Have a little Christian sympathy. It's two days before Thanksgiving."

Ms. Watson gave Frances a faint smile that seemed to imply that her plea for Christian sympathy was misdirected. "I have no choice in this matter, Mrs. Rosenfeld. I suggest you take your father home with you. Perhaps after the holiday, you know, things will have changed."

"He's had a *stroke*."

"Try to be patient, Mrs. Rosenfeld."

Ms. Watson glanced toward the old men in their windbreakers, who had been observing this altercation over the tops of their newspapers with a marked lack of interest, as if our little gun battle amid the brown chairs hardly registered in the high seas of incorrectly placed dinner trays. Then she looked hard once more at Frances, who dropped her arm.

"Mrs. Rosenfeld," she said quietly. "There is nothing I can offer your father tonight. You'll have to do what you can for him for the present."

"For the present?" repeated Frances, as if she had no idea what that meant.

At Ms. Watson's suggestion, we made a detour on our way home to stop at a medical supply shop in Watertown, where Frances rented a special stool so that my father could sit down in the shower, as well as a chrome contraption that fit over the toilet to give him railings to hold on to for support. Frances had neglected to bring along her cell phone when we left that morning, and we'd been too distracted at Greenswood Manor to think of calling from there, so we hadn't phoned ahead to tell Walter of the change in plans. By the time we got back to Concord and drove up the steep gravel driveway, it was almost six o'clock.

As we crested the dark drive, an odd thing happened: The house, fully lit, seemed to surge up at us suddenly like a stone steamboat, bearing down across a black river of lawn. Every window was ablaze, the curtains pulled back, light pouring out onto the dusky swells of surrounding shrubbery. A lavender plume of smoke curled from the chimney, drifting into the evening sky.

It wasn't until I'd turned off the ignition and leaned back in my seat that I remembered Sarah and her friend were expected to arrive that evening and that Walter must have wanted the house to look welcoming for them.

A thin, distant howl sounded from the woods.

"Coyotes," Frances said, from a dark pocket beside me.

"You're kidding."

"They've moved into the woods around here. We have deer and foxes, too."

I could see Walter and Jane moving past the unshuttered windows in the kitchen. Jane was lifting a pot of something from the stove. My dream about Mrs. Jordan and her story of the old man came back to me.

"So, besides the wild kingdom, who lived here before you?"

In all the years Frances and Walter had owned their house, I'd never bothered to ask this question. It was a wreck when they bought it: rotting windowsills, holes in the roof, squirrels in the attic. Frances had spent almost a decade restoring that house, and yet I'd never been curious about it. Houses were not in my purview, since I never expected to own one myself; also I suppose I was envious. The less I thought about Frances's house the better. Even now I was simply stalling before beginning the process of hauling out my father's wheelchair, unfolding it and persuading him to climb into it. Frances didn't move, either.

"Some people named Prence owned the house," she said. "An accountant and his wife. She died, then he did."

"Here?"

"In Florida, I think."

"Good place to die," said my father from the backseat. His breathing had sounded labored, almost stertorous, when we left Greenswood Manor, but it was more regular now.

"What?" Frances looked startled. "What did he say?"

I was surprised that she hadn't been able to understand him but decided that now wasn't the time to explain. "I think he's just glad to be here."

Frances nodded then craned her neck around to smile briefly at him. As she opened her door, the van's overhead light went on and the cool brisk scent of leaf mold and a whiff of skunk stirred in through the open door.

"So," she said, "I guess this is it."

But I could have sworn I caught a look of suppressed excitement on her face, the same expression that I'd imagined the day before, when she led me into the living room to show me her latest find.

SARAH HAD CALLED while we were on the Cape to say that she and her friend weren't coming until tomorrow; they would take a noon train from New York, after attending a rally of some kind at Columbia. By the time we received this explanation from Walter, without yet offering one of our own ("Later," Frances said, hardly bothering to glance up at him), we had parked my father in the living room and returned to the kitchen. Frances stood warming her hands over a pot on the stove. Clad in a sweatshirt and sweatpants, Walter was leaning his elbows against a counter.

"She'll be here tomorrow," he repeated.

When we'd first appeared at the back door with Dad in his wheelchair, that gangsterish fedora clapped on to his head, I'd had the impression that Walter was not entirely surprised to see him with us. This impression deepened as I watched him stand patiently in his running clothes, waiting for Frances to say something.

"There wasn't a room for him," I said finally.

Walter lifted his eyebrows at Frances.

"It's just for a few days," I said.

For dinner Walter had heated a rotisserie chicken he'd picked up on his way home from the hospital, which he served with peas and white rice on Frances's Blue Willow china. Frances had been collecting Blue Willow china, piece by piece, for years. She loved the calm scenes of willow trees and pagodas and curving footbridges, all uninhabited I realized, as I looked at my plate. Walter sat between me and my father on one side of the table, with Frances and Jane across from us. Jane had lit candles in the dining room and set the long cherrywood trestle table with cloth napkins folded into fans. Frances did not remark on her fan-shaped napkin but simply shook it out and put it in her lap.

Everyone was self-conscious, given my father's presence, but we all behaved well, at least for most of the meal. Jane went out of her way to be considerate, helping him from his wheelchair and into a ladder-backed chair, asking him repeatedly if there was anything he needed. It amazed me to see him sitting there like a ghost on the other side of Walter. The thin skin on his forehead was the spotted, vulnerable color of a dog's belly and his hair was so white it was almost transparent. If I'd found it hard to look at him without his moustache during that lunch in Barnstable, the sight of him was almost unbearable now.

Against the wall I was facing stood a mellow old oak dresser Frances used as a sideboard, its handles carved to look like acorns; according to Frances, it had once gone west in a covered wagon, only to come back again. Above the dresser hung a primitive oil of a jowly, tight-lipped woman in a mob cap, a lace fichu around her neck, her dark eyes as tiny as an elephant's. Long ago Sarah and Jane had dubbed her the "Common Ancestor"; they insisted her eyes followed you if you moved around the room. A few gaunt dignified old wooden farm tools hung on the opposite wall.

Everything in Frances's house had a charming story attached, usually of how it was rescued at the last moment from the trash or
from the hands of Philistines ("They were going to *paint* it!"),
and I reflected, not for the first time, that almost nothing in my
apartment had ever belonged to anyone else, or would be wanted
by anyone else, either.

Walter was trying to explain to me why managed health care
was a failure, perhaps to allow Frances to settle down and eat
her dinner. Not that she ate much. My father ate almost nothing.
Whenever he raised his fork, whatever was on it fell off. Jane tried
to help him by cutting up his chicken, but in the end she got up
from the table, with a scathing look at her mother, who was sitting
back in her chair with her eyes closed, and went into the kitchen.
A minute later she came back with a spoon and a carton of peach-
flavored yogurt. He didn't eat much more of that, but it was an
improvement over the odds he faced against rice and peas.

"There's no such thing as managed care in this country," Walter
was saying to me. "What we have now is unmanageable care."

Walter was doing a sturdy job of behaving as though my father's
arrival were no more inconvenient than if Sarah had come home
with a second college friend for Thanksgiving. My father himself did not participate in the conversation beyond a few grunts,
though he seemed perfectly alert, especially every time he looked
at Frances. Then a slow kindling would come into his eyes, and
half his mouth lifted, as though he were trying to smile.

Walter and I got up to clear the dinner plates; Frances followed us into the kitchen a moment later, leaving Jane alone with
Dad. As we were putting dishes in the sink I heard Walter mutter,
"How am I supposed to deal with this?" Frances turned to him
blankly, as if to say, Deal with what? She didn't assure him that

everything would be all right or insist that our father would just be staying for a few days, until Greenswood Manor had an opening. She simply said she'd take care of the dishes.

Walter gave her a hard stare, then shrugged his shoulders. But he looked worried. It was usually Frances who looked worried, while Walter maintained an ironic distance from upsets and inconveniences. Worry, to Walter, was something extreme and personal, what you did when you had a grave illness. He saw that kind of worry every day. Frances's generalized worrying, about terrorist plots and derailed elections and whether antiques were going out of style, made no more sense to him than her finicky concern with keeping the linen smelling fresh or whether she had shortbread cookies to serve with Scottish tea.

Even so, Frances's worrying usually came across as "just being careful" and wanting to "take care of things." She married Walter when she was barely out of college, arguing at the time that it was silly to wait, that she wanted "to get on with life," though now I wonder if she was worried that she'd never meet anyone else as handsome and successful. The same was true of the house, which she'd insisted on buying despite its decrepitude because she might never again find "such a bargain in Concord." She approached worry pragmatically, going at it straight on, the way a carpenter might plane a board that was not quite level. And yet her attempts to alleviate her fears—like trying to persuade Sarah to leave New York and come home—could rise to the heroic, all while she maintained an attitude of efficient purpose. Even tonight, even after that unfortunate mix-up with the nursing home and my father suddenly on her doorstep, Frances didn't seem so much worried as distracted. She had barely spoken during dinner. But as I watched her hesitate over whether to use dessert forks or spoons, it struck me that she was trying to figure out how to pretend that my father was an ordinary houseguest instead of an intruder.

Once we sat down to dessert (a store-bought pumpkin pie bought by Walter, with vanilla ice cream), conversation in the dining room faltered, until finally it stopped altogether. A minute ticked past. I found myself locking eyes with the Common Ancestor, turning my head from side to side.

Then Frances said abruptly, "Cynnie's book is wonderful."

"My book?" I said, caught off guard.

Everyone had turned toward me, even my father.

I smiled deprecatingly and picked up my wineglass. "It's still mostly just an outline. Frances read a few pages today in the car."

"Oh, come on," she cried, her face suddenly animated. "It's wonderful. You can tell them something about it, can't you?"

"It always sounds stupid when I start talking about it."

"Cynthia is writing about Mark Twain's daughters," Frances explained to Dad, who was across the table from her. She spoke slowly and loudly, although as far as I knew his hearing hadn't been affected by his stroke. "About him and his daughters and their life in Hartford."

"Well, that sounds great," Walter said kindly to me.

"Cynthia does a beautiful job of capturing them," continued Frances. "There were three girls, just like in our family, and they used to put on plays. They even did a play of Twain's *Prince and the Pauper,* as a surprise for him. And it was so good he made them do it again for all the neighbors and insisted on being in it himself."

"Well, I think he kind of *took over* the play," I interjected. "I'm not sure how the girls felt about it. There's this one bizarre photograph"—I turned to Jane, thinking she might appreciate some of the stranger aspects of the Clemens family—"of Twain dressed in drag, with a bonnet on his head. He's kicking up one leg and holding on to Susy, the oldest girl, who looks horrified. Actually, she looks more resigned—"

"Tell about Twain dressing up as Santa Claus." Frances's face was pink as she poured herself a second glass of wine. "It's the sweetest thing."

Walter shifted in his chair. "I heard Cynthia's going to go down to Hartford to see his house while she's here."

"I was hoping to go tomorrow—"

"A trip down memory lane," Frances said, fingering the stem of her wineglass. "Get Cynthia to tell you about the crazy notes the girls used to carry back and forth between the parents."

"They weren't crazy," I said, looking at her.

"Funny, I meant. His were funny."

I was beginning to feel dazed and immobilized, the way I imagine people must feel when they are about to be overcome by an allergic reaction to something they didn't realize they were allergic to.

"Twain was funny as a *writer*," I said stiffly, after a moment. "But at home he was kind of a monster."

"Oh, I'm sure he was difficult. But not a *monster*—"

"Mom," muttered Jane. "It's her book."

"But he *loved* those little girls. You have it all in your outline, Cynnie. The Christmas presents. The stories he made up for them—"

"Frances," said Walter gently.

Frances was usually the most diplomatic of conversationalists, perfectly attuned to other people's discomfort and restlessness, adept at switching to new topics, even if she had to resort to making fun of herself to do so. Which she did at just that moment by slapping a palm to her forehead and saying, "Oh, for Pete's sake. I'm sorry, Cynnie. Here I am going on and on like an old kook. I just got so excited. Their story just seems so *real*.

"It must be fabulous," she went on, her eyes gleaming in the candlelight, "to get to sit at home and figure all this out and choose what you want to tell from what happened."

I'd always known that at times Frances envied my freewheeling life, which could be arranged and rearranged and then left undisturbed—there was no one but me to knock my lampshades askew. Of course we both knew that I envied her life even more, for its settled commotion: the comings and goings of children, the husbandly phone calls about picking up something for dinner, the reliable everyday stir around meals and homework and clearing the table. Never in her life would Frances be greeted by a cold look of surprise, in an unfamiliar bed, on a morning when she had overstayed her welcome.

"You've always been such a good storyteller," she added placatingly.

"Well," I said, somewhat mollified, "in the *real* story Twain wasn't such a great father." I looked down at my plate, aware suddenly of my own father, sitting on the other side of Walter. "He was very unpredictable. He'd fly into terrible rages about little things, anything, like missing shirt buttons or the soup being cold. One minute he'd be laughing, the next minute screaming. I guess these days he'd probably be diagnosed as manic depressive."

"*These* days," repeated Frances, interrupting me once more. "These days everybody's got a diagnosis. I read the other day that Nabokov probably had Asperger's syndrome. And scientists all have obsessive-compulsive disorder. Anybody interesting has something wrong with him."

She picked up her fork and looked at the slice of pie on her plate as if she couldn't recall how it got there. Her ice cream had melted into a puddle.

"How about his wife?" she asked suddenly. "She was supposed to be lovely. Didn't she make Christmas baskets for poor people? Everybody loved her."

"Livy Clemens was an invalid."

Frances put down her fork reasonably. "But isn't that what a lot of women were in those days, especially if they had difficult husbands? Neurasthenics. I was just reading something about it."

"Livy was paralyzed for two years after going skating as a teenager and falling on the ice." I was annoyed at being goaded into divulging this information yet proud of knowing it. "She was never totally well after that. A faith healer finally got her out of bed by pulling up the window shades. But she died of hyperthyroid heart disease."

"Weird," said Jane, looking interested for the first time since this conversation began.

"As for the daughters," I went on, before Frances could interrupt me again, "the oldest died of spinal meningitis when she was in her early twenties. The youngest was an epileptic, who drowned in her bath on Christmas morning in her thirties. After staying up all night wrapping presents for her father."

Frances made a hoarse little noise. Then, as if to stop herself from further protest, she reached out to square a pewter candlestick.

"So what about the middle one?" Jane was pulverizing the pie crust on her plate, pinching it between her fingers. "Didn't you say there were three daughters?"

"Clara outlived everybody. She was the only one who got married."

I was watching Frances as I said this and caught a flicker of relief on her face.

"Did she have any kids?" asked Jane.

"One daughter."

"What happened to her?"

I tried to ignore the feeling that it was indecent to be talking about Mark Twain's daughters in this way. Trotting out my facts and nuggets. Showing off how much I knew about their troubles. When they had been private people, as private as I was myself, full of painful reservations about who they were and what was expected of them, not forthcoming to strangers who would, of course, have been curious. I could see them so plainly, standing in front of their fancy brick house, with its turrets and balconies and porte cochere. Wearing yellowed white dresses of eyelet lace, black stockings and laced boots, their hair tied back with ribbons, their dark eyes sharp and distrustful.

But Frances's insistence on talking about my book as a confection (which it was) and her obvious identification with those charming little girls sitting at Daddy's feet, begging for another story, infuriated me, so I said, "Clara's daughter killed herself."

"She did?" Jane stopped playing with her pie crust.

"None of the family is left?" Frances had gone pale.

"Why did she kill herself?" said Jane.

"Maybe it's time to change the subject." Walter rested a hand on my arm.

I stayed very still, aware of the warmth of Walter's hand through the fabric of my blouse. In all the years I'd known Walter, he'd never indulged in any patronizing flirtation with me, which I've seen other men practice like golf swings on the unmarried women in their lives. To his credit, Walter must have sensed my attraction to him, or at least wondered at my awkwardness around him, but he acted always in the same disinterested, avuncular way toward me, his wife's younger sister. I found myself wishing I were alone with him, so that I could pour us each another glass of wine and explain everything to Walter that couldn't go in my book. About the daughters who had once been lively, ambitious, and high-strung, like their father, but who for reasons both within and beyond their control had not done well, though their father had loved them so much he would have liked to stuff them in his pipe and smoke them like the most marvelous tobacco. And about their mother, who was always about to die but managed to hang on longer than anyone would have predicted. Whom their father had also loved, tenderly, consumingly ("Dear gravity" he'd called her); yet he was unable to stop himself from having rages in her presence and making terrible confessions, then begging her forgiveness with equal passion, subjecting her to an exhausting regimen of tantrums and absolutions that went on for decades. Until during her last two years, including her final months in a drafty Florentine villa, which the family had rented in an effort to save her health, her doctors wouldn't allow him to visit her in her room except on special occasions, and then only for five minutes.

Such an intricate life this family had led, with all their hopes and disappointments, all their strange negotiations with each other. But now the girls were just curiosities. Remarkable mostly for their sad endings. I would have liked to explain all that to Walter, to the careful listening expression on his face, though as he took his hand off my arm I was also irritated to think that he was listening so carefully to me for Frances's sake, which was also why he now wanted me to stop talking.

"Of course, they weren't *always* miserable," I began.

"Maybe *she* should be your narrator." Frances was leaning intently toward me across the table. "Clara, the one who managed to go on."

Perhaps this last interruption, and the presumption behind it, was what made me say, "Here's another tidbit for you. Twain had a thing for young girls."

Frances looked shocked. "What?"

"He collected girls when he was an old man. He called them his 'Angelfish.' He wrote them letters, invited them to his house for lunch. Got them to dress up for him. In harem outfits."

I figured this disclosure would stop the conversation dead, but by the time I stopped speaking Frances had already recovered.

"Oh, they say that sort of thing about everybody." She made a wry mouth. "The minute somebody's famous, he gets called a pedophile."

"Mark Twain liked little girls?" Jane's eyes were wide.

"Has everyone had enough dessert?" Walter reached for Jane's plate and stacked it on top of his own.

"All people want to do," complained Frances, "is find the cracks in things."

I smiled to myself. Pinned over my desk in San Francisco was a white file card, on which I'd typed out a quote from an essay by Virginia Woolf: "If life has a base that it stands upon," the quote begins, "if it is a bowl that one fills and fills and fills . . ." The card was pinned to the wall above my mother's cracked Wedgwood bowl. A clever comment, I used to think, on the nature of memory, until Carita stopped by one afternoon and gave this arrangement a pitying look, noting that mordant humor was out of style. She did, however, approve of my plan to write a book about Virginia Woolf someday, from the perspective of her "backward," possibly autistic half sister Laura, the granddaughter of Thackeray. Even cracked bowls have their uses.

"But what did Twain *do* with those girls?" Jane was asking.

"Well, as far as I can tell," I admitted, "he mostly just played cards with them. Although there *is* one story about a girl who—"

"Wait! I just thought of something." Frances began clinking her fork against her dessert plate. "Here's something I just thought of. What if *she* was one of them? One of Twain's little girls?"

We all looked at her in confusion, which she seemed to enjoy, because she paused to take a prolonged sip of wine before she said, "Dad's mother."

Jane stared. "*What* are you talking about?"

"Our grandmother, Cynnie's and mine. There's a story Dad used to tell," she said to Walter, "that Mark Twain gave the organ to her."

"The one in the living room?" said Jane.

"But Dad made that story up." My head ached as I leaned forward to peer down the table at my father. "Twain did have an organ, but—"

"Well, there must be *some* kind of truth to the story." Frances took another sip from her wineglass. "Otherwise why'd he tell it?" She smiled playfully and I realized belatedly that she had been teasing me and that everything she'd said tonight, all her bright comments about my book, had probably been nothing more than an attempt to lighten an uncomfortable evening.

My father had remained quiet throughout this discussion, watching Frances and pushing at the pie on his plate with a spoon. In the brief silence that followed, he lifted his head to look back at me.

"Mark Twain," he said, in his rough, gargly voice. "Leave 'em alone. Leave 'em all back there."

"Are you getting a cough, Dad?" Frances set down her wineglass, looking concerned. "Walter? What do we have in the house for a cough?"

I started to correct her and explain what he'd actually said, but by then I'd drunk several glasses of wine myself, and my father's angry gaze, suddenly turned my way, made me pause. Up until now, every time I'd glanced at him he had been looking at Frances, an expression of almost childish enjoyment lifting the mobile side of his face, while the other side sagged in a frown, like one of those old-fashioned tragicomic masks.

"It's time to get you to bed," she told him gently.

On the ride to Concord that evening, Frances and I had held a terse conference about sleeping arrangements, agreeing that our father would not be able to climb the staircase to get to the second floor. He would have to be put downstairs in Walter and Frances's bedroom. She and Walter would sleep in the study. Sarah and her friend would be in Sarah's room. I would move in with Jane, who had bunk beds.

Frances and Walter's bedroom was off the kitchen—it was the house's original kitchen, in fact. At one end was an enormous old fieldstone fireplace, big enough inside for a child to stand upright. Frances had put skylights in the ceiling and installed a set of French doors leading out to a brick patio at the back of the house. Otherwise the room was furnished only with an iron bedstead, painted white, and so tall that you needed a wooden step to climb onto the mattress. Two closets held Frances's and Walter's clothes, cabinets in the adjoining bathroom contained personal items. Frances wouldn't allow anything else in the room, not a clock, not a phone, not even a rug on the wide pine board floors.

Given Frances's affinity for objects, it was curious that her bedroom was so stark—though Carita once remarked that I myself lived like a Bedouin, hardly bothering to unpack my suitcases even after two years in my present apartment. "When you've moved around as much as I have," I'd told her, implying romantic quandaries and hurried exits, "unpacking starts to seem like an act of faith." But mostly I'd moved from apartment to apartment because I didn't have much reason to be one place over another, which made it hard to want to stay anywhere for very long. You could say just the opposite for Frances, and yet here was that vacant room, her "refuge," she often said, where Walter had told me she was lately spending entire days.

Walter and Jane stood up and went off to find their coats, preparing to go out to the van to carry in my father's suitcases.

"Coming, Cynnie?" Frances had risen as well and I had little choice but to stand up, too.

"Here we go, Dad." A moment later she was wheeling the wheelchair up to the table and leaning down to help him stand. "When Walter comes back in he'll help you get ready for bed. We're putting you in our room. It's quiet and it gets a lot of light in the morning. I think you'll like it. It's very peaceful."

"Because it's empty," I joked, in revenge for Frances's teasing.

"Yes." Frances smiled cautiously at me. "Now, will you give me a hand, Cynnie, by opening the door?"

The headache that had been gathering behind my forehead all day had built into a thundercloud by the time I transferred my things from the study into Jane's bedroom. Fortunately Jane insisted that I didn't need to change the sheets on the sofa bed for Frances and Walter.

"You look pretty clean."

"Appearances can be deceiving," I mumbled.

Her own room was small and dark and square, painted a dusky purple. In addition to the bunk beds against one wall, covered with zebra-striped nylon spreads, the room was furnished with a dresser and a desk and chair, all of which had been painted a sticky-looking black. A black plastic beanbag chair slumped in one corner beside a very dirty pink shag rug. A small Sony television sat on a plastic milk crate in front of the beanbag chair. On the walls were posters of rock bands, baleful-looking young men in black with names like Insomniac and the Strokes spelled out in Gothic lettering. Books, magazines, spills of school papers, hair elastics, gum wrappers cluttered every surface, accompanied by the smell of unwashed underpants, Patchouli perfume and bubble-gum, which rose up threateningly at me as soon as I crossed the threshold. It was exactly the sordid bedroom one would expect for a girl like Jane, yet its ugliness was unnerving, not just because it was deliberate but because it seemed so methodical.

"Mom hates this room," said Jane with gloomy pride.

I tried to respond, but when I turned my head I saw flashes of forked lightning.

"I don't care what she thinks. She's totally losing it." Jane sat down cross-legged on the other end of the bunk. "And she hates me."

"She does not," I managed to say, sitting down on the bottom bunk.

"She does. You should hear her on the phone to her friends." Jane dropped her voice in a good imitation of Frances's cool breathy register: "The *stress* is really getting to me. It's getting *worse*. I don't know how long I can *take* it."

"How do you know she's talking about you?"

"Trust me," said Jane. "I know."

Ordinarily I would have loved a moment like this, when I could play the wise, hip aunt in whom the girls could confide about bad boyfriends or drug experimentation, listening while they complained about their mother, who didn't understand anything, who was sneaky and tyrannical and deliberately obtuse, who read their diaries, and wouldn't let them go to friends' houses unless she knew the parents would be home, whose very being was inimical to the tentative, cherished, ill-advised visions they were forming of themselves. In other words, a mother I would have given anything to have had myself. But tonight I was having trouble even speaking clearly. A few minutes before, Walter had given me a vial of aspirin with codeine and I had taken four pills when he'd told me to take two. Mercifully, I could feel my eyes starting to close.

"I'm sure all your friends feel the same way about their mothers."

"I don't have any friends," said Jane, with the same proud gloom.

"Do you think you could turn that off?" With an effort, I pointed to the gooseneck lamp on Jane's desk, which was angled toward me and shining interrogatively.

Jane got up and turned off the lamp, then bent down and switched on a little blue glass nightlight shaped like a flower and plugged into the wall socket. Then she turned off the other lamps in the room as well, so that we were bathed suddenly in soothing blue light. "How's that?"

"Much better. Thanks."

Jane was quiet for a few moments and I began to get ready for bed, aware that she was watching me as I stood up to unbutton my blouse and clumsily pull off my jeans, then drag my nightgown over my head.

"Were you your mother's favorite?" she asked suddenly.

"*My* mother?" I said, taken aback. "I'd say Helen was."

"Not my mom?"

"She was Dad's favorite."

Jane pondered this information for a few moments, staring at her black beanbag chair. "Why do you think Aunt Helen never got married?"

"She didn't want to," I said. "She liked living alone."

"Why?"

"I think she thought it was simpler."

"Is that what you think, too?"

"Sometimes," I allowed, feeling that I was about to say something disastrously wrong. "I guess mostly."

Jane fell silent again. Then she asked, "So what was she like? *Your* mother?"

"I didn't really know her that well. She was sick a lot."

"Were you and Mom there, the night she died?"

I hesitated then nodded, not sure where this interview was headed, or what had sparked it, wishing only that it would end soon.

"So, what happened?"

It was then that I realized Jane had been saving these questions up for some time. That she must have asked Frances the same ones but hadn't been satisfied with the answers, and now that Helen was gone there was no one else left to ask but me.

"Well, she was in her bed," I told her slowly, "as she usually was, you know, because she was sick. That night we both went up to see her, and then the next morning she was dead. I think Frances felt in some way responsible," I added, thinking this might explain to Jane why Frances had avoided talking about our mother, "for not minding more."

"Not minding?"

"About her dying."

"You can have the bottom bunk," Jane offered, when I finished buttoning my nightgown. I thanked her a little too fervently.

"I sleep in the top bunk, anyway."

She continued to watch while I pawed around for my toothbrush, finally upending my stained old flowered toiletries bag, scattering tampons and a dial of birth control pills across the dark bedroom floor. Jane glanced with interest at the birth control pills as I began putting everything back in my bag.

"So do you think she killed herself?"

"Who?" I froze as I stooped to gather up my tampons.

"Your grandmother. Who we were talking about at dinner. The one who owned the organ. Mom says she was hit by a streetcar."

"She told you that?"

Jane nodded, biting a red-lacquered thumbnail, a pouch of soft babyish flesh folding behind her chin. "She said it could have been an accident or on purpose. She said Granddad was there and saw it happen. That's why he had such a hard time when your mom died."

"*He* had a hard time?" I wasn't sure I'd understood her correctly. "That's what your mother told you?"

Jane quit chewing on her thumbnail and began examining the split ends on one of her braids. "I can't really remember now. Something like that."

"But what did she say?"

Jane's eyes were crossed from staring at the end of her braid. "Oh, I guess that he was, like, traumatized by losing his mother. And so nobody should blame him for stuff he did later. I don't know," she said, dropping the braid and blinking cautiously up at me. "I forget."

"I didn't realize she was such a fan of pop psychology."

"Well, she's really into spiritual stuff. This 'free your mind' stuff. She's got all these dumb books now, like, *Every Moment Is Now* and *Take Life One Breath at a Time*." Jane gave an arch laugh.

"Your grandfather," I told her, "is hardly blameless."

"But it must have been really gruesome. Seeing your mother die like that." Jane immediately looked solemn, impressed at having such a terrible incident in her own family history.

After a moment she said, "Mom says your dad would have been

hit, too, but his mom pushed him out of the way at the last minute and saved him."

"Well, who knows what really happened. He was only seven."

"Gruesome," breathed Jane again.

"So what else has she told you?" I said, hoping to sound casual as I pleated the front of my nightgown.

Jane shifted on the edge of the bunk. "Oh, not much. She says you guys had a pretty happy childhood. That you took nature walks in the woods and stuff like that, and had a big house. That your dad was funny and told a lot of jokes." She shrugged. "I guess having your mom sick was hard, but she doesn't really talk about that. She mostly talks about him."

"Him?" I repeated. "She talks about him?"

"Lately she has been."

"Does she tell you about him and Ilse? And before Ilse?"

Jane shrugged again and began picking at a welt on her chin with her dirty painted fingernails. "Not really."

"So how does she explain why she never sees him?" I tried to seem amused, as if the whole idea of Frances talking about our father must be some sort of amiable prank. "If we had such a lovely childhood?"

Jane looked thoughtful. "She says for a long time she was mad at him. But then they made up."

"They made up?" My headache, which had begun to recede, suddenly redoubled.

"Yeah. She went down to the Cape to see him after Aunt Helen died."

"Ah," I said, pretending to have already known this.

Frances and I had long had a pact about my father, closely observed, that he was the source of everything that had ever gone wrong in our lives. My problems with men, Frances's obsessiveness, my headaches, her phobias about flying on airplanes. Anything we had trouble with, it was because of him. He was weak, selfish, cruel, just this side of venal, and even if he spent the rest of his life repenting the offenses he had committed, it would not be enough. The perfidy of our father was an absolute, like the speed of light.

I lay back heavily on the bunk and closed my eyes. "It's been a long day," I heard myself say. "I think I'm going to try to get some sleep."

"Okay," Jane said falteringly.

I wished she would leave, but she continued to sit at the end of the bunk, picking at her chin. At last the mattress springs creaked as she stood up.

When I opened my eyes, she was standing close to me, reaching for something on the upper bunk. The loose sleeves of the oversized shirt she was wearing had slipped back and I found myself staring at the inside of one of her forearms. Even in that dim blue light, a thin crosshatch of scars was faintly visible.

By the time I got downstairs for breakfast the next morning, Frances had clearly been up for hours. As I stumbled into the kitchen in my nightgown and a pair of Jane's wool socks, my head still aching, Frances was standing in the pantry rapidly opening and closing cabinets, concerned that she might not have enough food for Thanksgiving, now that Walter had invited the Egyptian resident and his wife and baby, who were Muslim, she was belatedly realizing, and might have dietary restrictions. It went without saying there'd be no driving to Hartford today. Not with my father in residence. Not with one of Frances's Occasions planned for tomorrow. Plus Sarah had sent an e-mail "reminding" Frances that her chemistry lab partner, Arlee, was a vegan.

"Which means, basically, nuts," Frances said. She opened another cabinet and rifled through the contents, pulling out a package of macaroni and tossing it onto the counter, where it joined a jumble of boxes and cans. "I mean, she can eat nuts. And grains and vegetables, but no refined sugar and nothing with eggs."

I pictured a hollow-cheeked girl, with long colorless hair and round granny glasses. Pale and morose from vitamin B deficiency and not enough sugar.

"Is she an animal rights activist?" I asked grudgingly.

Frances opened another cabinet, keeping her back to me. "Probably. Sarah only likes activists these days. It doesn't even matter what kind. Probably she's a poultry activist. Posing as a Thanksgiving guest."

"She'll probably try to free your turkey."

"Blow up my roasting pan."

We both laughed. Then I said, "Frances, why didn't you tell me that you'd been going down to the Cape?"

She turned around, but I couldn't tell whether I had startled her.

"Jane says you and Dad have 'made up,' whatever that means."

"I went down to see him a few times," Frances said quietly. "That's true. To check on how he was doing after Helen died."

"But why didn't you tell me?" I was horrified to feel my eyes begin to fill.

"I would have. I didn't mean to hide anything from you, Cynnie. But you seemed so angry with him after the funeral that I couldn't think how to bring it up. You told me you never wanted to see him again."

"But why did you care," I said, "how he was doing?"

Frances gave me a commiserative look. "He asked *me* to lunch, the first time. And I didn't tell you because I was worried you'd feel deserted or something, by my going to see him."

"But I would have understood," I insisted, though I was quite sure I would not have understood. I didn't understand now. How could Frances have wanted to have lunch with our father, alone, especially after the way he'd behaved toward Helen? Never visiting her in Vermont during her illness, never even calling her on the phone. Showing up late for the funeral, refusing to sit with us, dodging her friends, making excuses not to go to the private memorial service at her house. Who was *he,* to ask Frances to lunch?

"I'm really sorry, Cynnie, if this has upset you."

"It hasn't upset me." I looked down at my feet in Jane's socks. "I'm glad you and he have patched things up."

"Don't be angry."

"I'm not angry. I just don't like being lied to."

"No one's lied to you, Cynnie."

"So promise me you didn't arrange that mix-up at the nursing home on purpose."

Frances looked grave. "I would never do something like that."

"Fine. Then promise me."

"I promise I didn't arrange that mix-up."

For a minute or two neither of us said anything.

"Do you think Egyptians eat stuffing?" Frances had returned to her disorganized counters and shelves.

"I have no idea."

"What about cranberry sauce?"

"I think it's pork they don't eat," I said, crossing my arms and leaning stiffly against the doorjamb. "By the way, where *is*—" It seemed strange to refer to him easily as "Dad," as if we were a normal family, about to have a normal Thanksgiving, over which our normal old father would preside.

"He's in my room." Frances was reading the back of a box of rice. "Lying down. He's taken his medications and he ate a little oatmeal for breakfast."

"He asked you for oatmeal?"

"Jane made it for him. Before she left for school."

I hadn't even heard Jane leave that morning. The whole house had been awake and filled with industry and purpose, and I'd slept through it all.

"She asked him what he wanted and she said he said oatmeal." Frances looked up. "I offered to make him eggs or an English muffin, but I couldn't tell if he was saying yes or no."

The image of Jane in her black combat boots and dirty red fingernails serving oatmeal to my father was more than I could stomach, especially without a cup of coffee. Yesterday Walter had gone out early and brought me back a large coffee from town before he left for the hospital. Frances no longer drank coffee because she said it made her "jumpy."

Frances had moved to a bookcase beside the pantry. She began flipping through a cookbook. "I'm trying not to take it personally," she went on lightly, "that *I* can't get Jane to pick up a towel off the bathroom floor, but she'll make *him* oatmeal."

"So how does he seem this morning?" I resolved not to take it personally that no one had thought of coffee for me that morning. "Did he sleep okay?"

Cookbook in hand, Frances returned to her cabinet inventory. "Well, I think so. Walter says he thinks he did. I can't understand anything he says."

"It's not that hard to understand him."

Frances turned to me with a frown, as if I was being competitive.

"I can't believe it," she said, banging another cabinet door shut. "Walter *waltzes* off to work and now I have to go to the grocery store on the day before Thanksgiving, which will be a zoo, because he invited a horde of Egyptians for dinner, and *I'm* supposed to figure out how to feed them."

A zoo. A horde. Frances always exaggerated in a disparaging way when she was secretly pleased about something. Walter and the children were the *masses;* when I came for a visit, she told her friends that the house was *bursting with relatives.* In this way she created a whole world for herself, teeming with event, with just a few people.

"Oh Lord!" she cried, in mock exasperation.

"Do you want me to go?"

"Plus there's the centerpiece to do. And I can't find my table-cloth—"

"I don't mind going."

She stared down at the open cookbook she was holding. "I had everything so well *planned.*"

"Frances," I said. "I'll go."

Frances looked up at me almost blindly. "Really? You wouldn't mind? Because I've forgotten a couple other things, too. Are you sure?"

When I assured her that I was willing, she began naming all the things she needed from the store, including ornamental striped gourds for her Thanksgiving centerpiece. How quickly my plan of going to Hartford had become moot for everyone, I thought sourly. What's a little lost research when a Thanksgiving centerpiece is at stake? Though truthfully, I didn't mind going out. I could buy myself a large cup of coffee, and it would be good for me to get away from Frances for a while. A walk in town. A little fresh air. Maybe I'd even buy myself a pack of cigarettes to take outside and smoke behind Frances's potting shed, just like when I was a teenager, sneaking cigarettes behind the field house at boarding school. The adolescent sight of Wen-Yi smoking in his car the other day had reawakened old cravings.

"This is so great of you, Cynnie," said Frances, as I got up from the table. "Let me find my wallet."

"I'll take care of it. Will you be all right with—"

"He's asleep. At least, I think he is."

We paused for a moment in the kitchen, staring at each other, clearly having the same thought: *What if he's not sleeping? What if he's dead?*

"I'm sure he is," I said.

"Stop scaring me," said Frances.

"I'm not trying to scare you. Can he get out of bed on his own?"

"Walter rigged up a kind of railing for him with a couple of chairs." Her face darkened momentarily, perhaps at the idea of something being rigged in her house.

"And he has water? And—something to read?"

Again we stared at each other, lost in the immensity of our father's possible, unanswerable desires.

"I'm sure he'll be fine." Briskly, Frances reverted to her old capable self. She would find her tablecloth, folded with dried rose petals in a drawer. She would make extra cranberry sauce with orange rind and whole cranberries. She would joke about vegans. Although her voice sounded thin when she asked, "You won't be gone long, Cynnie, will you?"

IT WAS EVEN COLDER outside than the day before, but I was glad to be driving into Concord Village, past all those boxy, upright, old clapboard houses, with their raked yards and clipped privet hedges, past the parking lot for the Old North Bridge, swarming this morning with visitors wearing hooded Patriots football sweatshirts. In third grade at West Hartford Country Day, I stood by my desk one bright fall afternoon, watching particles of chalk dust float in a shaft of sunlight, and recited:

By the rude bridge that arched the flood,
Their flag to April's breeze unfurled,
Here once the embattled farmers stood
And fired the shot heard round the world.

I remember puzzling over how a bridge could be rude and how a shot could be heard all the way around the world, yet I never thought to ask for an explanation. My childhood was full of confusions like these, almost willfully acquired, since I would never admit when I didn't understand something. Not just because I was afraid of looking stupid but because the natural order of things appeared to me to include dusty obscurities, intended to remain unclear.

As I drove around the village that morning looking for a coffee shop, I admired the deep blue of the sky, which made the day look warmer than it was, shining above the tall white Congregational church, the prosperous storefronts and granite stoops, the tidy streets full of cars and vans and people in parkas walking along the sidewalks with shopping bags. It was a pretty town, and I liked the oldness of it, which was both convincing and unhaunted—a place where the past could be taken for granted because it was everywhere, from the enormous copper beech trees to the tilting slate gravestones in the cemetery just opposite a children's clothing store. And yet Concord's antiquity was why all those tourist buses sat idling in the parking lot of the Old North Bridge. Perhaps it was my years in California that made me appreciate Concord's achievement in being historic without being moribund or becoming a theme park; I never visited this town without feeling moved, though I would never admit it to Frances. With her, I pretended to think Concord was stuffy and quaint, full of Unitarians and women with frosted pageboys who became militant when a

Dunkin' Donuts was proposed for Main Street. Concord, after all, had banned *The Adventures of Huckleberry Finn* when it was first published (Louisa May Alcott priggishly scolded Twain for not providing "something better to tell our pure-minded lads and lasses"). But it was here that the Alcott girls once took long walks with their exciting, infuriating, improvident father, debating whether to give up wearing cotton, because it was picked by slaves, which would leave them in virtuous but scratchy wool all year long, debating whether to live on apples, debating whether God might be a woman. Stepping over horse dung in the street, quizzing each other on Greek vocabulary, waving to Mr. Thoreau, to Mr. Emerson, to Mr. Nathaniel Hawthorne, as carelessly as I said hello to my landlady when I passed her on the stairs. If I squinted, I could almost see them standing under an old oak tree, their cheeks pink in the chilly fall air.

It was four years ago, during my visit back east to see Orchard House, that Helen had telephoned one morning to tell Frances and me about her diagnosis, about which she'd known for some time, and to explain that she was treating herself. *Please don't worry.* Her voice was calm, tired, slightly impatient. The voice of someone already used to being sick. *I'm sure I'll be fine.* Perhaps I should have argued with her, as Frances did. Instead, later that same day, I stood in the front parlor of Orchard House, where Anna Alcott was married, "with lilies twined in her hair," just like Meg March in *Little Women,* and marveled at how little things had changed. Upstairs, Louisa's room still held her half-moon shelf desk, built by her father, set between the windows overlooking Lexington Road. In her bedroom, May Alcott had drawn figures in ink on the walls, defacing the woodwork and wallpaper; the drawings were still perfectly visible. She had also used a hot poker to burn decorative designs into a bread board, as a present for her mother. The bread board was still on display in the kitchen, the designs looking as freshly scorched as if they had been burned in yesterday.

At last I spotted a Dunkin' Donuts that had been unsuccessfully opposed. I parked the van and went inside. While I waited for my coffee, I reflected on how attached I had grown over the years to my historical characters, those unheralded sisters, May Alcott, Lavinia Dickinson, and Mildred Keller. More attached, in some ways, than to the people I knew. It wasn't so much that I identified with them—which of course I did—as I found them reassuring. Even inspiring. May Alcott, for instance, would always remain dear to me for her clumsy-looking bread boards and amateurish drawings. She'd persuaded Louisa to let her illustrate the first edition of *Little Women*, then to bankroll a sojourn in Paris to study art; she got married in Europe, got pregnant, then died a few weeks after childbirth, leaving her daughter for Louisa to raise. Her refusal to be ashamed of herself for not being as gifted, for mooching off her sister, for forging lustily on, demanding whatever she could get while she could get it, that's what I admired. May hadn't been anybody's favorite; she died young but not young enough to be glorified, like her sister Elizabeth, immortalized by Louisa as saintly Beth, "the family angel," while May wound up as selfish, prissy Amy March. Naturally, she deserved something back. That must have been her reckoning. Quid pro quo.

Then there was cranky old Lavinia Dickinson, whom I also loved, mostly for her crankiness. Lavinia must have had some reckoning to do herself, when she yanked open the bottom drawer of Emily's bedroom dresser a few weeks after Emily died and discovered a locked box full of poems hand-sewn into booklets, each one a perfect betrayal of their sisterly compact. For years, Lavinia had played Cerberus at the door, barking at visitors while Emily hovered like Persephone on the upstairs landing or watched from the windows, shrinking into the shadows, neither here nor there, grateful for Lavinia's protection. Or so Lavinia had thought.

> I never hear the word "escape"
> Without a quicker blood,
> A sudden expectation,
> A flying attitude.

Poor flabbergasted Lavinia. She must have sat right down on the floor in her apron and skirts, a hand over her mouth. Sat down and stared at those meticulous little pages, each one crammed with cryptic ecstasies and fierce meditations, most at first glance incomprehensible, all of them flauntingly unconcerned with rhyme or the usual pieties or even proper punctuation. Wondering how she could have been so cruelly duped. So *that's* what Emily had been doing, those tiresome years when Lavinia had been answering the door and making excuses. Delivering Emily's little notes and weird nosegays to the neighbors, trying to ignore their baffled expressions. Laundering those infernal white dresses. Haggling with shopkeepers, toting packages to the post office, shooing spying children out of the garden, being the drudge, the grump, surrendering whatever hopes she may have had of marrying and having children of her own, all so that Emily—pale, crepuscular Emily, watching everything with her sherry-colored eyes—could hide in the house, baking bread and growing heliotropes, demanding that most unreasonable of demands, to be left alone. And all this time Emily had been plotting jail breaks. Had been *having* jail breaks. No wonder Lavinia first considered burning those booklets.

As for mousy Mildred Keller, whom I loved least but perhaps understood best, I often imagined her sitting glumly on a parlor chair, swinging her feet, watching Helen scrabble words into people's astonished hands, peevishly wishing that she could go deaf and blind, too, so someone would notice her.

How to cope with not being the beloved? With not being the favorite, the brilliant one, the remembered one?

By getting your own back. By being cranky. By waiting on the parlor chair until it suddenly dawns on you that you are not deaf and blind, that you are not dumb, and that it's time to say something, even if no one is listening.

By acquiring, at all costs, a flying attitude.

AFTER BUYING WHAT Frances had requested at the grocery store, I put off returning to the house for a little while longer and drove around the countryish outskirts of Concord to look at old stone walls, another thing that you can't find in California. A man was standing on a ladder outside his house, hanging Christmas lights on a blue spruce. Which seemed preposterous, until I realized how late Thanksgiving was this year. On my way back through town, I stopped at a pay phone and, on an impulse, called Carita in San Francisco, forgetting about the time difference.

When she answered the phone she sounded sleepy and annoyed. "What is it?" she demanded. "Are you all right?" I could hear Paula murmuring in the background, so I said that everything was fine. "Why are you calling then?" And I was forced to admit that I did not know why I was calling, except that I'd wanted to hear, as I put it, "a friendly voice." "You're not all down in the dumps about *him,* are you?" she asked, referring to the bookstore owner. I answered truthfully that I'd hardly given him a thought. No, just the usual family tensions. "Grist for the mill," yawned Carita, which was what she always said when writer friends complained about their families. "Take notes." Perhaps if she'd been more awake, Carita would have questioned me further, and I could have said that I was regretting my decision to come east and missing the Thanksgiving she and Paula were hosting in their apartment on Alvarado Street, with the chili lights and the mariachi music and barking Prince Charles. Which might have made me believe, at least for the time being, that Carita's Thanksgiving *was* what I was missing. But instead she told me to "hang in there," then said good-bye and hung up.

I still wasn't ready to face Frances and my father, so I drove aimlessly around for a while longer, then pulled into the parking lot at the Old North Bridge and got out to have a look at the *Minute Man* statue. He is very good-looking, the Minute Man, in a noble, guileless, slightly numbskull way. I read somewhere that Daniel Chester French used a local gardener as his model, then fell in love with him. Unrequited. Though at least French had his statue to admire whenever he wanted and someone bronzed and attractive to gaze permanently back at him.

Finally I walked across the bridge (not the original Old North Bridge but a copy that is now itself old and historic) and sat down on a bench overlooking an empty field full of frozen ruts.

The field reminded me of a vacant stretch of land across the street from our house in West Hartford. An abandoned potato field that bordered a stream, left over from the days when Stone Ridge Farms, as our development was called, had actually been a farm. Neighborhood children used it mostly for warfare; it was where we poked each other with sticks and pulled down each others' pants, shrieking with rage and excitement, pelting each other with mud. During one of these battles, someone unearthed a scatter of rust-colored bones by the old stonewall: a femur, some ribs. Most likely the remains of an animal, but rumors quickly spread that a child had been buried in the potato field, then later that several little skeletons had been found. Soon the field became known as the Bloody Lot. Screams were imagined, then heard, and piteous weeping. The piteous weeping was especially audible during loud thunderstorms. Dogs began to bark. Everyone heard it then.

One summer evening I was playing with a small band of children in the field when we dug up some sort of tubers at the far end, maybe they were potatoes—knobby, thin, yellow potatoes. We decided to roast them on sticks over a little fire made of twigs and kindled with someone's father's silver butane lighter. When we ate them they tasted of dirt. Bloody dirt. A few of them fell into the fire and had to be clawed out with sticks. We ate the potatoes ravenously, even the charred ones, rushing out into the arterial dark to dig up more, out in the dark where treacherous ruts could make a child fall and twist her ankle and be left maimed and helpless, prey to escaped convicts and child murderers, until dawn broke, when a search party of parents would find her, asleep and filthy, probably violated, covered with dew. But no one fell. No one called us in to go to bed, either, though it was late.

"Bloody Lot!" we shrieked, capering around the fire, thrusting our sticks into the air. "We have conquered the Bloody Lot!"

Eventually parents did come out to call their children. They stood on the edge of the field swinging flashlights, calling indulgently at first, then more urgently, in some cases angrily—noticing the embers from our fire—until all the children were gone. Except me. No one came to call for me, not even Mrs. Jordan, and in the end I ran across the dark muddy field by myself. When I opened the front door, out of breath, dirty and red-eyed, shirt torn, my face streaked with soot, Frances and my father looked up from where they were playing Scrabble in the living room.

"Pomegranate," my father was saying, "does not have an *i* in it." He was an excellent speller, despite never reading books, and encouraged games of Scrabble because the rest of us were not.

For a moment they regarded me with identical surprise.

"Well hello, Cynthia," said my father at last, going back to the game. "Shouldn't you be in bed?"

When I returned to the house it was almost noon. Frances and my father were seated in the kitchen at the round oak table, apparently listening to the dishwasher, the shutters closed, a plate of untouched-looking dry toast between them. Frances leapt up to meet me.

"*There* you are," she called out, her eyes unnaturally wide.

I explained that I'd got lost.

"Did you?" she said, still in that unfocused way.

My father had also turned to look at me, his whole body shifting in his wheelchair. "Where have you been?" he asked, clearly enough.

"It's Cynthia, Dad," Frances told him patiently. "She's just come back."

I smiled and set the grocery bags down on top of the stove. "I've been shopping. Sit down, Frances. I'll put these away."

"Oh no," protested Frances. "You've been out all morning. I'll do it." Smiling, she got up to carry the two bags into the pantry. But she lost her grip on the second bag as she hoisted it up and two cans of cranberry sauce came tumbling out onto the floor, rolling away toward the sink.

"Klutz," she scolded herself, stooping to retrieve the cans. Then she added in a scandalized voice, "*Canned* cranberry sauce? It's full of preservatives. Cynnie!"

"For emergencies," I said. "In case Egyptians eat preservatives. All those mummies, you know?"

Frances grimaced, then took the bags into the pantry. The counters, which had been a mess when I left, were now immaculate, everything back in the cabinets, the section with the marble pastry top scrubbed, appliances standing at attention, metal surfaces gleaming like artillery.

My father peered at me from his seat at the table, his eyes still keen and discerning in that half-stalled face, with something of their old marauding glint.

"She," he said slowly, under the dishwasher's pensive sloshing, "is a wreck."

Or maybe he said, "I can't eat this dreck," meaning the dry toast. Exactly the sort of thing, in the old days, he might have said.

"Oh, she's okay," I said softly.

He lifted both hands, letting them hang trembling in the air.

I understood that he had noticed it, too, the way Frances's fingers shook. I also understood why he was noticing. What had apparently begun in my infancy as a trembling in my mother's left arm, a twitching of her fingers, had gradually crept into the increasing exhaustion and clumsiness that so often characterize Parkinson's, until by the time I was in elementary school she spent most of her day in bed. Though there had been swift, surprising respites, too, weeks and months when she flexed her fingers more easily and walked downstairs by herself, leaning on the bannister.

"Psychosomatic," I told my father, who was watching me closely. "She's very suggestible. Especially with you being here."

"Hah?" he said.

I was bending down to repeat myself when Frances came back through the pantry door. "Well—" she began.

But whatever she meant to say next was lost as she stared at the two of us, my father and me, leaning toward each other, in the middle of what must have looked like a shared secret.

Two

My father did not believe in God. And after being married to my father for a while, neither did my mother, who believed instead in him, surprised and grateful that he'd married her when she was well over thirty, and beholden to him the way plain wives often seem beholden to handsome husbands. He was also witty and smart and energetic, and he'd sprung her from her girlhood home, that dull, prim house on Belknap Road, where my grandparents continued to live into their eighties, with its ugly but "good" Empire furniture and its three sets of "good" china, though no one, in my memory, ever went there for dinner, including us.

My father's family was not "good," or even particularly acceptable, and he didn't like to talk about them. He was the son of a Jewish pianist from St. Petersburg (Fishel became Fiske at Ellis Island, something I didn't learn until I was in college), who floated up the eastern seaboard looking for work as a music teacher, eventually landing in Hartford and setting himself up as a piano tuner. In Hartford he met red-haired, blue-eyed, Protestant Miss Adele

Timms, paid companion for an elderly woman who had a house on Asylum Hill.

My father always maintained that his parents met through an acquaintance who worked at a concert hall, but I imagine them each walking alone one afternoon on Prospect Avenue, kicking through fallen leaves. A streetcar rattles past, carrying no hint of its dark role in my grandmother's future. The sky is cobalt. The breeze is sweet with rotting leaves. Migrating geese fly honking overhead, filling the air with that lonely exhilarating autumnal sound that when you're young makes you feel as if anything could happen to you but also that nothing will. Adele wears a wide-brimmed straw hat trimmed with a black bow the size of a pair of garden shears. Pausing at the same intersection to watch the geese, my grandparents strike up a conversation. She remarks on his accent. He remarks on her hat. Music is mentioned, a shared fondness for Tchaikovsky discovered. Adele's father, a saloon owner, once had gentlemanly pretensions—before Prohibition ruined him—and had doted on his pretty daughter. As a girl, Adele had been given lessons on a rented pianola. She was also taken occasionally to concerts in New York, then treated to tea at a shop. Poor Adele. Just pampered enough to believe that life should include music and fancy hats and that one should hope for love, not money. Otherwise she would have known better than to linger for a streetcorner chat with Leo Fishel.

As they continue to stand on that curb in Hartford, but no longer with the excuse of migrating geese to hold them, Leo—sensing a kindred dissatisfied spirit—reveals his disdain for piano-tuning, and Adele makes several unflattering remarks about her elderly employer, who is not the lady she pretends to be. After another few minutes of vivid but mannerly complaint, they discover that

on Sundays both enjoy a stroll in Bushnell Park. Perhaps one afternoon . . . ?

The elderly woman was where the organ came from: she gave
it to my grandmother as a wedding present because Adele used
to work the organ for her in the evenings; probably the old lady
hadn't liked its wheezy, funereal music any more than I had and
was glad for an excuse to get rid of it. She had been a secretary for
Mark Twain's friend Charles Dudley Warner—the sole basis for
my father's story that Mark Twain had owned the organ and given
it to my grandmother. From a mustard seed of truth sprout the
most egregious lies. And, of course, the most enduring stories.

After they married, Leo and Adele lived in a tenement on
slummy Front Street, in a narrow three-room apartment next door
to a quarrelsome Polish family with seven children. Adele hung
up white net curtains, which quickly browned in the sun, and
insisted on having tea at four o'clock every afternoon while the
organ played "The Wedding March" from *Lohengrin*. She had
liked, my father once told me, "nice things." In that apartment my
father was born, and there my grandmother gave up on white net
curtains and *Lohengrin,* switched from tea to cooking sherry, and
took to lying down every afternoon with a washcloth over her eyes.
Until one day she stepped, accidentally or on purpose, in front of
a Hartford streetcar. That's as much as I know about my father's
parents, and half of that I've had to invent.

After his mother died he went to live with a distant cousin,
an elderly spinster he was instructed to call Miss Rush. The only
thing he liked about Miss Rush was her house on Westerly Ter-
race, which had soft carpets, a crystal chandelier in the dining
room, and always smelled lushly of furniture polish, instead of
boiled cabbage, the prevailing scent in the apartment on Front

Street. And for his thirteenth birthday, she gave him a copy of *The Adventures of Huckleberry Finn,* which he read, famously, all the way to the end. Otherwise, Miss Rush made him go to church and sent him to an all-boys school on Asylum Hill and tried to do her best by him, but he was a disappointment. A *scapegrace.* That was the old-fashioned word my father used to describe himself in his tales of Miss Rush, from whom he escaped at the age of fifteen when she died of peritonitis. He did odd jobs on the Front Street wharves; he smoked; he drank. He played in crooked card games arranged to set up other players, whom he referred to grandly as "marks" and "sitting ducks." He supported himself this way for several years, before being drafted in World War II. He also "chased skirts." Especially when he was on leave from the army, when he looked so dashingly respectable in his khaki uniform. But the day he set eyes on my mother, coming uncertainly down the steps of the Hartford Public Library in a pink belted dress from Bonwit Teller that did not suit her, carrying a stack of five books, one of which she dropped, he reformed.

Because she was the one. From the moment he retrieved that book to hand back to her, Edith Wharton's *Age of Innocence* (I'm inventing this, too, but it's the kind of book she would have been checking out of the library, for the second or third time), from the instant he eyeballed her calfskin gloves with the tiny pearl fastenings, then watched her tuck in her long chin, blushing and stammering in apology, he knew: the ultimate sitting duck.

He believed in necessity, he often told us, without explaining what he meant. But it wasn't hard to figure out: A handsome man without money, brought up with an appreciation for "nice things," needs to marry a rich woman. Since good-looking rich women weren't likely to bother with him, he'd try for a plain one. At least Elizabeth Seymour was a plain educated one, conveniently dwindling at home, waiting on elderly parents. My parents had not been badly matched. Her money, her good manners, her knowledge of the right people, the right way to behave at dinner parties, the right house to buy, had, for a while, appeased and encouraged him. And his unsentimental regard for necessity made him well suited for selling insurance, a business in which he was set up, reluctantly, by her father, who had been president of an indemnity company.

As for the sleeping dragon of his former appetites, he believed in exercise.

EVERY SUNDAY MORNING, no matter what the weather, while everyone else on Woodvale Road attended services at either the Episcopal or Congregational church, or slept late, or watched cartoons in their pajamas, my father dragged his three daughters out of bed, gave us each a slice of cold buttered toast and an apple, and herded us into his black Lincoln Continental, reminding us not to touch the leather upholstery with our fingers, and drove us to a state park for a nature walk. This weekly exercise was to keep us "trim," a goal made more urgent by his failure so far with me. But most of all, he loved being out in the woods. He should have been a trapper or maybe a forest ranger. He had a collection of topographical maps covering southern New England that he pored over in the evenings, looking for hikes we might not have yet taken. Often we'd drive half the morning to get to a trailhead he had determined on earlier that week. Once there, he would leap from the car, while we clambered over each other in the backseat, pinching and squabbling, arriving outside just in time to see him march off, his old fishing hat quickly disappearing into the trees. Usually he was out of sight before we started walking. But his thick-soled yellow boots left waffle-patterned footprints in the dirt or mud or snow, and he would often whistle show tunes, to keep our spirits up and to let us know where he was if he got too far ahead. Or he would sing out joyfully in his chocolatey baritone:

Oh my darlin', oh my darlin',
Oh my darlin' Clem-en-tine,
You are lost and gone forever,
Dreadful sorry,
Clementine.

Sometimes when we stopped for a rest, he would entertain us with grisly claims filed by people hoping for insurance money: thumbs severed by blender blades, hands macerated by garbage disposals, noses blown off by exploding camp stoves. But always the story was more complicated than it at first seemed. Always there were extenuating circumstances. Carelessness on the part of the injured person, faulty judgment, plain bad luck. "Don't be too quick to assign blame," he would caution us. "Don't forget to accuse the accuser." Or he would reminisce about World War II, when he was a corporal in the infantry, the best time in his life, he insisted, because it was so straightforward.

"Shoot or be shot," he might say, with horrible though unconvincing relish. "Eat or be eaten."

"That's a cliché, Dad," I would say.

This was the signal for a "cliché war," where I dueled with my father using pat phrases; the idea was to shout clichés as quickly as possible, jumping off from a word used in the previous cliché, until you ran out. The spouter of the last cliché won. *One bad apple spoils the whole barrel! The apple never falls far from the tree! Can't see the forest for the trees! Can't step in the same river twice!*

Twice burned, never forgotten! It was my father's game, created to spite Miss Rush, whose speech had been stuffed with platitudes, repeated endlessly, probably because he never listened to her. I had taken to this game with enthusiasm; it was the only time I can recall having my father's full attention.

Often these cliché wars led my father to quote Mark Twain's maxims, which he insisted would never become clichés because they were true, whereas true clichés were only obvious. *The human race consists of the damned & the ought-to-be damned. Be good & you will be lonesome.* And his favorite maxim of all: *You can straighten a worm, but the crook is in him and only waiting.*

I was good at cliché wars, but only Frances, with her long legs, could keep up with my father on a nature walk. She enjoyed his outrageously flinty assessments of the human condition, and once she was awake and warmed up enough she enjoyed walking. The two of them often pointed out birds to each other; they could identify trees even by the twigs.

Helen was not interested in birds or trees, or in my father's World War II stories, or in his "eat or be eaten" philosophizing, which disgusted her even when she knew he was kidding. By the time she was in high school, she usually found ways to get invited to other girls' houses on Saturday nights.

I was not so lucky. While my father and Frances tramped ahead, I stumbled along in my scratchy red wool coat, left to follow those waffle-patterned tracks as best I could, tripping over roots, whipped in the face by thin tree branches, my pants' legs muddy from falling into leaf-choked streams. Hoping desperately to avoid his impatience, which in spite of his many moments of high good humor was always rumbling, always threatening to erupt into a fulminating, explosive, all-consuming rage. At my

chubbiness, my laziness, my sulkiness, my stubborn failure to be as
smart as Helen or as athletic and well-behaved as Frances. Rages
that he frequently regretted but rarely restrained.

"WHAT'S WRONG WITH your mother?" neighborhood kids
used to ask. "Is she crazy?" Frances hit one of them in the mouth
once, a short devious wet-eyed boy named Kirby Harper, and split
his lip, though she'd been aiming to hit him in the stomach.

"Nothing's wrong with her," she spat, "except she has to live on
the same street as your mother."

"What's *wrong* with her?" Frances asked my father.

"Well, pretty much everything," he might answer, with a sad,
supple smile behind the black bowl of his pipe. Other times he
might sigh, "Nothing's wrong with her that a miracle wouldn't
fix."

To the same question, Helen would have answered: "My father's
what's wrong with my mother."

Helen loved our mother, who had not been sick when Helen
was little and whom, like me, Helen called "Mama." She often did
her homework sitting on the chaise lounge in our mother's room,
chewing on a pencil eraser, interrupting her trigonometry calculations to ask if Mama needed anything. She carried up cups of tea,
and bowls of chicken broth, lukewarm, which during bad peri-
ods Helen spooned into her mouth. ("Open wide," she sometimes
said, unforgivably.) One humid July evening when our mother
complained of the heat, Helen took an entire box of Kleenex and
floated each white tissue out of the bedroom window. The next
morning, the lawn was covered with snow.

The wings of Helen's nostrils were always red. Even in summer,
her lips looked chapped. If anyone asked what she was thinking,
she smiled and said, "Oh, you know."

Frances avoided our mother, whom she called Mother, when she called her anything. No cups of tea. No bedtime kisses. She disliked the distinction of having the only sick mother in the neighborhood, a mother who lay in bed all day and sometimes drooled. Such a parent implied something abnormal about the child as well, some festering possibility.

ONE AFTERNOON WHEN I was about eight, all the children on the street were running through the sprinkler fan in our yard, playing hide-and-seek. My hiding spot was behind the chaise lounge in my mother's room, where no one would ever bother looking for me. I'd been there for what felt like hours, and no one had noticed me yet.

"And that wasn't the only time."

Peering around the back of the chaise lounge, I could see my mother smiling faintly, propped up in bed. She was talking to Helen in her slow, raspy voice.

"When I was a girl," she was saying, "sometimes when I was taking a walk, I'd look up and suddenly it would seem like everything in front of me was moving. Trees, houses, fences, driveways. Sweeping by me, like in a flood."

"Probably an optical illusion," said Helen sagely.

My mother paused for so long that I could hear the rattle of her breath in her chest. Then she said: "But the strange part was, the only way I could get it to stop was to picture myself as a grown woman. Holding up my hand and saying 'Stop.' The first time was by accident, but then I tried it again, and it worked. I'd look back at myself, say 'Stop.' And it would all stop."

After a moment, Helen asked, "What did you look like?"

"What'd I look like?"

From my hiding spot, I saw my mother lurch sideways in

surprise. Fingers of sunlight pushing past the mustard cretonne drapes, illuminating busy constellations of dust motes revolving in the air. For another long moment she was silent; then her lips began to move once more. But by then I was no longer listening, struck by an appalling, fascinating thought: What if you looked into the future and didn't recognize yourself? What if you saw someone else looking back at you instead?

HIDING WAS A GAME at which I excelled. One of my favorite hiding places was inside the enormous leathery rhododendron that grew near the back steps, where I could sit cross-legged on the mulch with dirt clinging to my knees and watch whatever went on in the backyard while bees buzzed around my ears. I must have been about ten when one afternoon I spied on my father and Frances during one of their "chats," often conducted on warm Sunday afternoons in the glider, during which they congratulated each other for being so alike.

"With the two of us," he was telling her that afternoon, taking a slow pull on his pipe, "the important thing is to keep going."

"But why wouldn't we?" Frances kicked out her legs to make the glider swing faster. I swatted at a bee. Frances was not a very good student, for all her other stellar qualities, but she was starting high school and in a few years would have to apply to college, and even at the time I understood that my father was trying to find an encouraging way to tell her to buckle down.

He blew two smoke rings, which hung bluely in the air.

"Sometimes things get in the way. All I'm saying is that you have to keep going no matter what happens." His voice was suddenly stern. "Otherwise you'll wake up one day and find you haven't gone anywhere, and then it's too late."

"It'll never be too late for me," declared Frances.

"No," he agreed, blowing another perfect smoke ring. "We'll make sure of that."

Then he said, as he often did in those days: "The two of us have a special bond."

Frances had just impressed him by identifying a bobwhite quail by its call, then whistling to it and getting the quail to call back from a grassy thicket. *Bob-white! Poor poor bob-white!* As a boy, he revealed, he used to whistle to bobwhites himself when he and his friends hiked out to Talcott Mountain, where they hunted for caves and tried to trap minnows with their hands, and the rest of the time threw rocks at each other. He described how a female bobwhite would pretend to have a broken wing if a fox threatened her chicks and drag herself across the ground as a decoy. When Frances asked if the male bobwhite would do the same thing, he said he didn't know.

By then my father had taken to sleeping a few nights a week at his office in Constitution Plaza. He was working on an insurance project, he told Frances that day in the glider, as they coasted back and forth, shoulders gently bumping, hand in hand. Something very involved, a project having to do with surety claims and trusts.

Be good & you will be lonesome.

MY MOTHER GOT WORSE, then she got better. Then she got worse again. Meanwhile Helen grew smarter and smarter, while Frances became skinnier and more athletic, and I stayed pretty much the same, except that by the time I was eleven my baby fat had begun morphing into breasts, a good year or so ahead of my classmates. Boys discovered me, and I discovered that if I let them push their hands up my shirt, they would mutter endearments like "You're really great" into my hair. This gave me a previously unknown feeling of importance, and I became mildly addicted to the tight warmth in my chest when a boy asked hoarsely if I'd like to "go for a walk," though I tried not to overdo it. Then Helen was eighteen, Frances was sixteen, and it was time for Helen to go to college.

Helen didn't want to apply to college, despite her admirable grades, but according to my father Helen had her life to consider and wasn't going to be allowed to ruin it. Education was a necessity. He wanted her to become a doctor. A famous brain surgeon. So when I was thirteen Helen went off to Wellesley, which was where my mother had gone to college.

Conversation at dinner, never lively, now almost stopped altogether. My father ate quickly when he was at home, which was increasingly seldom, then went into the living room and looked at his maps while he smoked his pipe. Often he went out again. Frances sometimes didn't show up for dinner at all, deciding to ride her bike to a friend's house for dinner instead. On those nights I ate in the kitchen with Mrs. Jordan, then went up to my room to read. We did not own a television set; my father called them "idiot boxes" and wouldn't allow one in the house. A shame, as a lot of what happened that fall might have been less absorbing to me if I'd had something else to watch.

A FEW WEEKS AFTER Helen left for college, my mother enjoyed one of her surprising respites. Some mornings Mrs. Jordan helped her downstairs and left her to sit on the living room sofa. Once she tried to braid my hair. Another day she asked Frances for a bowl of potato chips. Though Frances pretended not to understand her. Frances was less well behaved lately. My father had spoken to her several times about doing her homework, which she kept neglecting.

It was around then that Mrs. Jordan began assigning my

mother small tasks. Sorting silver, rinsing lettuce. Mrs. Jordan
spent considerable time arranging these tasks beforehand, pulling all the leaves off a head of lettuce, for instance, so that all my
mother had to do was swish the lettuce around with her hands in
a sinkful of tepid water. Often my mother made a mess of these
tasks, splashing water on the counter, knocking silver to the floor,
upsetting a collander of green beans. Mrs. Jordan praised her anyway and declared that she did not know what she would do without my mother's assistance. I found it galling that Mrs. Jordan was
treating my mother the way she used to treat me when I wanted
to help her bake cupcakes. But my mother didn't seem to notice,
or if she did, she didn't mind; she would sit for an hour or more
in the laundry room, handing up napkins and pillowcases to Mrs.
Jordan to be ironed.

Mrs. Jordan was the color of coffee beans. She had a gold front
tooth and a black wig that looked like a turban, and wore a white
uniform, although my parents did not require this, and white orthopedic shoes, which I sometimes tried on because they made a
pleasant squishing sound when I walked in them, like the sound
of walking through spring mud. Somewhere in the deep foliage
of her genetic history she must have had pygmy ancestors, because I towered over her, and Mrs. Jordan claimed that her mother
was even shorter and her father had been able to fit under her
mother's arm.

Mrs. Jordan was from Greensboro, Kentucky, and belonged to
the River of Life Church, which met in a storefront at the corner of Mather and Vine, and worshipped, as she put it, "the God
within." Sometimes she left religious pamphlets around the house:
pages printed in purple ink from a ditto machine, stapled inside
thin floppy pastel covers, with titles like "Have You Saved Yourself
Today?" and "The Lord's Love Touches You No Matter Who You

Are." A small room in our basement had been made over to Mrs. Jordan and had acquired her distinctive peppery scent of perspiration and the lacquered smell of the fixative she sprayed on her wig. There was also an adjoining little bathroom that had ochre walls and a torn shower curtain the color of egg yolks that gave me the horrors when I was younger, though sometimes I visited Mrs. Jordan's bathroom just to look at it. She'd been hired through a friend of my mother's, because she needed "a change of scene." That was the explanation I was given for how Mrs. Jordan got from Greensboro, Kentucky, to West Hartford. I once saw her without her wig and was astonished that she wasn't bald, as I'd assumed, but had perfectly ordinary hair, although it was parched-looking and gray.

Frances claimed that Mrs. Jordan "was not all there," but Mrs. Jordan did all of our cooking and cleaning, and greeted me when I came home from school with a plate of Pepperidge Farm cookies and a glass of chocolate milk, even though at thirteen I realized that I should have been drinking Tab and eating celery sticks, like Frances. In my opinion, Frances was the one who wasn't all there. In the last few months she'd gotten so thin that her period had stopped, though no one else knew this but me, inveterate investigator of bathroom trash baskets.

Mrs. Jordan never paid much attention to Helen and Frances, beyond telling them to get out of the kitchen or to stop trimming their bangs and leaving hair in the bathroom sink. She was nicer to me and sometimes sat at the kitchen table sipping a cup of Postum while I had my snack and asked about my day. But the one she really loved was my mother. Loved her with a frank intensity that I found surprising at the time, not understanding what my mother could possibly offer to anyone, stuck upstairs in her bedroom all day long. Mrs. Jordan had no children of her own.

She often washed and dressed my mother and combed her hair, once my mother was unable to do those things easily for herself, so perhaps her affection had a maternal aspect. But their relationship also involved a service my mother had rendered to Mrs. Jordan in hiring her, a service that had never been defined for me but was important enough to have placed Mrs. Jordan permanently in her debt.

Mrs. Jordan was always distraught when one of my mother's respites ended. Each time she truly believed, despite all evidence to the contrary, medical and otherwise, that her prayers had been answered, and that my mother was finally getting well.

As soon as Helen left for college, Ilse started appearing at our house every afternoon to prepare Frances for the math section of the SATs, which Frances would be taking for the first time that year. If Ilse was still in the house when my father came home from work, he would invite her to stay for dinner. Soon it became clear, at least to me, that Ilse was taking extra care with Frances's SAT preparation, inventing new problems for her to solve, prolonging their struggles with geometry and Algebra II until past six o'clock, when my father's voice would be heard in the front hall, demanding that someone come "say hello" to him.

"Hello," Ilse would call out, before anyone else had a chance.

It was also around then that Mrs. Jordan had begun calling my mother "the Mistress," in a deliberate tone, though she had never done so before, and despite repeated efforts by my father to discourage her.

"Who do you think you work for," he'd say jokingly, "Emily Post?" But soon this new formality got on his nerves. After breakfast one morning, he followed Mrs. Jordan into the kitchen and said in a challenging voice, "So if she's the Mistress does that make me the Master?" Mrs. Jordan stared at him impassively, then scraped leftover eggs and toast into the garbage pail.

Every morning she massaged "the Mistress," tending to her stiff arms and legs, rubbing them with an oil made from juniper berries that was supposed to stimulate circulation. "The Mistress is lying down," she would inform Frances, whenever Frances banged into the house after school. "So you be quiet."

"I'm not making any noise," said Frances, dropping her books on the floor, rattling plates, breaking a glass.

By Halloween, my mother suddenly could no longer see well enough to read, not even large-print books, and reading had long been her great consolation. Since I felt the same way about reading myself, I volunteered to read aloud to her when I got home from school. For our debut selection, I studied my bookshelf, rejecting anything that looked depressing, and finally chose *Cherry Ames, Student Nurse* over my nearly complete collection of Nancy Drew mysteries. I was a great fan of Nancy Drew, mostly because of her boyfriend, Ned Nickerson, with whom I was secretly in love. Ned had a fresh outdoorsy crewcut manliness entirely missing from the pimple-faced ninth-grade boys at West Hartford Country Day who were so eager to put their hands up my shirt. My father might have once been something like Ned Nickerson, I thought, if he'd been less hot-tempered and more law-abiding. But my mother didn't like mysteries, so in the evenings I read about the medical challenges surmounted by Cherry Ames in her white apron and blue-striped dress while my mother ate a few green grapes or sipped broth from a cup.

"Nothing like a good book for company," Mrs. Jordan often commented afterward, washing dishes at the sink. Or maybe she said "the Good Book." In Mrs. Jordan's view, lack of prayer was the chief reason for my mother's decline. This was the opinion she offered to me, anyway. Of course by then my mother's illness, though incurable and degenerative, had become an almost reasonable state of affairs, or at least accepted, as anything will if it continues for long enough. One night I overheard my father telling someone on the telephone that my mother could "go" at any moment. Although, he added, lowering his voice, she could just as likely linger on for years.

ANOTHER RELAPSE. This one happened at the beginning of November, and it was worse than all the relapses before. Once again, my mother lay in bed all day, sometimes breathing in fishlike gasps. She'd caught a bad cold and a cough, which threatened to turn into pneumonia. A thick fug of menthol and steam from two vaporizers filled her room, part of Mrs. Jordan's attempts to ease my mother's breathing. Mrs. Jordan's tall black wig was now often askew; she was up and down the stairs all day, carrying liniments and oils, rubs and salves, syrups and pills, cups of chicken broth. The rest of her housework went largely neglected and when my father wasn't home we had cold cereal for dinner. She hardly noticed me. Even when I asked her to sit with me in the kitchen while I did my homework, she was on her feet after a few minutes, remembering something she'd forgotten to do for my mother.

To no one in particular, she declared that she would not let the Mistress suffer.

Helen came home for a weekend and had to be forced to go back to college; my father literally pushed her into the car to drive her to the bus station. Frances claimed that my mother's loud breathing was driving her crazy, that the smell of menthol was driving her crazy. She insisted on trading bedrooms with Mrs. Jordan, who was happy to move to the room next door to my mother's. I began waking in the night, hearing my mother calling out for Mrs. Jordan. Her voice was rough and demanding, weirdly mannish. *Please!* she sometimes shouted. Even when I pulled my pillow over my head, I could hear her. But then abruptly she would stop shouting, which was almost worse, because then I lay in bed waiting for her to start up again.

A few times when I got up to go to the bathroom I passed my mother's door and each time there was the shadowy figure of Mrs. Jordan in her pink flannel nightgown, standing by the bed. Once my mother was lying across Mrs. Jordan's lap. Mrs. Jordan was crooning to her, stroking her lank hair. Someone had pushed the curtains back for once, perhaps to open a window briefly and let in some fresh air. Moonlight illuminated my mother's long pale arms, hanging limply over Mrs. Jordan's dark legs, the one woman so big and pale and ungainly, the other so small and dark. In the glimpse I had of my mother's white face, her open mouth was almost square.

FRANCES TOOK UP residence in the basement, spending hours locked in the bathroom with the torn yellow shower curtain. She was failing math. She was probably failing English, history, and social studies as well. She'd been kicked off the field hockey team because she kept fainting during games (the school thought it was drugs; I knew it was celery) and because her grades were so poor.

Where was my father for most of this time? At his office, at a meeting, out with clients. Off fishing, out hunting. Sometimes he slept at his office, claiming that my mother's coughing kept him awake, too. The next evening he would return home distracted, either hugging me too hard or forgetting to say hello, mawkish one moment, irritable the next. I was used to these uneven displays from him, which generally signaled "a busy time at work," and did not pay much attention. But for the first time that I could recall, there were no Sunday morning nature hikes, no twilight walks with Frances around the neighborhood. No discussions, either, about their special bond.

ONE NIGHT JUST BEFORE Thanksgiving, when Mrs. Jordan was out at her weekly prayer meeting—at that point, one of the few times she would agree to leave the house—my father asked Frances in a quiet voice if she would take a bowl of soup upstairs to my mother. Frances was sitting in the living room, playing solitaire instead of writing a term paper on the Salem witch trials.

My father said, "She hasn't eaten anything since lunch."

Frances laid out another card.

"How long are you going to keep me waiting?" he asked.

Frances looked at him then, a long, steady look.

A rare thing, I remember thinking that night, to have my father at home for an entire evening, turning the pages of a bird guide on the sofa, smoking his pipe. He seemed to be making a deliberate effort to sit there with us, forcing himself not to leap up and find an excuse to drive off in the car for a quart of milk, which he might come back without, or the evening paper, which he would then forget to read. He'd even taken off his shoes. Outside it was snowing—a sleety, nasty snow. It felt almost cozy to have him there in the living room in his stocking feet, puffing on his pipe, his legs crossed, one foot gently bobbing. He had not criticized me at dinner when I ate a second slice of key lime pie for dessert. He smiled when I announced that I'd finished all my homework, unlike Frances, who hadn't even started hers. To impress him, I'd taken *Walden* from the bookshelf and sat down with it on the other end of the sofa, though I'm sure my father had never read *Walden* himself; it must have been my mother's book. I didn't understand what I was reading and kept skipping around, although I lingered over the line, "It is an interesting question how far men would retain their relative rank if they were divested of their clothes."

Frances laid out another card, then another.

"Frances."

"I'll do it," I offered. "I went up to check on her earlier," I told him obsequiously. "She seemed okay."

"Frances can do it," said my father.

He watched her as she left the room. He watched her all the time lately, whenever he was home. He seemed to have something on his mind to tell her, but he hadn't said anything out of the ordinary, except to make her drink a glass of milk at dinner and to demand to know why she wasn't doing her homework. He'd been going through her school things, finding penciled comments from her teachers: *Please come talk to me about this paper. It seems that you gave up before you even got started . . .*

If I caused him any concern, he didn't show it.

Frances trailed into the kitchen, swishing her ponytail. My father hadn't been past the doorway of my mother's room in weeks, ever since she started that cough. If my mother got any worse she'd have to go to the hospital, and she was terrified of hospitals. "Whatever happens," she used to tell my father, "don't let me end up in the Plague Plaza." Or the Morgue Marriott. Or La Casa des Corpses. In the old days, she'd had a cheerfully sardonic sense of humor, not unlike his own.

Mrs. Jordan had told him to stay out of the master bedroom. "You are too excited, Mr. Fiske," she said. He could never sit still during his visits, but paced around the bedroom, accidentally knocking over books and medicine bottles, swearing at himself, forgetting to leave his pipe downstairs, filling the room with fragrant noxious blue smoke. So instead of visiting, in the last few weeks he'd taken to writing her notes on three-by-five-inch file cards. Notes about the weather, how we were doing in school, what was for dinner. Notes that were supposed to be light and newsy, though often he couldn't stop himself from mentioning small worries. (*Frances is neglecting her homework . . . A boy came by asking for Cynthia I didn't like the look of . . .*)

Touchingly, and rather surprisingly, given his usual irreverence, he would sometimes add an inspirational saying at the bottom of the file card, sayings you might find on a daily calendar, like the one Frances had given him last Christmas. *Tomorrow Is Another Day. Patience Is the Art of Hoping.* My mother always looked pleased to get one of his notes on her tray. It was perhaps the central confusion of my childhood, my mother's abiding love for my father. An attachment that in his own way he encouraged, which she must have taken for love in return, and perhaps it was. There had been many women in his life during their marriage—even as a child I knew that—and yet there had never been any one woman but her.

Mrs. Jordan would read my father's note aloud, in the same furry contralto she used to read *Cherry Ames, Student Nurse* after I lost interest; then my mother would hold the file card for a few minutes. Often I examined these notes before the tray was taken upstairs. Several times when my father had written a note to my mother but neglected to add an inspirational saying, I tried scribbling one myself at the bottom of the card. But the only sayings I could ever recall were Mark Twain's maxims, impressed upon me during those enforced Sunday hikes through the woods.

I am only human, although I regret it.

It didn't occur to me until recently how those maxims must have sounded to my mother:

You can straighten a worm, but the crook is in him and only waiting.

An uneasy conscience is a hair in the mouth.

Be good & you will be lonesome.

Up they went, to her dark bedroom, to be trumpeted by Mrs. Jordan, who read like a person hard of hearing, and did not notice the different handwriting at the bottom of those three-by-five-inch cards.

What must my mother have thought, lying in bed, listening to what she could have only assumed were declarations made to her by my father? Even if she recognized Mark Twain's maxims—and she may not have, since she didn't care for Mark Twain—they would have been easy to misinterpret. She must have known something about Ilse by then, who'd been in and out of our house for months. Did she think he was finally telling her that he'd waited long enough? That it was time for her to fade out so that he could marry someone else? I don't know and never will. My mother and I were not close enough for confidences, though she might have tried to talk to Helen, or possibly even to Frances. But Helen was away, and Frances avoided her room like the Plague Plaza.

However no notes had gone up on the dinner tray in the last few days. My father had been away until just that evening on a business trip. Coincidentally, during those same few days Ilse had stopped showing up to coach Frances in math and to drive us around in the VW Beetle.

On the back cover of her green social studies notebook, Frances had written in crabbed letters: *I wish she would die so that he would stay home.*

When I stepped into the kitchen to get a glass of water, I found

Frances setting the white wooden bed tray with folding legs, as we'd seen Mrs. Jordan do so often: a shallow china bowl, a spoon, paper towels, a plastic bib. She took a pot of soup out of the refrigerator. Just a little broth left in the pot, no more than a cup. My mother would never tolerate canned soup; she claimed she could taste the tin can. Usually Mrs. Jordan took pains to make a fresh pot of soup every other day, since chicken broth was now about the only thing my mother would eat. But Mrs. Jordan, overburdened with so many extra demands, was becoming forgetful.

Frances wrinkled her nose, commenting that the broth had an "off" odor. Should she throw it out, find something else? But there wasn't anything else, not that my mother could eat. So she heated what remained of the broth on the stove, while I went back to the living room and to Thoreau's chapter on solitude.

At around ten o'clock, my father told me to go up to bed. Frances had long since disappeared into the basement. On my way to the bathroom to brush my teeth, I stopped to look into my mother's room and found her awake, propped up in bed by three or four pillows to help her breathe. A couple of the pillows had slipped down, pitching her awkwardly to the side and too far forward. The sight of her large bony frame half toppled over was alarming enough that I stepped all the way into the room.

On either side of the bed, vaporizers whispered, sending up ghostly twists of steam. Only a small lamp by the chaise lounge had been left on. No sign of the bed tray; Frances must have carried it back down to the kitchen. A jumble of medications crowded the top of the nightstand, one empty vial lying on its side, next to one of Mrs. Jordan's church pamphlets and a box of Kleenex, from which a wad of tissues had been pulled out and then dropped on the floor. The pitcher of water that always sat by the bed was almost empty. A glass tumbler lay on the rug. Frances hadn't bothered to refill the pitcher or pick up the glass. I felt a momentary satisfaction in being the one to notice these small derelictions and looked forward to mentioning them tomorrow to Mrs. Jordan, as further evidence of Frances's carelessness and inconsiderate behavior.

"Good night, Mama."

My mother didn't answer, but she gave me an unblinking stare. Which was the way she often looked at people. Like a sad basilisk.

Her coughing, at least, had stopped for the moment. I could smell my father's pipe smoke, which had traveled all the way up the stairs. I could also smell my mother. Urine, unwashed hair. And something else, a dank exhausted smell, not entirely masked by gardenia dusting powder. Moved by guilty repugnance, I went up to the side of her bed. But there was nothing I could do, except fix her pillows and try to push her back into place, then pick up the glass tumbler that was lying on the floor. Something was happening in this room that had been happening for a long time, something as obvious and inescapable as it was incomprehensible, something that should shock no one, and yet it had reduced me to an embarrassed bystander, an onlooker—not daughter, not child, but someone unrelated to the person in that bed, and utterly, utterly beside the point.

I leaned toward her and whispered, "Sleep well."

At that moment my mother suddenly plunged forward like a jack-in-the-box and seized me by the wrist. It happened so fast and so unexpectedly that for an instant I couldn't understand what had taken hold of me. A bracelet of pressure increased to a vise around my wrist. Her thin fingers were surprisingly strong, taut as piano wires.

"*Mama*," I cried.

For another instant, she retained her grip. Then she muttered something and collapsed back against the pillows. Although, curiously, she looked not so much exhausted as out of patience.

"Don't watch" was what I thought I'd heard her say.

But later it would seem to me that I stood by her bed for hours, staring at a crust of dried spittle, like salt, at the corners of her mouth.

Eventually I took the pitcher into the bathroom to fill it with water, peering out of habit into the wastepaper basket, which was empty except for a white plastic cap. Back in the bedroom, I set the pitcher on the nightstand. Once again I fixed the pillows behind my mother's shoulders, busily plumping them in the overbearing way of nurses in hospital movie scenes. I imagined her looking up at me with grateful eyes, thanking me for being such a loving child. I even took a Kleenex and dusted the nightstand. My mother was staring in my direction, yet she didn't appear to be seeing me, or really anything in the room. She might have been gazing at the girl she used to be, that smart, self-conscious, long-chinned girl on Belknap Road, hunched on an Empire chair with a library book, or sweating in a wool cardigan and scratchy kneesocks, taking a forlorn walk around the neighborhood under the elm trees, watching the world melt and rush away from her.

I considered giving her a kiss on the forehead. But her hair was so dry. Her forehead was clammy. Her pale face looked like a face in a snapshot, one of those old brownish photographs left loose in the back of a family album, not good enough to fix on a page because the subject was captured in the act of turning away, her expression indistinct, irreclaimable. Caught forever in a moment of not paying attention.

OF COURSE I REALIZED that something was wrong with my mother that night. I even realized that she might be dying. But since she had been dying, more or less, for years, and since I was angry about once again not figuring in anyone's calculations, especially my mother's, who looked as if she wished someone else had come into her room instead of me, Mrs. Jordan probably, I closed the bedroom door and went down the hall to my own room without calling down to my father, or to Frances. I read for a little while, then undressed, got into my nightgown, and climbed into bed.

Serves them all right, I remember thinking.

FOR DAYS AFTER my mother died Mrs. Jordan dragged herself about the house praying aloud, muttering and weeping, continuing to neglect her cleaning and vacuuming, so that the whole house retreated further and further behind a gray scrim of dust. "Loved that sweet lady," she wailed from time to time, stretching out her thin, corded neck. She fixed her eyes on Frances or my father, who might be sitting at the kitchen table trying to have breakfast, my father eating eggs, toast, and bacon, Frances eating half a grapefruit, and leaving half of that.

"It was time for her to go," said my father automatically.

"Loved her right to the end," wept Mrs. Jordan.

By then we all knew that my father was in love, too, with Ilse.

This was discovered only a week or so after my mother's funeral, after Helen had returned to Wellesley even though the college gave her permission to stay home and take her exams following the Christmas break. Since the end of September, it turned out, he and Ilse had been meeting in secret. He gave us all the details, announcing lugubriously (a hand over his eyes) that he had something to "confess." Hiking in the woods around Cromwell and Middletown, going to the movies in Storrs (buying tickets separately, standing separately in line, sitting in separate parts of the theater, then finding each other in the dark), having dinner at little country inns as far away as Litchfield.

Helen called my father to say that she would not be home for Christmas, that she intended to stay in Boston with her room-mate's family. She blamed herself for "not being there," she told Frances, in a separate telephone conversation, to which I listened undetected from the upstairs extension; the next moment she de-clared she was never coming home again. But Frances and I had nowhere else to go. In a stunning display of callousness, or care-lessness, or as a further "confession," my father invited Ilse to move into our house as soon as he could get the master bedroom "ready." In the meantime, she appeared nightly at our dinner table, blonde and bespectacled, and sat stolidly in her chair, eating everything on her plate.

At school, Frances and I began receiving curious, probing, not altogether sympathetic looks. Frances was more bothered by these looks than I was—in a perverse way, I found it vindicating to have people suspect that something beyond ordinary loss had hap-pened to us. When my father announced on Christmas day that he was sending us both to boarding school, Frances seemed relieved. About our mother's death, she claimed to feel nothing.

"REMEMBER HER THE WAY she was when you were lit-tle," my father advised me one cold December afternoon when he discovered me sitting in my mother's room on the chaise lounge, staring out the window at the dark furled leaves of the rhododendrons.

But whenever I tried to picture my mother as she'd been when I was younger, I recalled unfair punishments and minor betrayals: how she had slapped Frances once for hitting me when I was actually crying about bumping my head on the underside of the dining-room table, and the way she used to tell me not to climb on her, that she was not a tree.

HEART FAILURE, SAID the coroner's report. Though no autopsy was conducted. My mother's heart had been weak for several years and it was not as common as it is now to get a second opinion on such things, even if the circumstances seemed slightly suspicious. Or maybe forensic science was simply less advanced back then. Except in truly nefarious cases, if someone died then she was dead, and that was pretty much all there was to it. I wouldn't say death seemed more expected in those days, but it was somehow less surprising to people.

BEFORE MY MOTHER DIED, Mrs. Jordan took to scorching my father's shirts with the iron, singeing toast, burning the fried chicken she made for dinner. If he objected, she would fold her short arms and give him an empty stare. Once she flashed her gold tooth.

"Not the only thing's going to burn around here."

The rancid soup, the empty medicine vial, the water glass on the floor. Not a reader of Nancy Drew mysteries and *Cherry Ames, Student Nurse* for nothing, it didn't take me long to wonder whether my mother's heart had failed on its own.

"It was a blessing," Mrs. Jordan told me the night after my mother was buried in Cedar Hill cemetery, in the same plot near some mulberry trees where her own parents were buried under a granite obelisk engraved SEYMOUR. In the summer the obelisk was covered with purple splotches, left by birds that ate the mulberries. We were sitting in Mrs. Jordan's room, the room that used to be Frances's, both of us on the canopy bed. The corners of Mrs. Jordan's eyes were webbed with tiny red lines.

"It was what she wanted, praise the Lord."

"What did she want?"

Mrs. Jordan leaned closer and took my hand, pressing it between her hard dry palms. She ate a clove of garlic every day, for health and digestion, and what she said next hit me with a raw blast: "Her release. She'd asked God to release her from her torment. And God heard."

"She asked God?"

Mrs. Jordan nodded. Her face, usually remarkably furrowed and folded, like three baked potatoes pressed together, suddenly became smooth. The River of Life flowed through her, babbling with the voice of the God within.

"She asked and He heard. She asked for God's help. We prayed on it together."

I pictured those tasks Mrs. Jordan had so carefully arranged, so that my mother could think that she was "helping" by rinsing beans and drying lettuce, sorting the silverware by herself. I pictured the empty medicine vial by the bed.

I said: "I thought she didn't believe in God."

Mrs. Jordan didn't answer but continued to gaze ecstatically at a pink wicker wastebasket with raffia butterflies in one corner of the room.

"Does my father know?" I asked, following her eyes, picturing now the white plastic cap in the bathroom's wastebasket. "About God?"

IN THE WEEK FOLLOWING my mother's death the singeing and the burning got worse. Frances complained about Mrs.
Jordan's staring at her. She complained that the laundry wasn't
getting done; there were bugs in her bed. When Mrs. Jordan
started doing the laundry again, Frances claimed that Mrs. Jordan
was using soap powder that gave her a rash. She claimed Mrs.
Jordan purposely let the milk go sour; she let eggs go bad and
then scrambled them for Frances. Mrs. Jordan, she insisted, was
putting spiders in her pillowcase.

An uneasy conscience is a hair in the mouth.

"IT'S TIME FOR HER to *go*," Frances told our father angrily
one night, after I was supposed to be in bed. All that first week he
had stayed home, though he was often on the phone. There were
many details to be attended to. The master bedroom was being
repainted a light leafy green, the mustard curtains replaced by
bamboo shades. My mother's clothes were being given away. He
was ordering new furniture.

To Frances, he murmured that he would see what he could do.

"There's nothing wrong with Mrs. Jordan," I informed my father,
the next morning. "There's something wrong with Frances."

Frances had stopped sleeping. At night she roamed around the
house, turning on all the lights. Her teachers reported that she fell
asleep at her desk. Her friends had stopped calling and dropping
by. Her bike stayed parked in the garage. My father watched her
all the time now, a deadpan look on his face.

TWO WEEKS AFTER my mother's funeral, Mrs. Jordan left
the house on Woodvale Road, taking with her only an old plaid
cloth suitcase with a stubborn zipper, wearing a black raincoat and
her shiny black straw Sunday hat, with the little net that came

down over her eyes. A taxi pulled into the driveway to transport Mrs. Jordan to the Hartford bus station. She planned to take a Greyhound bus to Greensboro, where she had a previously unmentioned niece with "grandbabies."

Before she went, Mrs. Jordan gave me a hug and said, "You be a good child." She didn't give Frances so much as a glance.

THE MORNING AFTER Mrs. Jordan's departure, I was halfway down the backstairs that led into the kitchen when I heard my father and Frances talking at breakfast. He was saying that Mrs. Jordan's husband had been a wife-beater.

One night Mr. Jordan came home drunk, gave Mrs. Jordan a black eye, then passed out in their bed. Mrs. Jordan put on the kettle. She took all the dishcloths from the kitchen and used them to tie her sleeping husband to the bedposts. As soon as the water in the kettle boiled, she took the kettle off the stove, carried it into the bedroom and poured boiling water down the length of Mr. Jordan, starting with his feet. Then she called the police. The police took a look at Mr. Jordan, then at Mrs. Jordan's black eye, and cited her for "disorderly conduct."

A year and a half later, after months of suffering, Mr. Jordan died of cancer, an ordeal through which she nursed him faithfully.

The crook is in him and only waiting.

"Why did you hire her?" Frances sounded aghast.

"Your mother liked her. She said she was a poor soul who deserved a break and that a clear conscience wasn't everything."

"She tried to kill her *husband*."

"She was protecting herself. Mrs. Jordan was a good woman," my father added. "And she needed someone else to take care of. But your mother's illness was too much for her, by the end. As even your mother seemed to realize."

"She was cracked," said Frances flatly.

"It was your mother's idea," he insisted.

THAT NIGHT FRANCES came into my room while I was reading *The Secret of the Old Clock* for the third time. She sat down on the end of my bed and related the story of Mrs. Jordan and Mr. Jordan, dropping her voice to a whisper when she reached the part about the knotted dishcloths, then again when she repeated what my father had said about Mrs. Jordan "needing someone else to take care of."

After she finished, I smiled at her with pity and hatred.

"That's what he wants you to think."

"What's that supposed to mean?" Frances was paler than I'd ever seen her, as pale as one of Mrs. Jordan's pamphlets with their limp purple pages. Her long hair hung in dirty strings. Under her eyes were bruise-colored thumbprints.

"Use your head. Mrs. Jordan is religious."

"So?"

"So she believes in God. As in hell."

"What does that mean?" Frances was beginning to look scared.

"I know what he's hiding. I went up there that night."

Again I saw the empty vial, the tumbled water glass. Smelled again the pipe smoke in the hall.

"After you were there." I dropped my voice to a whisper, just as Frances had a few moments before. "The night she died. She was still alive, and she *knew*."

Frances's lips twitched. "Knew *what*?"

My mother lunged forward, seizing my wrist with her bony fingers, leaving angry red marks. Again I confronted those staring eyes, not staring at me. What *had* she known? Clearly she'd known something, if only that she was about to stop knowing anything. Perhaps if there'd been a hint of relief on that face, a shade of composure, some consoling smile summoned for my benefit, or at least a frank look in my direction, I might not have continued on and said what I said. But there had been no relief, no composure. Only a monstrous indifference.

I said: "I saw what he did."

"What?" Frances was hardly breathing. "What did he do?"

As I looked into Frances's frightened eyes, a terrible calm spread through me, a fatalistic calm, not unlike what I felt poised at the end of the high-dive board at the West Hartford Country Club, staring down for a few seconds at the sunburned, half-naked bathers below, who could not help me, once I launched myself into the air above that turquoise cupful, any more than I could help myself. And it was in this same suspended moment that I glimpsed the true power of mendacity: you can always be persuaded to doubt your own certainties but never your own lies.

I pretended to hesitate, the reluctant bearer of ill tidings.

"*What?*" Frances reached out and grabbed my wrist, squeezing hard, exactly where my mother had gripped me.

"That soup you gave her?" I said. "Do you remember how it smelled?"

Frances nodded doubtfully.

"Do you remember an empty bottle of pills on her nightstand?"

"No." Frances's eyes were shrinking green dots.

"And a water glass on the floor, that had been knocked over? As if maybe someone had been in a hurry?"

"I don't remember."

"Why do you think Dad asked *you* to take the soup up to her?

"Because he knew you wouldn't notice anything," I hissed triumphantly, when she didn't answer. "And if you did, he knew you wouldn't care. You're too out of it to notice anything these days."

Her face had turned to clay. My own cheeks were hot. How neatly I put the clues together. Ned Nickerson would be amazed. Except that I'd added a couple.

"I'll ask him," she said in a small voice.

"Go ahead," I shrugged, as she stood up. "But he'll just say she was sick and give you his sad look. And then he'll start talking about your special bond."

Frances stepped back as if I'd shoved her.

"Time for her to go," I mimicked my father's voice. "Do your homework, Frances."

LATER I TRIED to take it all back. My mother was wrong about conscience, and Mark Twain was right.

"That wasn't true," I told Frances, a few days after Ilse moved in. My father had installed Ilse in the master bedroom, along with a new king-sized bed made of blond wood and equipped with a mirrored headboard. A bit of furor had accompanied the arrival of this bed; the frame was too wide for the front door and it eventually had to be disassembled on the sidewalk, under the gaze of several neighbors.

I found Frances in the basement, in the room that had been Mrs. Jordan's, lying in bed with a sheet pulled over her head.

"Go away," said Frances, from under the sheet.

"I need to tell you something."

"Go away."

"What I said about Dad wasn't true. I was joking."

But by then it was too late, as I must have known it would be. I never said anything to my father about what I'd told Frances and how she'd reacted. I didn't care about him, especially not once he and Isle began their travels and left us at school. Although Frances and I soon made up, of course.

 Three

Frances was fretting over the striped gourds I'd bought for too much money at the supermarket. They did not make a festive enough centerpiece, arranged in a wide milky green glass bowl, even when she added miniature ears of Indian corn and walnuts, chestnuts and filberts, heaping the nuts plentifully. Something was missing. The gourds looked measly. She should have asked for bunches of russet and gold chrysanthemums or some pepperberry branches. Or clementines and pears for a fruit pyramid. But when I offered to go out again, Frances said not to bother, even though she'd also forgotten to ask me to buy Wondra for making gravy and would have to use flour tomorrow instead, which meant lumps. And she couldn't find the bag of fresh cranberries she was sure she'd bought, so now we'd have only the canned cranberry sauce. But it was after four, and the roads would be getting icy.

"And, anyway, I'll just forget something else," she added, smiling regretfully.

Jane and Wen-Yi Cheng were in the dining room for their tutoring session, murmuring over equations. Rather, Wen-Yi could be heard murmuring. Jane was silent.

"Did you two have a nice chat last night?" Frances asked, coming away from listening at the door. "Before you went to bed?"

"I had a headache."

Frances looked relieved. "You've always been her favorite aunt, you know."

"Well, she doesn't have any others," I said disagreeably.

"If she does want to talk to you. You don't have to tell me about it. Whatever she says."

"You'd just like me to give you a hint."

"No." Frances looked at me. "I'd just like to know that she's talking to someone."

I pretended to stare out the window at the snow. Our father was once again napping. Walter had said he would pick up Sarah and her friend from the Route 128 train station at five, which meant they would get stuck in rush-hour traffic. There was so much to do, Frances kept saying, turning a gourd over and over in her hands.

"And those Egyptians," she said finally with a little laugh. "How could Walter have invited a bunch of Egyptians to dinner? What was he thinking?"

As I watched Frances arrange and rearrange the striped gourds in the glass bowl, I wondered if she had any idea what Walter did or thought about all day. She seemed resigned to having no clue about what Jane had on her mind, or certainly what was going on with Sarah.

"Damn," said Frances dropping several gourds onto the floor.

As she bent to pick them up, I noticed again that her hands were shaking.

"Have you gone to see anybody," I asked, "about your hands?"

She glanced at me. "I told you, I'm just cold."

"Turn up the heat then."

"This is an old house." One by one, Frances put the gourds back into the bowl. "It's drafty. And it would cost a mint to keep the heat above sixty all day. Walter thinks I'm being stingy, but I really don't mind the cold. It's sort of like eating what's in season. If it's summer, you should be hot and eat berries; if it's winter, you should be cold and eat squash."

"And if you have a weird family, you should be weird."

"I suppose." She gave me a tired smile. "If you're talking about Jane."

"Well, it's also too dark in here."

"Is it?" said Frances, straightening up.

"You should get track lighting."

Frances made a face. She counted track lighting as one of the great sins of the modern world, along with nuclear power plants, chemical warfare, and preservatives.

"I was joking," I said.

She smiled at me again, and I saw that there was no point convincing her that her house was dark and cold, because she was already perfectly aware of it and had decided, for whatever reason, that she liked it that way, perhaps because it seemed more authentic.

"It's supposed to snow again," she said.

"I didn't hear anything about snow."

But when I folded back the window shutters, I saw that it had indeed begun to snow, very lightly, already collecting in the rhododendrons, coating the leaves with a white skin of frost.

• • •

"LESSONS NOT GOING well for Jane."

The math tutoring session was over. Wen-Yi was sitting in the kitchen with Frances and me, warming his hands around a cup of tea. Although she had so much to do that she couldn't possibly get all of it done, not to mention that someone should look in on our father who'd been asleep for what was beginning to seem a very long time, Frances had decided to sit down and have a cup of tea, too. Jane had disappeared upstairs as soon as her tutoring session was over.

"She don't want pay attention."

"She's been having some trouble at school." Frances offered Wen-Yi a plate of green apple slices.

He shook his head. "She say algebra is stupid."

Snow was now falling thickly from a sky the color of an old pie tin. In the distance a neighbor's dog had started to bark: a piercing, hysterical, frenzied barking. Maybe a coyote was bothering the dog.

"Algebra is very important," said Frances soothingly.

She and Wen-Yi were sitting close together on one side of the round oak table. Clearly this wasn't the first time Wen-Yi had complained about Jane's lack of focus, but from the ardent way he peered at her over his teacup I decided it might be the first time he'd sat so close to Frances.

"But it's hard for her," Frances was saying.

"She not pay attention," said Wen-Yi stubbornly.

"Maybe she doesn't think algebra is relevant," I offered. "I mean, for her life."

"Of course algebra is relevant." Frances frowned at me.

To change the subject, I asked Wen-Yi which province in China he was from, then didn't listen to his answer, convinced that I wouldn't remember it. He peered at me for a moment, before turning away to examine Frances's bowl of striped gourds, inquiring whether they were for Thanksgiving dinner.

"Oh no," Frances smiled, "they're just for decoration."

Wen-Yi looked slightly shocked. Frances had told me that sometimes he sat on the edge of the kitchen table while she chopped vegetables for the evening meal, asking what she was making, how it would be prepared. Food was of great interest to Wen-Yi. His other topic was DVDs. He was always asking if she'd seen this or that DVD (he had a taste for thrillers and crime movies), affecting amazement when she hadn't. He himself had apparently viewed hundreds of DVDs, all in the last year. "Oh, you must see *True Lies*," he might tell her. "You must see *The Usual Suspects*."

Frances sighed and sat back in her chair. "Well, I certainly appreciate all your patience, Wen-Yi. I know it's not easy, trying to explain things to someone who doesn't want to understand."

Wen-Yi seemed dissatisfied with the direction the conversation was taking. I could see him casting about for what to say next.

"Jane say her grandfather move here."

"Only temporarily." I wished Wen-Yi would leave. I didn't like his hangdog attentions to Frances. "And speaking of Dad," I added significantly. "Shouldn't we—"

"He here now? Your old father?" Wen-Yi actually glanced around the kitchen, as if expecting to see an apple-cheeked grandpa in suspenders and a red flannel shirt sitting in a rocker by the stove, whittling clothespins.

Frances explained that our father was waiting to move into a nursing home. He'd had a stroke, she told Wen-Yi, and also now he was getting a divorce. "At eighty-two."

"Eighty-two?"

I couldn't help feeling irritated at the disapproval that briefly clouded his face. In China all aged grandparents probably lived with their dutiful children for years, smiling peacefully over their rice bowls until one day they fell into them.

Wen-Yi was smiling again at Frances. "Thank you for tea. I see you tomorrow. Dinner at four thirty?"

"Yes," said Frances. "My older daughter will be here, too."

"Wait till you meet Sarah," I told him, making an "okay" ring with my thumb and forefinger.

Frances frowned at me once more, then turned back to Wen-Yi. "She's coming home for Thanksgiving. She's at Columbia," she said proudly.

That morning while I was getting dressed, I'd found a pencil sketch of Wen-Yi under some textbooks on Jane's desk. The likeness was quite good and must have taken her some time—she'd caught in particular the sensual plummy curve of his mouth—but then she had drawn a thick red circle around his head and a slash across his face.

I pictured Wen-Yi Cheng sitting across the Thanksgiving table from Sarah, his narrow face aglow, those delicate nicotine-stained fingers brushing hers as he passed her the mashed potatoes while Jane watched. You like cranberry, Sarah? More butter, Sarah? More bread? Sarah, in college what you study?

"What a nice young man," said Frances, when he was gone.

"I've seen a lot of nice young men," I told her, "and he's one of the nicest."

"What's wrong with him?"

"Just don't keep too much cash in the house."

"You're a paranoid person, Cynthia. Did you know that?" Frances stood up abruptly and began gathering up cups and saucers from the table. "Look, it's almost five. I need to pull together something for dinner. And we need to wake up Dad." She clattered the dishes into the sink, loudly enough to wake the dead. "Do you want to do it, or should I?"

Instead of answering, I said: "Frances, did you really make a mistake about the nursing home?"

She stared at me. "What?"

"Did you *want* to have Dad here?"

Frances turned on the faucet, testing the water with a finger until it turned hot. Then she held her hands under the running water as she filled the sink. Still not facing me, she said, "All I want is for this to work out. Everyone being here together for Thanksgiving. That's all I want. Just a regular old-fashioned family holiday."

I snorted.

Frances continued to hold her hands under the running water. "So if there's any way you could loosen up. I mean, please, Cynnie. It's just a few days."

"I'm not *not* loosened up."

She picked up a cup, rinsed it, and set it in the dish rack. Then she said in a small deliberate voice, "I wonder sometimes if you even know why you're writing about Mark Twain's daughters."

"Of course I know why," I snapped. "It's my job. Don't be patronizing."

"Fine." A long troubled glance at me. "Did you realize," she asked after a moment, "that every year, on December 16, the day his mother died, Dad used to go to Cedar Hill and put flowers on her grave?"

"No. And I'm not sure I really care, either."

Frances continued to rinse cups and saucers and stack them in the dish rack. At last she said with a faint smile, "All right, we'll go wake him up together."

"He's been sleeping a lot," I observed.

"Well, he's an old man." Frances turned off the faucet and reached for a dish towel to dry her hands.

"So maybe we should let him sleep," I said. "What does he want to be awake for, anyway?"

"Whatever's left," she said.

"Are you really so sure?"

"What kind of a question is that?"

"You saw what was in that bag with his medications, that statement Ilse put in about what he wants if anything happened."

Frances grimaced and waved her hand as if someone had blown smoke in her face. "After all this, you're going to believe Ilse?"

"He signed it, Frances."

She looked at me frankly. "Are you really so sure?"

Even before the front door had opened, I could hear Sarah's clear ringing voice. "It's not like she's disturbed or anything," she was telling someone. "She's just kind of out of it."

Fortunately only I was in the hallway at the time—I could hardly bear to imagine how Jane would react to being described this way—but the next instant the door flew wide and everyone was crowding inside, first Walter, then Sarah followed by another girl, who had her head down, both of them wearing blue wool coats and knitted hats, tracking in snow and a draft of frosty air before slamming the door shut, then Jane and Frances hurrying in from the kitchen, Frances exclaiming over how cold everyone must be before giving Sarah a quick, hard embrace. Sarah was apologizing for being so late. The train was delayed almost two hours; someone had reported an unclaimed Barney's bag in one of the entrances to Penn Station, and the police had evacuated the whole station, though the bag turned out to contain only packages of panty hose.

Sarah was still talking while she hugged Jane, then turned to me. I felt the brief press of her cold cheek against my own and breathed in the wintergreen scent of her shampoo and the brisk smell of snow trapped in her wool coat. Followed by a hard jab from the black umbrella that protruded from her leather satchel bag. She was taller, thinner, very pale. In the dim light of the front hall, she so strongly resembled Frances at the same age that I forgot about the umbrella pressing against my rib cage and thought my heart was contracting.

"Hi, Aunt Cynnie," she said, pulling away first. "It's great to see you."

"Great to see you, too. What a nice umbrella," I added witlessly.

"Oh, everyone in New York carries an umbrella."

Then she introduced her friend, who was standing just behind her, obscured by the coatrack. Who was not a girl, it turned out, but a boy of about eighteen. Arlen. Arlen Lee Evans. Arlee. Short, portly, black. (I saw Frances draw a quick breath, then force herself to smile, and saw Sarah notice this with a small dry smile of her own.) Arlen's hair, when he pulled off his hat, was in neat cornrows. He had a tiny diamond stud in his nose, a downy wisp of a moustache, and a large gap between his front teeth. Under his coat he wore a satiny cherry red track suit and several gold necklaces. Arlen had brought Frances a white paper sack of salt bagels from Zabar's, which he presented to her in the hall as though he were handing her a bouquet of roses, along with a little bow that managed to be comical and courteous at the same time.

"Why thank you, Arlen," said Frances, smiling gamely. "How thoughtful!"

More thoughtful than Sarah, who declared she'd brought nothing but a duffel bag full of dirty laundry.

"I keep giving away all my change on the street," explained Sarah. "So I never have quarters for the laundry machines."

"Never?" repeated Frances, recovering herself.

Arlen laughed, then so did the rest of us. It was just like Sarah to turn an apparent lapse into a virtue. It was also just like Sarah not to tell anyone beforehand that the lab partner she was bringing home for Thanksgiving was male, not to mention gay and black. By her studied casualness, it was clear that she was pretending to herself, as much as to the rest of us, that such particulars did not signify, and we should be ashamed of ourselves if we thought they did. It was a little early in the visit for Sarah to fling down the gauntlet of her new independence, but I suppose she felt it had to be done immediately, if she was going to manage it at all.

Snow was melting into little puddles on the floor. "Could we all please move out of the hall?" said Walter in a beleaguered voice.

Frances ignored him, turning the full wattage of her charming smile on Arlen. "I'm *so* glad you could come for the weekend," she said. "We're always telling Sarah that we're dying to meet her friends."

Touché, I thought, glancing at Sarah. Frances could be a formidable adversary when it came to adjusting particulars, especially in her own house, something that Sarah would do well not to forget.

Frances remembered that our father was sitting a few steps away in the living room, installed in his wheelchair by the fireplace. "Sarah, darling," she called, "could you come with me for a minute? Look who's here, waiting to see you. Arlen, come meet my father, Robert Fiske."

I heard my father grunt a few words in response to Sarah's greeting. He even produced a sinistral smile when Arlen seized his hand. In a cheerful treble twang, Arlen announced that he was from West Texas and that this was his very first time seeing snow. My father made a wry gasping noise and bobbed his head genially. He had always been hard to shock, to his credit, and this evening at least he was agreeing to play the part of the lovable old tolerant grandpa.

Walter lugged the duffel bags upstairs. Jane was still hanging about uncertainly in the hall when we returned from the living room. She couldn't take her eyes off Arlen, who had several times smiled warmly at her, but she seemed unsure of what to say to Sarah. Jane and Sarah had an edgy relationship. As I understood it, Jane resented Sarah because Frances didn't criticize her, while Sarah was convinced that Jane was the only one Frances ever worried about. I pictured both girls, years from now, lying on the couch in an analyst's office. "My mother preferred my sister," they would each say, confidently.

"I have a new iMac," Jane announced.

"Cool," said Sarah. Having only just arrived, amid tokens of her new exotic life—an umbrella that all New Yorkers carried, bagels from Zabar's, a black lab partner with a diamond nose stud—she could afford to be generous. Jane smirked nervously.

"Hey, is there a bathroom around here?" asked Arlen.

"Of course there's a bathroom," said Frances, a little sharply.

"This way, Arlee," said Sarah, with a tiny note of triumph.

She directed him to the downstairs bathroom off the kitchen, then headed upstairs after Walter, trailed by Jane. Frances disappeared into the pantry. For dinner that night, she had prepared a large salad of red leaf lettuce, arugula, and slivered almonds in a shallow wooden bowl, to be served along with couscous. At Jane's suggestion, she'd also ordered a pepperoni pizza, which might be easier for Dad to eat, as he wouldn't have to employ a knife and fork.

While everyone dispersed about the house, I went back into the living room where my father was still sitting in his wheelchair.

"So," I said. "What do you think of Sarah's little friend?" My father shrugged. He was not interested in Sarah or her friend. Instead he was gazing at the old player organ in the corner, muttering to himself.

Eventually I realized he was asking, "Does it still work?"

"You tell me."

My father cocked his head in a questioning way.

"I thought it was gone," I told him.

He favored me with his lopsided smile. "Gone but not forgotten."

I gave him a hard stare; he stared back at me.

I wasn't surprised that he remembered our old game—my father had always had an excellent memory—but I was surprised he'd have the nerve to try to play it again.

Together we pondered the organ for a few moments. Earlier that afternoon, Frances had rubbed the wooden surfaces with lemon oil and put an old Spode vase of dried marsh grasses, twigs, and cattails on top of the organ's cabinet in an effort to harmonize the organ with the rest of the room. These decorations had failed to make any improvement. If anything the organ looked more out of place than before, when it had had at least a temporary, just-here-for-the-time-being air, like something she'd picked up for a client at an auction. Under that fragile vase of grasses, the organ loomed dark and disruptive, with its greasy wood and yellowed keys, its overdone fretwork and those grotesque scrolled legs ending in clawed feet. Nothing about it, not a single element, belonged in this comfortable, intelligent room of beautiful old things.

As if he agreed with me, my father sighed gustily.

Elsewhere in the house we could hear laughing, the sound of the refrigerator opening, Frances calling to Walter to bring her

a bottle of wine from the basement. The house was filling up.
Tomorrow it would be even fuller, crowded with Egyptians and
hungry Chinese graduate students. The phone rang twice. No one
came into the living room.

We sat on together for perhaps five minutes more, transfixed
by having nothing to say, when suddenly a strange arid wheezing
erupted from my father, and I realized with a start that he was
laughing. At first I couldn't understand why, until it came to me
that he was laughing at the predicament we were in. At our being
related but having nothing to relate to each other, having nothing
in common but mutual discomfort. After a moment, I laughed,
too. He was just an old man. An old man who had suffered and
been afraid, who had lost almost everything. An old man who
was here to spend the holiday with his family, what was left of
it. Why bother blaming him for anything now, when he was just
an old man, whose greatest crime, in the end, had probably been
impatience?

I stopped laughing and looked away.

"Here today," I heard him mutter, "gone tomorrow."

He winched himself around in his wheelchair to peer at me.

"Tomorrow is another day," I said.

DURING DINNER THAT EVENING, Sarah and Walter had
an argument about the recent election. Though previously a Demo-
crat, this time Walter had voted for President Bush, to Sarah's
pronounced distress.

"How could you be such an idiot, Dad?"

Patiently, Walter listed the reasons why he had voted for George
Bush, which all added up to national security.

"You're an ostrich!" declared Sarah.

"Listen," replied Walter evenly. "You need to learn that people can see things differently and both be right."

"Not in this case," said Sarah.

Frances, who had never been interested in politics, asked them several times to stop arguing, then finally left the table and went into the kitchen, my father watching her with his half-frozen grin. She was followed a few moments later by Arlen, solicitously carrying his plate. After dessert, Sarah asked coolly if she could borrow Walter's car, and she and Arlen and Jane went to a movie in Lexington.

Walter wheeled my father off to help him get ready for bed while Frances sat at the kitchen table polishing silver and I lay on one of Frances's carmine and cream Knole sofas, reading a vampire novel someone had left in the living room. Vampire novels have never appealed to me—I always empathize with the vampire, as you're supposed to, which I find manipulative—but I was too tired to go upstairs and find my copy of *The Prince and the Pauper,* which I was reading for background material. I stopped reading when I realized that Walter had returned to the kitchen and that I could hear him talking to Frances.

Once again she'd had quite a lot of wine at dinner, and the last time I passed through the kitchen a bottle was on the table with a half-filled glass next to it.

"I don't know *why* you had to get into it with Sarah tonight," she was saying fretfully. "You could see she was exhausted. She looks terrible."

"She does not," said Walter. "She looks fine."

"She's too skinny. Did you see the bags under her eyes?"

"Frances, she's a college student. None of them sleep enough. And if she was so tired she wouldn't have gone out to a movie."

"She went out to escape all the tension in the house after that argument."

"Don't be ridiculous. If there's tension in this house, it's not from what was said at the dinner table."

"That boy doesn't have bags under *his* eyes."

"Arlen seems like a nice guy," said Walter firmly.

Frances went on as if he hadn't spoken. "Sarah's put him in the other bed in her room. She didn't even *ask* me if it was all right. Though there's nowhere else to put him. But I have to say, he's not someone I'd have imagined Sarah picking for a friend."

"Why not?"

"He strikes me as a little . . ." But then instead of saying what I expected to hear, Frances said, "Nosy."

"Oh come on," Walter said, "he's just being friendly."

"I don't know what Sarah's told him. But while you were arguing about George Bush he came into the kitchen and kept asking how I felt about having Dad here."

"Well, he did say he wants to major in psychology."

"Why," said Frances, her voice beginning to spiral, "*why* do you never take anything I say seriously? I just said I thought Sarah didn't look well and you dismissed me without even considering what I'd said."

"Oh come on. I did not *dismiss* you. But for godssake, Frances, you're always worried about something. If I took every single one of your worries seriously—"

This was unwise on Walter's part, to go on the offensive. He was not by nature a bully, and whenever it came to arguing with Frances and the girls he was something of an innocent, blundering into ambushes he should have anticipated. Like most men who rarely question themselves, Walter didn't understand how to be evasive, either.

"Oh really?" demanded Frances. "Just how often do you bother to wonder *what* I'm worried about?"

"Frances, calm down."

"Don't tell me to calm down."

I wondered if I should try to intervene, pretend I was wandering into the kitchen for a glass of water. But I recalled that I'd told Frances I was going to bed early while she and Walter were helping my father get settled for the night. Afterward I'd changed my mind and decided to sit in the living room without anyone's realizing I was there. It would look like I'd been purposely eavesdropping.

"Don't do this," Walter said.

"Do what? What am I doing?"

"I don't know," he said heavily. "Confusing things."

"Confusing?"

"Imposing things. Making things happen that weren't supposed to."

Frances was silent for a moment. Then I heard her say, "Like what? What am I *imposing*, Walter?"

Another pause, this time while Walter figured out what to say next. Finally he said: "This is about your father, isn't it?"

"I *knew* that's what you'd say." Frances sounded icily victorious. "You and Cynthia. The two of you. You're in league."

"Frances, ever since you asked me if he could live here—"

I sat up on the sofa, my heart thumping painfully.

"I *told* you, there wasn't room for him at the nursing home—"

"I mean before, when he first had his stroke. When you asked back then, and I said no." Walter paused again. He seemed to be struggling to figure out not just how to explain himself but how to understand what he was explaining. Finally, with an air of starting over, he said, "Ever since he had his stroke, it's like you've been hoping—"

"Hoping what?" said Frances, when he didn't go on. "What, Walter? Can't you even *say* what's on your mind?"

"All right. Why'd you insist on inviting her to Thanksgiving?"

"She's alone. No one should be alone on Thanksgiving."

"What about friends—"

"She doesn't have any. Not that I ever hear about, anyway."

"But you knew it would complicate—"

"It's not *her* fault," she interrupted. "I'm not blaming *her*."

Walter made an exasperated noise. "But can't you see what you're doing? Pushing people together like this? Have you even considered that you could be wrong?"

A long pause, during which I felt light-headed and slightly sick. Who were they talking about, me or Frances's assistant? And was that what Frances had wanted all along? To have Dad live with her?

Whatever they said next was obscured by the loud beating of my heart, but then I heard Walter say, "It's all the same thing. Maybe you *want* me to have an affair. That's what Cynthia thinks."

"That's disgusting," Frances said coldly.

But she must have finally realized that she could be heard all over the house, because after that she dropped her voice, and a few minutes later I heard both of them go upstairs, leaving me alone in the living room.

Walter was the one on the sofa the next morning when I came downstairs a little after seven. I hadn't slept much the night before and he didn't look as if he had, either.

"Morning," he said thickly, reaching for his glasses.

Then he pretended to me that he'd caught Frances's cough—he even coughed, once or twice, to prove it—and said he had slept in the living room to avoid waking everyone else. He looked cold and stiff and almost elderly, struggling to sit up on the sofa, wrapped in an old green plaid flannel bathrobe with his gray hair sticking up.

"Well, happy Thanksgiving," I told him, trying to sound light-hearted, as if Walter's sleeping on the sofa was just the begin-ning of a harum-scarum day full of unpredictable demands and concessions.

Together we went into the kitchen, where I folded back the shutters and turned up the heat. While Walter went out in his slippers to look for the paper in a drift of snow, I made coffee for both of us, using the ground coffee and the plastic filter that I'd bought for myself in town the day before. I even found proper mugs at the back of a cabinet. Outside it was again snowing lightly. Snow weighed down the topmost branches of a big Douglas fir by the shed, dislodging in powdery drifts when a crow lifted up from a branch and flapped into the ash-colored sky. A soft blue-gray light shone in through the windows and despite my sleepless night, and my uneasiness about last night's argument between Walter and Frances, I experienced one of those miraculous reversals that can accompany daylight. So what that Frances had wanted my father to come live with her? She felt sorry for him. She was a generous person, even if her generosity was sometimes inconvenient. As for her suspicions about Walter and her assistant, they were clearly unfounded. She'd reached middle age; she was rattled by having a daughter go off to college; her business wasn't what it had been; she was feeling left behind. There was nothing to worry about when it came to Frances and Walter. They'd survived too much over the years to be hurt by a silly argument, any more than Walter and Sarah had wounded each other by arguing over politics at dinner. I sat holding my coffee mug, warmed by my own reasoning, appreciating the simple quiet of the old house and the snow falling outside the windows.

Eventually we could hear my father stirring in the big bedroom off the kitchen. Walter went in to help him get out of bed, which my father could not do easily on his own, and into the bathroom. I made more coffee and put on some toast while they shaved and dressed together, Walter shaving my father. Then Walter wheeled him into the kitchen and while everyone else slept on into the morning, the three of us sat drinking coffee and reading the paper and looking out the window at the snow. Until Frances suddenly appeared, tense and wraithlike in a pair of gray sweatpants and one of Walter's white button-down shirts.

"Walter," she demanded, without greeting any of us. "Where is the turkey?"

"The turkey?"

"I asked you yesterday to take out the turkey. Where did you put it?"

"You didn't ask me to take out the turkey."

"Yes, I did. Yesterday morning."

"Frances—," he began.

"Oh my God," she said, raising her hands melodramatically. "Don't tell me the turkey is still in the basement freezer."

Here it was, almost ten o'clock on Thanksgiving morning, with eleven people expecting to sit down to dinner at four thirty that afternoon. Frances kept repeating these particulars as Walter carried the turkey up from the basement and dropped it with a stony thunk on the kitchen table. Twenty-seven pounds of solid ice.

"Would it fit in the microwave?" I wondered.

Frances was holding the base of her throat.

Walter glanced at her irritably. "We'll buy another turkey."

"All the stores are closed."

My father said nothing but sat in his wheelchair peering around with an expression of unfathomable satisfaction, while the rest of us stared at the frozen turkey, whose gelid condition seemed to have lowered the temperature in the kitchen by ten degrees.

Arlen ambled into the kitchen, again wearing the red track suit. He said good morning, yawned and patted his mouth, then looked with interest at the table.

"Frozen bird? That happened to my mom once."

"Really." Frances tried to smile. "What did she do?"

"Put it in the bathtub." He gave a gravelly laugh.

"The *bathtub*?"

"Then I used a hair dryer on it."

"Is that why you're a vegetarian?" I asked.

"That's why he's a psychology major," said Walter, not looking at Frances.

"Heh-heh," laughed Arlen, fingering his downy moustache.

Frances was the only one who didn't look amused. "Well, did it work?"

HALF AN HOUR LATER, I was kneeling on the cold blue ceramic tiles of Frances's bathroom floor, submerging the turkey in the Jacuzzi. According to Arlen, there was some danger that the skin would soften faster than the rest of the bird and depart from its corpus. Gentle massage, he said, was key.

I turned on the Jacuzzi jets and the steaming water began to bubble like an enormous cauldron. Even so, my hands ached from trying to hang on to the cold turkey, which kept slipping away from me and clunking to the bottom of the tub. Arlen had elected to keep me company in the bathroom. He supplied the information about massage, plus the word *corpus,* surprisingly without reproach, especially for someone who did not even eat eggs. I was reminded of Mrs. Jordan, who had also been a vegetarian, though she was in no other way, except the most obvious, anything like Arlen. Mrs. Jordan had often prepared meat for us without comment, expertly frying hamburgers and broiling steak, but never got over her habit of asking us how we would like our "flesh" cooked.

In the kitchen, Walter was calling all the grocery stores in the area. My father had been left to the ministrations of Jane, who was making oatmeal again for his breakfast, while Sarah and Frances got to work on the rest of dinner. Arlen lowered himself down beside me on the tiles.

"Your hands must be freezing," he said. "Let me help."

While we took turns floating the turkey back and forth between us, Arlen told me that he had asthma and that being a vegan was the only thing that had helped. His mother was a dietician. His stepfather was a security guard at an oil refinery. Arlen himself intended to get a PhD in clinical psychology, then go home to West Texas.

"Therapist to the oil wives," he said, giving the turkey a push. "That's my plan. They have the worst problems."

"And why is that?"

"Well, for starters, all that guilt over their money and big houses, and being skinny and beautiful? People thinking they have no right to get depressed? It's got to be terrible."

I must have looked genuinely taken aback because he smiled and said, "I'm just fooling with you. I want to work with kids."

He would make a wonderful therapist, I assured him, if he could get a frozen turkey to soften up, which made Arlen laugh. He laughed easily, I noticed, and often, with a throaty appreciative chuckle. No wonder somber Sarah liked him. Though there was something a little too canny about his eyes, a kind of prudent watchfulness, which I figured had to do with spending his formative years being a gay black boy with asthma in West Texas. I began to enjoy kneeling in the big steamy bathroom, the two of us passing the turkey back and forth, guiding it under the frothing water. After a while I found myself telling Arlen about the Sisters of History, and about San Francisco—which he said he dreamed of visiting—and about the fog, and my neighborhood on the edge of Noe Valley, and Carita and Don. It was such a relief to talk about my life in San Francisco, and Arlen seemed so interested, that I went into more detail than I'd intended, especially when I began describing my research on Mark Twain's daughters. I hit all the high points: Susy's early death, Clara's neurotic ailments, Little Jean and her uncontrollable rages. How as Jean got older, and her epilepsy got more severe, she grew convinced that her father didn't love her, that no one really loved her. She became obsessed by the thought that she would never marry or have children. As a result, she was excessively devoted to animals. Though in my book, I added, Jean was just "quirky." A kind of nineteenth-century Harriet the Spy, who snoops and listens in on family conversations, and knows everything about everyone, without being quite able to put it all together. Back and forth floated the turkey, blanched and puckered and prehistoric-looking, like something chipped out of a glacier.

"Wow," said Arlen, sitting back on his heels. "That's some family you got there."

Jane appeared in the doorway, sent by Frances to check on our progress.

"Gross," she remarked, gazing down at the turkey in the Jacuzzi.

"It's in a transitional phase," I told her.

"Yeah, right." Jane rolled her eyes. "From bad to worse." Then she said, "By the way, Ilse just called."

"Ilse." I stared. "What did *she* want?"

Jane shrugged. "Sarah talked to her. I think she was just checking on Granddad."

"My father's wife," I explained to Arlen. "Who didn't bother to tell him that he was supposed to be going to a nursing home. How did she know he was here, anyway?" I said to Jane.

She shrugged again.

"Well, that's strange," I said, when Jane had left. I pictured

Ilse's drawn face, her pale straggling topknot, the curt way she'd muttered, "He never cared so much for me." Why would she call to check on him? To make sure we weren't sending him back?

But thinking about Ilse, especially while kneeling on a cold bathroom floor, was a sure way to bring on a headache, so I asked Arlen what we had been talking about before Jane interrupted and he reminded me that we'd been discussing Mark Twain.

"I read *Huckleberry Finn* in high school," he said disapprovingly. "I thought it was racist."

"You have to read it in context," I told him. "People often make the mistake of judging Twain by contemporary standards."

Arlen looked unconvinced. For a few minutes we pushed the turkey back and forth, dangling our wrists in the hot water. Eventually, he wanted to know what was wrong with old Mr. Fiske.

"A long life." I sighed.

Arlen looked sympathetic.

"Plus he's had a stroke."

"That's too bad." Then he asked, "How'd your mom die?"

Long ago I made it a rule never to inquire about people's bereavements, beyond the most commonplace questions. It seems intrusive, for one thing, to be openly curious about someone else's afflictions, and also risky. In my experience, people's sorrows are always in danger of bursting out; it's only through careful inattention that they can be contained. But Arlen appeared to have no such reservations.

"Was it sudden?"

"Yes and no." Reluctantly, I explained about my mother's long illness, first the Parkinson's, followed by the heart ailment. The respites and the relapses, which got progressively worse. Then the bad cold she contracted. The fishlike gasps. One night Frances had taken her up some broth on a tray. The next morning, she was dead.

"So Frances was the last one she saw? That must've done a number on her."

"Actually," I said, "it was me."

"Sorry?"

"I was the last one to see her."

He shook his head. "It's so hard on kids, when they lose their moms."

"Not if they barely had one in the first place."

Arlen winced, then paddled his plump hands in the water while the turkey bobbed up and down. After a moment he said softly, "How about your dad? Where was he? Wasn't he there?"

"He was there. Part of the time." Then I said quickly, "Frances tries to make him seem like a nice old guy, but he wasn't so nice back then. In fact, he was cheating on her right up to the night before she died."

We both listened to the bubbling of the jets. In the bright light of the bathroom, the tiny diamond in Arlen's nose glinted and glittered. I was aware—I'd been aware all along—of where this conversation was going. Sarah must have asked Arlen to root out information about her mother and grandfather over the holiday, had perhaps even banked on the surprise of him to get everyone talking.

Or maybe not. Maybe the presence of Arlen was designed instead to shut everyone up. Maybe Sarah had dragged him along as a distraction, a deflection. Something to ward off her mother. (What assurances and promises had Frances tried to extract from Sarah, during those October phone calls?) The more I thought about it, the more I became convinced that Walter was probably right, that Arlen had been brought along by Sarah for "protection" from her family. Except that Arlen's own curiosity was getting the better of him.

IN THE KITCHEN, Sarah was peeling potatoes. Walter stirred the gingered carrots, while brussels sprouts roasted in the oven and a tall stainless steel pot of water simmered on the stove. Frances had prepared two kinds of stuffing, one with sausage, port, dried cherries, and hazelnuts; the other with corn bread and sage. Already the kitchen smelled savory and complex, a mix of butter and garlic and onions and different herbs. Exactly the way a kitchen is supposed to smell right before Thanksgiving.

As I walked in, Sarah was telling Walter that she was going to declare herself as premed, although this announcement did not seem to surprise Walter. Their differences of the night before seemed to have been forgotten. Neurology, Sarah was thinking, would be her specialty.

"What do you think, Dad?"

Frances was not taking part in the conversation. As I filled the kettle to make myself a cup of tea, Frances hardly glanced up from her station near the sink, where she was polishing her Waterford crystal goblets. Eventually, I noticed that she was polishing the same goblet over and over.

"Are you okay?" I said in a low voice.

"Of course," she said, not turning around. "I'm fine."

Uncharacteristically, Frances had given up on her centerpiece and let Jane take charge of the table, which she'd covered that morning with a heavy white damask tablecloth. When I looked into the dining room, I saw that Jane had again folded the napkins into fan shapes. She'd also done a clever thing with the striped gourds, grouping them with the nuts and the Indian corn around the base of each of Frances's six silver candlesticks, placed at intervals down the middle of the long table. For a centerpiece, she'd taken a fluted silver dish and filled it with pinecones, interspersed with a few sprigs of bittersweet she'd clipped from the spray on the front door. The pinecones carried a fresh lively scent of sap.

"That looks really nice," I said as Jane hustled past me with forks and knives. "Very abundant."

She nodded, moving around the table with her fists full of silverware. In the interim since she'd visited us in the bathroom, she'd twisted her red hair into a bun, bristling with bobby pins, and changed out of her black cargo pants into a tight moth-eaten black silk dress worn over torn fishnet stockings and her combat boots, to which she'd added a pair of elbow-length black gloves. With her hair in a bun, her tattoo was on full display.

"Very nice," I repeated.

"Thanks," she said, not looking up.

When I returned to the kitchen, Frances was still polishing goblets. I reminded her that we needed to prepare a rice dish for Arlen, and the Egyptians if it turned out they didn't eat turkey. I also reminded her that, as a vegan, Arlen would not eat butter, and so we should serve margarine as well. Frances didn't respond. Sarah and Walter were now discussing premed requirements and whether she should take Chem II in the spring or wait until next fall. Sarah had decided to quit playing JV field hockey, so that she could have more time to study. Walter wasn't sure this was a wise idea. She was only a freshman, after all, and exercise was important. As far as I could tell, they still hadn't asked Frances's opinion about Sarah's plan to become a neurologist or whether she should quit playing field hockey. In fact, they seemed to have forgotten that she was there.

But just as I was going to mention the rice dish and margarine again, Frances put down the crystal goblet she was polishing and went to stand close beside Sarah. Sarah and Walter continued talking. After a moment Frances put a hand on Sarah's shoulder.

Sarah stiffened.

"Whatever you do, darling"—Frances was smiling tensely— "just keep going."

Sarah gave her a mystified look. I was startled myself to hear Frances use that particular phrase, until I realized that it must have been the most encouraging phrase she knew. Perhaps she was using it now to encourage herself as much as Sarah.

"You just *keep going*," Frances repeated.

"Okay, Mom," said Sarah in a humoring tone.

It had to be confusing for Frances, I thought, as I watched the three of them continue to stand awkwardly by the stove. Sarah withdrawing into her life at college, Jane so moody and critical. No longer little girls in handmade cotton smock dresses, clamoring to bake Christmas cookies or sew Halloween costumes. Even Walter was changing, now that he was head of his department at the hospital and had achieved more or less all that he was going to achieve. I had the impression that middle age was chafing at him and that what Frances saw as cantankerousness was his increasing restlessness, especially with her intense domesticity—the candles, the tablecloths, the Thanksgiving hubbub—which he'd once looked upon proudly but now found constrictive. And yet he must have recognized that to ask her to behave differently would not only be cruel, by now it would be impossible. Keep going, that's what was left.

"You know, there's probably still time for you to take a nap, Mom." Sarah dropped her shoulder under Frances's hand but in such a way that she might have just been shifting her weight. "You look totally done in."

I hadn't noticed before, but Frances did look exhausted. In fact, she looked like someone who hadn't slept in days.

"Go ahead, Frances," urged Walter. "We can handle the rest."

Walter and Sarah smiled at Frances. Frances stood there for another moment, going pale, her hand hovering a fraction above Sarah's shoulder.

"I'm *fine*," she said.

"Ah So," said Jane, spying the battered Datsun from the kitchen window. "Here comes Mr. Chopsticks."

"Oh no, he's early," Frances cried.

But when Sarah and I opened the front door, it was to the deep elegiac blue of snow at dusk. Across the driveway, a line of tall junipers stood like the crenellated towers of a castle into which snow fell dreamily. A single light shone in the distance from a neighbor's window. Against this tranquil backdrop stood Wen-Yi on the front steps, in a thin black coat, an orange wool watch cap, and black tasseled loafers that looked brand new but had already been ruined by his walk from the driveway through the snow. In one hand he carried a boxed pumpkin pie.

Fortunately, I'd just managed to put on lipstick and mascara and change into the long claret-colored velvet gown I had worn the Thanksgiving before, at a dinner at Don's house. I had bought the gown one afternoon when Carita and I were shopping at a vintage clothing store in Berkeley; it had tight sleeves and a low-cut neckline, trimmed in gold thread, which was flattering on me, and the dark velvet showed up the auburn highlights in my hair. Yet as I glanced down at myself now in the doorway, I realized that what had been charmingly vampy in San Francisco looked garish in Concord, and suddenly I worried that I was as ridiculously dressed as Jane.

Sarah had also changed, into a high-necked white blouse and a long black skirt made of some soft, knitted material, and a pair of black suede boots. Her smooth brown hair was swept back, held behind her head with a tortoiseshell clip.

Wen-Yi stared at us mournfully, then looked down at his soggy tasseled loafers.

"Would you like to take them off?" asked Sarah. "I could get you a pair of slippers. I'm sure my dad has an extra pair."

He considered this offer for a moment, torn between comfort and propriety, or perhaps worried that the black dye from his wet loafers had bled onto his white socks. Then he shook his head and declared that he was "very happy." I introduced him to Sarah and he surrendered the boxed pie to her, then handed me his coat and orange cap.

Arlen was sitting at the kitchen table, drinking a cup of tea and eating a handful of raw cashews, still clad in his track suit. Wen-Yi's eyes widened at the sight of Arlen, who grinned in return. Walter had a dish towel slung over his shoulder and his sleeves rolled up. He was putting the turkey, thawed at last, into the oven.

"A small miscalculation." Frances gave Wen-Yi a panicky smile as he entered the kitchen. "I'm afraid the turkey's going to be a little behind schedule." But as if to make up for this tepid greeting, she made a show of bustling over to Wen-Yi and giving him a kiss on the cheek, then looping her arm through his. She hadn't changed out of the clothes she'd been wearing since morning and they made an odd-looking pair, Wen-Yi in a blue suit and a yellow striped tie, Frances in sweatpants. Wen-Yi glanced nervously at Walter, whose eyeglasses had steamed up from the heat of the oven.

"Did you meet Sarah?" asked Frances animatedly. "And this is her good friend, Arlen. You know Walter, of course."

"Of course," said Walter, straightening up.

Walter had done some quick thinking. By calling a neighbor for advice, he had found out about a special plastic turkey bag in which the turkey would roast in half the usual time. Walter had walked through the woods to the neighbor's house to get one of those bags while I was upstairs dressing. Roasting plastic would release toxins, Walter explained now to Wen-Yi, taking a pull from a bottle of beer, but what the hell.

Frances noticed Wen-Yi's damp shoes and asked if he'd like to sit by the fire. I followed as she led him by the hand to the living room, where Jane was working on a jigsaw puzzle she'd spread out on the coffee table while my father watched. Frances must have asked Jane to find something to engage him. My father, too, was wearing a coat and tie; Walter had helped him get into them.

Jane said hello to Wen-Yi and my father nodded while Frances introduced them, then Frances found a plaid shawl on the back of a chair and insisted on winding it around Wen-Yi's shoulders. She made him sit down on the sofa beside Jane.

"That should warm you up!" she exclaimed.

Wen-Yi looked relieved when Frances said that she had to get back to the kitchen. Gone was his usual pouty smolder, and I saw that Frances had offended him with her fussing. In his new black tasseled loafers, he'd done his best to look debonair and sophisticated, a proper doctoral candidate. But now Frances had gone and bundled him in a hairy old plaid shawl. As she left the room, Wen-Yi was leaning over the jigsaw puzzle with his elbows on his knees, pointedly not watching her go.

THE EGYPTIANS ARRIVED late because of the snow, toting their almond-colored baby, half swallowed in a white snowsuit and steadfastly asleep in his padded car seat. Walter introduced them as the Fareeds, Kamal and Amina.

Right behind them was Mary Ellen Gunderson, Frances's assistant, Walter's supposed inamorata, who drove up in her car at the same time they did. They'd already met out in the driveway.

"How nice!" said Frances, who had changed at last, into a Japanese-looking gray silk dress, made of several long filmy overlapping panels that floated diaphanously whenever she moved. A beautiful dress but in its own way as overdone and theatrical as mine. She seemed to be floating now as she greeted her guests, asking for their coats, cooing over the baby, hoping that they weren't frozen from their trek across the driveway.

While she and Walter attended to the Fareeds, I took Mary Ellen's camel's hair coat and the pricey bottle of Calvados she'd brought Frances as a hostess present. Mary Ellen was less New Agey than I'd pictured her, about thirty-five, solid and muscular-looking, wearing a strand of seed pearls and a bright turquoise wool skirt and sweater set. Her dark hair was chopped at chin length, framing a square, sallow, good-humored face speckled with tiny brown moles. Her one startling feature was the color of her eyes, an unusual pale blue, which the turquoise outfit was obviously meant to enhance. Hovering in the doorway, she apologized to Frances for being late, saying that she'd been on the phone with her aunt in New Jersey.

"I usually go to her place every year, but my uncle's been sick. My aunt's arthritis is acting up, too. I offered to come down and do the turkey, but she said she just didn't have the energy for it. I hope this isn't too much trouble, having me to dinner."

Frances smiled from beside the mourner's bench, piled now with coats and hats, then graciously assured Mary Ellen that of course it was no trouble and said how wonderful it was that she could come, thanking her twice for the Calvados, which would go so well with the pie. Though Frances's back was to me, I could see her face reflected in the cloudy old mirror. Two hectic spots of color had appeared on her cheeks.

"It's *wonderful* that you could come," she repeated, reaching for Mary Ellen's hand. "Have you two met? Mary Ellen, this is my sister, Cynthia. The famous writer. Visiting from California."

"Cynthia. *Hi.*" Mary Ellen's face crumpled with enthusiasm. "I've heard so much about you. Your sister talks about you all the time."

"Oh no," I said before turning to say hello to the Fareeds.

Kamal, the young husband, was tall and slightly overbearing, with a big imperious nose and thick shiny black hair combed back off his forehead. His wife had a small apologetic face, gently rounded, with large soft brown eyes. She wore a green headscarf, a loose amber-colored silk blouse, black pants and neat little black fleece-lined snow boots, which she removed and set in the corner by the door, then replaced with stylish black pumps she pulled out of a plastic grocery bag. They both spoke perfect English, almost accentless in Kamal's case. But they'd arrived overloaded with baggage—a cloth bouncy seat with a bar of brightly colored plastic toys, a portable crib in a rectangular carry case, a baby monitor, a swollen quilted diaper bag ("How long are they staying?" I heard Jane whisper to Sarah and Arlen)—and also more pies, homemade, with perfectly crimped crusts. Two pumpkins and an apple.

"Who needs turkey with so much pie?" Walter said too loudly, toasting the pies with his beer bottle, red-faced above his blue Oxford shirt.

Eventually everyone was persuaded to move into the living room, where Wen-Yi and my father were sitting in heavy silence. My father peered up at the new arrivals truculently, one of his eyelids half closed. Frances excused herself to check on the turkey. The rest of us perched on the two sofas and chairs, trying to look interested in Jane's jigsaw puzzle, while Walter took drink orders, then followed Frances into the kitchen. I sat next to Wen-Yi. The puzzle was of Rousseau's *Sleeping Gypsy,* always so mysterious, with that huge lion pacing either hungrily or protectively behind the prone figure of the gypsy, who looks almost fatuously uncon- scious. Jane had already fit together most of the pieces around the edges. She and Wen-Yi were working together; every so often he proffered a piece between his long fingers that would prove to be just the one she was looking for. The Fareeds' baby, whose name I didn't quite catch (Ahmad?), was also a welcome diversion. Though the baby appeared to be perfectly comfortable asleep in his car seat, Kamal insisted that he be taken out and exhibited in his yellow pajamas, before he was put to bed in his portable crib. Kamal and Amina carried the crib upstairs, led by Jane, to assemble in Sarah's room, while Sarah sat on the edge of the sofa holding the baby, her face tensing with responsibility when he drooled onto her shoulder.

"So," I said to Mary Ellen, who looked disappointed not to be the one holding the baby. "You work with Frances?"

"Oh, I'm just her assistant." She turned gratefully to me. "I'm not a designer. Not yet, anyway."

"But is that what you'd like to do? Be a designer?"

"I'd love to be like Frances. She's a genius at what she does." Mary Ellen leaned toward me, smiling. "And she's not wild about going out and spending people's money, either, like some of these decorators. I really respect that. Half the time she just uses what's already there, just changes things around so it all looks better. Like this upholstery?" Mary Ellen patted the carmine and cream floral cushion she was sitting on. "Well, it's just inside out on the other sofa. Frances had bought all this fabric, but then she decided she didn't want both sofas to match, so rather than buying a bunch of new fabric she reversed what she had for one of them. Isn't that smart?"

I agreed that it was.

"She always says that when things match up too well they don't appeal to the eye. It's contrast that appeals to the eye. Isn't that interesting? Being an interior decorator has a lot to do with understanding human nature," she went on. "It's a lot more than just knowing better than other people what things should look like."

"Are you planning to start your own business?" I asked, hoping to get off the subject of Frances.

"Right now I'm not really into making plans," she said, stroking the sofa cushion. "My mom died not too long ago. So right now I'm just kind of living for the moment."

"I'm sorry," I said.

"Well, thanks," said Mary Ellen. "She'd been sick for a long time." She seemed on the brink of saying more when Walter reappeared with a tray of wineglasses, trailed by Kamal, who'd come back with Jane for the baby.

"Sarah's decided to be premed," Walter was telling Kamal.

Jane sat down with Arlen beside a shelf of carved wooden birds, leaving Wen-Yi to work on the puzzle alone.

"Hey, good for *you*." Mary Ellen turned to Sarah. "That's so great."

"Thanks," said Sarah briefly.

"Are you a doctor?" Mary Ellen asked Wen-Yi.

Wen-Yi stared back at her, elbows tucked into his sides, still wrapped in the plaid shawl. Taking pity on him, I explained to Mary Ellen that he was getting his PhD in mathematics at Tufts.

"Topology," he offered finally.

"Top what?" Mary Ellen smiled encouragingly.

"String theory." He pulled off the shawl and began explaining string theory to Mary Ellen and Sarah. Which left me with no one to talk to but my father, sitting silent and shrunken in his wheelchair, one clawlike hand drawn up against his chest.

"That's such a neat old piano," I heard Mary Ellen say next.

Jane and Arlen were having an earnest conversation in a corner, their foreheads inclined toward each other. "Actually, it's a player organ," Sarah said, watching them.

"Does anybody here play it?"

"No one has so far," I said. "Want to give it a try?"

"*Oh* no." Mary Ellen lifted the palms of her hands in mock distress. "I'm no musician."

"You don't have to be," I reminded her. "You can make it play by itself, or you can play it like a regular organ. Either one."

"Oh." She straightened up, looking a little flushed. "Well, maybe I should get one for my aunt with arthritis. My aunt loves piano music."

Frances came in at that moment. "I haven't had a chance to

show you, Mary Ellen," she said gaily, the pearl gray panels of her dress drifting behind her. "It came just last week. Our last remaining family heirloom, *snatched* from the abyss. It used to belong to Mark Twain."

"It did?" said Arlen, looking up from his conversation with Jane. "For real?"

"Well, that was the *story*." Frances smiled. "Anyway, the organ gave Cynthia the idea for her book, the one she's working on now. Isn't that right, Cynnie?"

"Not that I know of."

Mary Ellen laughed awkwardly. "Well, that's really neat," she announced, "I mean, however you got the idea," turning her pale eyes on me as Frances excused herself once more to go back to the kitchen.

I smiled back at her, ashamed for being rude to Frances, who after all was just making small talk, though that remark about the abyss had been ill chosen, given that our father was sitting right there. But I resented being turned into one of Frances's pieces, with a charming story attached.

Mary Ellen began asking questions about my books and the subject of family heirlooms was dropped.

"Gosh," she exclaimed eventually, "I'm just so impressed. I mean, it must be such hard work, coming up with all those ideas."

"Probably no harder than anyone else's work."

"Hey, don't sell yourself short." Mary Ellen reached out to give my arm a little shake. "What you're doing is really amazing."

Frances was crazy, I decided, to think Walter could be interested in Mary Ellen. She was the sort of woman about whom married friends sighed and said, "Poor Mary Ellen, I just don't understand *what* the problem is." But they understood perfectly well what the problem was. Mary Ellen gave the fatal impression of Making the Best of Things, with her seed pearls and her turquoise outfit, her plucky efforts at carrying on conversations with uncooperative people. She was a Good Sport, who Lived for the Moment. Few things are more off-putting than the sight of someone reduced to such a hand-to-mouth existence.

When Kamal and Amina returned from settling their baby, followed by Walter carrying a bottle of wine, I got up to see if I could help Frances. Who was herself a good sport, of course. The ultimate good sport, who could take bad luck and reverse it, the way she'd transformed our rotten old father, hunched like a bat in his wheelchair, grumpily waving away a glass of wine, into a bit of decorator's gold: a nice old man by the fire on Thanksgiving.

A bottle of cabernet and two bottles of Sancerre were opened on the table, with two more cabernets breathing on the sideboard. By the time we sat down at the table we'd already gone through several bottles of wine and it was almost six o'clock. The dining-room windows, left uncurtained, were black.

"House rules: No talking about politics at dinner," announced Frances, the last to pull out a chair. She wagged her finger in comic admonishment at Walter and Sarah. "We don't want indigestion on Thanksgiving."

Everyone laughed good-humoredly as Walter and Sarah picked up their napkins and pretended to wave them in surrender.

"To our kind host and hostess." Kamal rose as Frances settled into her chair. "To Walter and Frances. Thank you for including us at your fine table." He regarded them both solemnly, as if being included at a table decorated with gourds and pinecones were a grave initiation. "Many blessings."

Crystal glittered as everyone raised their glasses; even Jane had a glass.

"To all," echoed Amina.

"To all," we said.

"To having dinner at all," said Walter.

"Amen," said Arlen.

"What a cute table," said Mary Ellen.

We all smiled at each other, every face bathed in the friendly, emotional glow of candlelight. In addition to the white tapers in the six silver candlesticks, Jane had collected all the candles in the house, tea lights and votives and five or six thick white pillar candles, placing them along the windowsills and the oak sideboard, even balancing one between the wooden prongs of an antique rake on the wall. She'd found glass holders for the tea lights and votives; the white pillar candles she put on china saucers.

"Lovely," agreed Amina.

Only Frances looked slightly dissatisfied. She had worked out a careful seating arrangement while everyone else was in the living room and she and I were hurrying back and forth through the kitchen's swinging door, lighting candles, opening wine bottles, setting out the food in her Blue Willow serving dishes. But in the end, she'd left the kitchen too late to oversee who went where. The Fareeds were sitting together instead of being split up. Mary Ellen was to have been seated between my father and Jane, but now the girls were sitting with Arlen at the end of the table and Mary Ellen had wound up between Kamal and Walter, who was pouring her a glass of Sancerre. Frances and I were next to each other, with Wen-Yi on the other side of me.

"Would you like some wine, Wen-Yi?" I asked, leaning toward him.

"No thank you," he said gruffly.

"Not a drinker?"

"No," he said.

"How about some butter? Or are you more of a margarine man?"

He turned to give me a baffled look.

From the wall, the Common Ancestor watched with her elephant's eyes, surveying the gingered carrots and the brussels sprouts, the dish of cranberry sauce, the two kinds of stuffing, mashed potatoes, baskets of bread, two silver gravy boats, and the rice pilaf, of course, in an overlarge bowl. The turkey, bronzed and glistening, had emerged from its plastic shroud and now rested majestically on a platter in front of Walter. We all took a moment to admire it, before Walter, standing officially at the head of the table, took a bone-handled carving knife from its velvet-lined wooden box and began to carve. Silver and china gleamed in the candlelight as, one by one, we passed our plates up to him and he served us slices of turkey, asking us whether we wanted light or dark meat. Then everyone started to talk at once and the room filled with the lively, optimistic sound of polite laughter and the clink of silverware.

Glancing up from the table, I tried to imagine how this scene would look to anyone passing by outside—the long white table laden with food, the candles, the lit faces of so many people—although no one would be passing outside, except maybe a coyote. How sad, I thought, already a little drunk, to be a coyote in Concord.

From her end of the table, Sarah was confessing to Amina that she was afraid of babies. Amina laughed, her hand splayed on her chest, admitting that before she had one herself, she too had been afraid of babies. (And why not be afraid of babies? I wondered, holding the mashed potatoes for Sarah. Little time bombs, ticking with futures no one could predict. Who, for instance, could have foretold that baby Emily Dickinson, red-faced and squalling, spitting up her supper of mashed egg, would become the world's most reclusive poet? Or that adorable blonde little Helen Keller would get scarlet fever before she was two years old and wake up one day deaf and blind—*or* that this catastrophe would be the making of her? How could anyone bear so much uncertainty? And yet I couldn't stop watching Amina's soft face across the table and the way she dropped her eyes as she talked about her baby, like someone trying to be casual when mentioning a lover.)

Wen-Yi was talking to Jane—he'd finished off his turkey and stuffing before most of us had got started—telling her that he had studied piano in China and won a competition. When he first came to Boston from China he played a church organ for Saturday evening services at a Catholic church in Medford that had lost its regular organist. The priest was a friend of his landlady. Wen-Yi went to all the church suppers, where spaghetti was often served. Lasagna. Italian dishes.

"Didn't they taste weird to you?" Jane wanted to know.

"Free," shrugged Wen-Yi.

Walter was telling Kamal about a new MRI the hospital was leasing, the most recent model from GE. "I hear it's a marvel." The gingered carrots were still going around the table, followed by the brussels sprouts like little green planets in their blue dish. Twice Wen-Yi pressed against my arm as he reached for the bowls and dishes that were passed to him. Conversations reeled around me, orbiting separate topics; faces leaned in and out of the candlelight. Now it was no longer babies and MRIs being discussed but embryonic stem cell research, the outrageous cost of housing in Boston, and the television show *Fear Factor* on which minor celebrities allowed themselves to be covered with scorpions or dropped into snake pits. ("It's a reality show," Jane explained to Frances, who had never heard of *Fear Factor*.) At the far end of the table, Arlen asked my father a question about the insurance industry, and after some hesitation my father appeared to be answering. Such marvels, I thought, lifting my wineglass. Such wonders. Even little Whatsisname, asleep upstairs in his portable crib, his wheezes and snuffles broadcast from a lozenge-shaped white transmitter plugged in by the door. Doing our best to enjoy ourselves, to blend in, to be a part of this gathering, to pass dishes and choose between butter or margarine. Deciding for this one evening to ignore the coyotes outside the window and to concentrate instead on the bright table laid before us with old silver and lovely old china and bowls of fragrant food, surrounded by the gleam of cheerful company. It was all there on the table, everything a person could ever want. And I realized that I was glad to be in Frances's house, that I had been right to come. I would not, at that moment, have wanted to be anywhere else in the world. I sipped my wine and watched the faces around me talking and laughing, while the candles glowed and flickered and threw shadows on the walls.

FRANCES WAS TELLING Sarah and Arlen about a Thanksgiving she remembered from our childhood. Casting laughing glances at our father, she described how he had carved the turkey so painstakingly that finally our mother told everyone at the table that they were eating Michelangelo's *Turkey*.

"And *cold* as marble, too!" concluded Frances. "By the time he got done with it.

"Remember that, Cynnie?" she said, turning to me.

I must have been about nine during the Thanksgiving she was describing. While carving the turkey, my father had had trouble with the electric carving knife he'd received for Christmas the year before and was wielding for the first time. My mother kept begging him to use an ordinary carving knife, but he refused. While the knife buzzed angrily, jumping around on the turkey, he hacked off bits of bone and gristle, his mouth twisting each time he swore at himself, his face turning red. In the end, he'd thrown the whole platter of turkey to the floor, snarling that he was no "goddamn Michelangelo," then he refused to allow anyone to pick the turkey up off the carpet, even when Molly, our fox terrier, began to gnaw at it. Though my mother tried to save the evening by laughing and saying that if my father was no Michelangelo, at least he had an artistic temperament.

"You've got a much better memory," I told Frances, "than mine."

"Oh, I don't know," she said, smiling at me. "I seem to be forgetting everything these days."

Then she turned her smile on our father, who lifted half his mouth in a gallant attempt to smile back at her. From his end of the table, Arlen sent me a sympathetic look. It gave me some comfort to realize that he'd heard it, too, the false note, the wistful unreality of Frances's story.

"Did you get enough turkey, Cynnie?" Frances was asking.

"More than enough," I answered, turning away.

WELL ALONG INTO the evening, after six or seven bottles of wine (Jane had drunk her glass, plus half of Arlen's, and now her head lolled against the back of her chair), the talk turned naturally enough to gratitude, it being Thanksgiving. Mary Ellen proposed that we go around the table and say what we were all thankful for in our lives, which is what they did each year at her aunt's house in New Jersey. But then Sarah proposed instead that we each describe something we were proud of having done for someone else. Because, she said gravely, activism was not promoted enough in American culture.

A draft had slipped into the room and I shivered, trying not to yawn. Turkey always made me tired. I'd also drunk too much and spilled gravy on my red velvet dress.

Thankfully, at first the answers were facetious: Kept my hair, offered Walter, so that Frances didn't have to be married to a baldy. Arlen announced that he was proud of not eating any turkey so that there could be more for the rest of us, for which he received light applause from everyone but my father and Wen-Yi, neither of whom seemed to be following the conversation. I gazed at Jane's centerpiece of pinecones and bittersweet and thought of saying that I was proud of not having done anything for anyone so that nobody had to feel indebted to me. But now the tone had shifted, the candles flickered and became serious as everyone refilled their wineglasses and looked into their plates.

Amina spoke first, saying that she was proud of her decision to come to university in America to study law even though her parents had wanted her to stay in Damascus. Recently Amina had set up a free advocacy service at the hospital, for other Middle Eastern women living in Boston, wives of residents and medical students, who were having immigration troubles or complications with their visas. Though some were very depressed and came to talk more about their worries than their legal problems.

"It's very difficult for them," Amina said with a mindful glance at Frances. "These women have done nothing, but still they are afraid.

They feel guilty for leaving behind their mothers, their sisters. They're afraid for their children. They don't want to go back, but back there is all they think about. It's like they never left."

Everyone at the table nodded and looked thoughtful. Sarah leaned forward and promised to send Amina a book she was reading for her freshman seminar on the political oppression of women. Amina smiled back at her, but clearly Sarah did not understand what she was talking about, as even Sarah, sitting back suddenly in her chair, seemed to realize. Kamal had put an arm protectively around his wife's shoulders. He was proud of spotting a spinal tumor in a woman who the chief resident had said was pretending to be sick; if she'd been sent home she would have been paralyzed within a month.

One at a time, each person at the table spoke. Walter, too, had solved baffling and near-fatal cases, and, it went without saying, he was proud of having provided for his family. Mary Ellen was proud of having left Boulder, Colorado, where she'd settled because she loved to ski, and moved back to Peabody to care for her widowed mother, who had died the year before after suffering for nearly a decade from early-onset Alzheimer's. By the end Mary Ellen's mother had forgotten her own name. What a faithful daughter, I thought when Mary Ellen finished speaking, especially as her mother wouldn't have noticed if she'd disappeared. Along with everyone else I smiled at Mary Ellen compassionately, though it struck me there was something impervious about her steady good nature. All that well-meaning chitchat, her bright outfit, those sturdy muscular arms and legs. Having cleaned her plate and contributed a worthy anecdote, she now sat up straight in her chair, regarding the turkey carcass with her pale blue eyes, appearing to ask nothing except to be thought of as a nice woman who'd appreciated her dinner. Yet here she was, next to Walter, getting the first choice of meat, getting her wineglass filled first. It was almost smug, this business of carrying on as if she didn't mind having thrown her youth and vitality away on someone who didn't remember her from one minute to the next.

Now it was my father's turn to reveal what he was proud of having done for someone else. For a long moment he looked down the table at Frances; finally he mumbled something and waved his hand, pass on, pass on—but amiably, modestly, the patriarch with too many epic sacrifices to choose one. Sarah and Arlen were both proud of volunteering as mentors in an inner-city literacy program on the Lower East Side. Then it was my turn, and unable to think of anything else, I said that I was proud of the social contribution I was making by writing books for girls that weren't about teenage movie stars and diet fads. Wen-Yi was proud of his math tutoring. Of helping young people, "like Jane," understand that mathematics was a remarkable world of theory and calculation, not just meaningless problems. (Jane smiled dreamily at this and closed her eyes.) People saved, people cured. Pinecones in a dish.

Even Jane woke up to say that she was proud of having organized a petition at school to protest the ban on wearing baseball caps in the classrooms, though she did not wear baseball caps herself.

Frances was the only person who had not yet spoken. Her face was flushed as she gazed at the old dining-room windows, where candle flames were reflected and repeated in the wavery rectangles of each dark pane. How youthful she looked in the candlelight. So fair and fine-boned, so unfaded, hardly older-looking than her own daughters, though of course in daylight she looked quite different.

She was caring and good, a truly good person, I thought, with the tired fondness brought on by the end of a long day of shared labor. Look at what a nice dinner she'd made, what a lovely evening she had orchestrated. I even forgave her for that Thanksgiving story. She just wanted things to look the way she wanted them to look, that was all. No crime in that. Meanwhile, the pause was lengthening and becoming conspicuous. Frances sighed deeply, yet even then she held back from speaking for another moment, fingering her wineglass.

At last she said quietly, "What I am proud of is being able to bring my whole family together tonight. We've been kept apart, some of us, for a long time by misunderstandings. But all that's now in the past."

She turned her head to look first at me, then at our father. "And I'm just grateful there's still time for us to recognize what we have in each other."

There was a long, draping silence.

Then I laughed. Frances was refusing to leave the earlier conversation, I realized; she was being facetious. Teasing, once again. But no one else laughed. Instead a murmur of approval rippled around the table.

Kamal actually bowed to her from his chair, pressing his buff-colored palms together. He was, I thought, in spite of his princely looks, an asinine young man. Someone who would wake up a sleeping baby to put it to bed. But at his end of the table, my father was also raising his hands. Tremulously, he clapped them, twice.

Misunderstandings?

She smiled at me with that enchanting smile.

The next moment I had lurched to my feet and started to clear the table, clattering dishes together, spilling wine, upsetting Jane's harvest arrangement so that nuts rolled across the tablecloth. My eyes stung and I could hardly see what I was doing.

You conniver, Frances, I thought furiously. You cheat. Luring me out here, pretending to need my help. Pretending to put *him* in a nursing home. Knowing that if you told me the truth, that you wanted to pretend we were all one big happy family, having a nice big happy family reunion in your nice big house, I would never have agreed to come. My feelings didn't matter. My memories didn't count.

I picked up a stack of Frances's Blue Willow plates, imagining how satisfying it would be to drop them on the floor.

Fortunately at that moment the baby began to wail upstairs, his urgent cries vibrating through the monitor. Amina jumped up to hurry to him, and a moment later Walter followed to see to the fire in the living room. Sarah and Jane had already risen to help me clear the dishes. Everyone else began shifting, blinking, looking foolish, like people who've been sitting in the dark when the lights come on.

But just as they were all rising from the table, scraping back chairs and stretching and folding napkins, there came the sound of a person clearing his throat, and I heard my father say distinctly: "Proud to be here."

A pause. Encouraging smiles in his direction. Nice old guy, the rest of them were thinking. Unfair to be so disabled, to be so *old*. Must have been quite a figure in his day, and still sharp as a tack. Good to have the voice of experience chime in to remind us all of what's really important.

Arlen was looking at my father in his chair. "And what makes you so proud of being here?" he asked gently. "Mr. Fiske?"

"Her." He raised his good hand to point to Frances.

"What?" Frances was smiling gauzily. "What did he say?"

"Her," he repeated, now looking at me.

"He's so hard to understand." Frances shook her head. "Really, that's the hardest thing about a stroke. Though we're making progress, isn't that right, Dad?"

"Hah," he said, still looking at me.

Amina was yawning behind her hand on one of the sofas, while the baby gazed imperturbably from her lap, his hair spiked into tiny black exclamation points. Kamal had already dismantled the portable crib, leaving it folded beside the rest of their paraphernalia in the front hall. Jane was back at work on *The Sleeping Gypsy*, looking sleepy and rumpled herself, sitting cross-legged on the floor, her black dress tucked up around her knees. She'd brought in most of the candles from the dining room and set them on top of the organ, around the vase of twigs and grasses, making the room glow with suggestive warmth.

Sarah and Arlen sprawled on the carpet on the other side of the coffee table. Sarah had rolled up her white sleeves, exposing the big elbow joints on her thin arms, looking very like Frances had as a girl, propped up by her elbows, staring at the fire. I was still furious with Frances but had recovered myself enough while I was in the kitchen, rinsing dishes, that I was able to sit collectedly in the living room. Walter had brought out the bottle of Calvados Mary Ellen had given Frances, which he was pouring into thimble-sized sherry glasses, while Mary Ellen watched from a hard leather hassock next to my father's wheelchair. The snow had stopped, Wen-Yi reported after stepping outside for a cigarette. A cold front was coming in from Canada, said Kamal; he'd heard the weather report on the radio in the car. But still everyone sat on, half stupefied, unwilling to surrender the warmth of the living room for the cold outside, though no one had said anything sensible for the last twenty minutes and in fact had resorted to talking about the baby, sure sign of a dying conversation.

Only Wen-Yi, once more helping Jane with her puzzle, seemed alert, even hungry, frowning at a half-eaten piece of apple pie on someone's plate, left balanced on the arm of the sofa. He'd hardly spoken during dinner and seemed intimidated by the flow of talk around him. Arlen had at first sat next to him in the living room and tried to ask about the night life at Tufts ("Do you go out to clubs?"), but Wen-Yi looked at him with such offended alarm that Arlen quickly gave up and went to sit on the floor with Sarah. Twice Wen-Yi had gone outside to smoke a cigarette in the driveway.

When he went out a third time, I joined him. We stood in the lee of the potting shed, protected from the wind, and I let him cup my hands between his as we lit our cigarettes. I took a deep drag and felt the smoke burn my throat. When I stopped coughing, I took another drag and stared up at the tangle of branches, suddenly bare, over my head. The sky had cleared and looked black and glassy above the white dovecote and the copper weathervane on top of the house.

"Cold," remarked Wen-Yi.

He seemed very young to me, as he stood in his thin black coat smoking in the snow. Young and seedy and famished, like a crow with his floppy dark hair and bony shoulders. He didn't belong in Frances's house any more than I did. It was entirely possible that once his tutoring with Jane was done he might never step inside such a nice house again.

"Freezing," I said.

When we finished smoking, we dropped our butts into the snow. Then without exactly meaning to, and perhaps moved less by lust than by a confused maternal impulse, I leaned toward him and kissed him on the mouth. His lips felt thin and chilly against mine, but I pressed against him anyway, hoping to carry the thing off now that I'd started it, trying to ignore that he did not lean toward me in return and that when his hands closed around my elbows it was to move me gently away.

Once we returned to the living room Wen-Yi and I sat on opposite ends of the sofa with Kamal, who looked to be falling asleep, between us. No one seemed to notice my red face. Perhaps revived by our encounter by the potting shed, Wen-Yi immediately became more talkative, returning to his doctoral dissertation, which he wanted to explain to Kamal. Amina made the baby clap his hands. Walter excused himself to watch the last few minutes of a football game upstairs on the TV in his study.

Wen-Yi's voice began to rise while talking to Kamal. As he spoke, he made small persuasive circling gestures with his narrow hands. K theory and group theory. Both parts of one theory, a theory of grand unification, Wen-Yi explained in his choppy English, using the same insistently helpful tone that Frances had used a few minutes ago when she was telling Amina how to make soup stock out of turkey bones and a bay leaf.

Yes, yes, yes, nodded Kamal, his eyes beginning to close.

Wen-Yi must be jealous of Kamal, I realized, who was about the same age, another foreigner, but without an accent, and with a family, plus a late-model silver Volvo sedan parked in the driveway.

"Noncommunicative geometry," Wen-Yi was telling Kamal, his tone becoming more aggressive.

"Ah." Kamal suddenly opened his eyes.

"You see?" demanded Wen-Yi. He continued to stare hard at Kamal.

"Fascinating," muttered Kamal, belching discreetly.

"All forces of universe all aspects of same thing, all going, same time. Nothing ever finish." Wen-Yi handed Jane a piece of the gypsy's mandolin. "You see?"

Kamal nodded groggily again. Wen-Yi gave a fierce little smile.

"Well, *I* don't," said Arlen affably from the floor. "What are you saying, Wen, there's no such thing as time passing? That yesterday and today are the same thing, and we just *tell* ourselves they're different?"

"Yes," said Wen-Yi.

"Well, that's crazy," Arlen declared. "I'm glad I'm not making travel plans for some romantic getaway with *you*."

Wen-Yi stared at him in consternation, but Arlen was gazing into the fire, the tiny diamond in his nose glittering, serenely enjoying his revenge for Wen-Yi's aghast look earlier. Beside him, Sarah was trying not to laugh.

Adored Sarah. Slender, athletic, mostly well behaved. A girl who admired her father, but couldn't bear to let her own mother put a hand on her shoulder.

When I looked up, I saw that Frances was looking at Sarah, too. We exchanged a glance that was carefully blank.

"My personal theory of the universe," Arlen was saying, "is that we're all stuck in it."

Mary Ellen blinked, then said, "That is so true," as Kamal said, "Amazing, isn't it?" before turning to Amina to murmur that the baby needed a change and that maybe she should nurse him before they left. They excused themselves to carry the baby upstairs. From the sound of footsteps overhead a moment later, it seemed that Kamal had decided to join Walter in front of the football game.

Only my father, sitting quietly in his wheelchair, was watching Wen-Yi, apparently waiting for him to continue his discussion of string theory, waiting for some connection that had not yet been made. But Wen-Yi had given up. For a few minutes he focused sulkily on the jigsaw puzzle, handing Jane pieces so that she could be the one to put it together.

Then perhaps to forestall going home, he looked at me and asked with dignity, "May I play your organ?"

"Not mine," I said ungraciously.

"Hasn't been restored yet, I'm afraid, or tuned," Frances called out to Wen-Yi, smiling from the other sofa.

Wen-Yi shrugged. If she could serve toxic turkey, that shrug implied, and allow her daughter to have a gay black boyfriend, then she could listen to an out-of-tune organ.

I poured myself another thimble of Calvados. Wen-Yi settled onto the piano bench and frowned at the organ's dark gummy-looking fretwork. He pumped the footboards and fiddled with a few of the stop knobs. Finally he cracked his knuckles and began to test the yellowed keys, making the pillar candles flicker above him. He was going to play Beethoven's "Moonlight Sonata," he informed us, then tried a few rapid scales that were completely dissonant, all the notes flat when they should have been sharp, and vice versa. But Wen-Yi continued to run his fingers doggedly up and down the keyboard. The organ wheezed and boomed and groaned, and at last a Frankenstein version of "Moonlight Sonata" lurched into the room.

Everyone flinched. It was like listening to a dirge piped into a cave. Upstairs the baby began to cry. I found it actually disturbing, the way the notes vibrated within my chest, as if such an awful noise could be coming from me.

My father was very pale, his skin almost translucent in the firelight as he sat calmly listening to Wen-Yi. But the music was irritating Frances. Her mouth was pulled down, eyes narrowed; she looked appalled. There was no way to excuse this music or to pretend it was something other than it was, which was an abomination.

Happily, the organ was too badly out of tune. Wen-Yi could not play it after all.

"Very sorry," he said, quitting abruptly.

"Oh, but that was *wonderful*," cried Frances at once, clapping her hands together.

The fire had died down; the room had become very cold.

"Gosh," said Mary Ellen, stifling a yawn on the hassock.

"Next time," promised Frances, "it'll be all ready for you."

Wen-Yi shrugged and stood up. He gave Frances a little bow, then glanced around the room, pausing for a frown at me, as if he were once more considering that leftover piece of pie.

"Sorry," he repeated, shrugging again.

THE FAREEDS LEFT FIRST, full of profuse thanks, refusing to accept foil-wrapped packets of leftover turkey and stuffing, or even extra slices of their own pies, obviously relieved to climb into their Volvo with their almond-milk baby and drive back to their apartment in Brighton. I imagined them turning to each other in the car, faces alight with relief at their escape. Such an odd assortment of guests! They would carry this feeling of deliverance all the way home and then into bed, startling each other with a playfulness and passion that had been missing ever since little (Omar?) was born.

Mary Ellen and Wen-Yi were also standing up to leave when Frances stopped them, insisting that everyone needed another glass of Calvados. Walter had rejoined us by then.

"They have to drive, Frances," he objected.

"Well, they need some hot cocoa," she replied, not looking at him. "And I want Cynthia to tell them about her book."

"Oh no," I said, backing into a copper tub of firewood.

"But it's so *interesting*," she persisted, turning to Mary Ellen. "Please sit down. Don't listen to boring old Walter. Have another drink."

Frances had seated herself in the middle of the sofa and was pulling on Walter's wrist, so that either he had to sit down with her or make a scene by shaking her off. No one else seemed to know what to do, so Mary Ellen perched again on the leather hassock and when Frances patted the cushion next to her, Wen-Yi reluctantly sat down on her other side. The girls and Arlen stayed where they were on the floor.

"I'd like to hear about your book, Aunt Cynnie," said Sarah.

"Me too," said Arlen.

"There isn't much to say," I objected. "It's just a book for girls."

"Just!" cried Frances.

Walter laid his hand on her arm.

"I'm taking Cynthia down to Mark Twain's House in Hartford."

Frances put her hand over his, then turned to Mary Ellen. "It's been completely restored to the way it was when he lived there. Down to the Tiffany wallpaper. Hand-stenciled," she added.

"How do you know that?" I asked, too astonished to object to her claim that she was "taking" me to Hartford.

Frances glanced innocently at me. "I looked up the Web site to see when the house was open. It's so fascinating," she told Mary Ellen, "the idea of being able to re-create an entire era in such detail."

I decided that the only way to end this evening was to get it over with. So I sat down in the Hitchcock chair by the fireplace, fixed poor Mary Ellen with a baleful look, and began describing Mark Twain's daughters by starting with Susy, the oldest. The brilliant one. Her father thought she'd make a great writer and praised her lavishly, but Susy had insisted on being an opera singer instead. She and Twain had once been close, so close that at thirteen she wrote an adoring biography of him, which begins, "We are a very happy family!" (However, she quickly goes on to mention Twain's bad temper and his incessant smoking, noting deftly, "He has the mind of an author exactly, some of the simplest things he can't understand.") But as Susy got older there had been resentment on her part, perhaps abetted by her father's excessive encouragement of her, which had gone to her head. A dislike of being Mark Twain's daughter. A feeling that her father, with his antics and tantrums, was more clown than great man, that he lacked seriousness and kept her down and was the source of all her insecurities.

"But tell about the Christmases. His Christmas letters." Frances was frowning impatiently as she poured herself more Calvados, splashing a little onto the coffee table. "The kitten named Sin. And the stories he made up about the bric-a-brac—"

"Meanwhile," I continued, ignoring Frances, "the youngest daughter, Jean, was an epileptic. Not many people know this. First Susy died, then the mother died. And then Jean's epilepsy got worse. Twain couldn't handle poor Jean. They had never been close. She had fits, you know, in embarrassing places, like at people's dinner parties, so he sent her away."

"Oh no," said Mary Ellen, staring palely up at me from the hassock.

"The *cherubs*," prompted Frances in a stage whisper, holding a hand to one side of her mouth. "Cynnie, tell about the cherubs." When I made no response, she turned to Mary Ellen and said assertively, "Twain bought this bed in Venice that had carved cherubs on the bedposts, which could come off, and the girls would take them down—"

"*Mom*," shushed Sarah.

"By then Twain was living in New York, with his secretary," I went on, raising my voice. "A young woman who wanted to marry him, that was the secretary, and she wanted his daughters out of the way. That's what Jean and Clara thought, anyway. They hated the secretary."

"Was she, like, really mean?" asked Jane, gazing at me from the floor.

"No." I pretended to pause thoughtfully. "She wasn't mean, exactly, but she knew a good meal ticket when she saw one."

"Although in the end Twain took Jean back." I resumed my ironical tone. "After the secretary was out of the picture. It turned out she'd been stealing his money, or that's what Clara accused her of doing. So finally he decided he wanted his daughters around him again. He missed the old days. He wanted them to be one big happy family. But then, alas, Jean died suddenly one night.

Drowned in her bathtub, during a fit, naturally, so they didn't have much time together after all."

"But you're not telling about the *girls*," protested Frances, frowning at me. "You're just describing them when they were grown up. Tell about your book, about when they lived in Hartford, and the funny stories they'd get Twain to tell them, and all the famous people they met—"

We exchanged another look, expressionless on my part, imploring on hers. Drunk as I was, I understood perfectly well what Frances wanted from me, there in the living room with our father and her whole family listening: the tale of Mark Twain's daughters and their pleasantly eventful childhood. She wanted what everyone wants—what even I wanted—a good story with a reasonable ending. But she'd gotten carried away, as she always did, with the decor. With the kittens and the cherubs and the Christmas letters. And so I was forced to brandish the sorrows of Mark Twain's daughters to keep Frances from snatching them up, to save them from becoming bric-a-brac and bedposts.

"Wait," interrupted Sarah. "What about the mother?"

"Wasn't she there?" Jane chimed in. "While the girls were growing up?"

"She was there," I said. "But I'm leaving her out. She was sick all the time and uncomplaining. Her part's not that interesting. Anyway, then there was Clara, the middle one. She was the Survivor."

I heard Walter make a restive noise and paused, having briefly lost track of which story I was telling. Everyone sat regarding me for several moments.

"What happened to Clara?" Sarah was asking, in a polite tone that suggested she'd had to repeat this question.

"Oh, she was fine." I roused myself. "More or less. She got married. She found religion. Eventually she died. And that was the last of Mark Twain's daughters."

"But what about *her* daughter?" Jane stared down at the coffee table, playing with one of the scattered pieces of the jigsaw puzzle. "The one you told us about the other night. Isn't there anything else about her?"

"Not really," I said. "Drugs, depression. Life's not worth living and no one cares about me. The usual. When you kill yourself, that's pretty much it."

"She killed herself?" said Arlen. "Wait, who're we talking about?"

"Mark Twain's *granddaughter*." I frowned at him. "She overdosed. In a hotel off Sunset Boulevard. After spending time in a mental hospital. Pretty grabby stuff, huh? Nobody knows about her, either. Maybe she'll be my next book." I mimed holding up a book and reading the cover. *"The True Story of Mark Twain's Granddaughter, an Insane Drug Addict.* Or: *No Matter How Sad Your Life Is, Hers Was Worse. Historical Fiction for Middle-Aged Girls."*

Mary Ellen gave a little moan of dismay. The rest were silent. Outside the wind had picked up and was blowing against the windows, rattling the panes.

For my part I sat staring at the twisting patterns in Frances's Persian carpet, wishing that I were back in San Francisco, sitting alone in my apartment with all the shades pulled down. It was clear to me that I was behaving badly and had been behaving badly, to varying degrees, all night, though no one had called me on it. But in the last ten minutes I'd crossed the line and now my behavior could no longer be ignored. I'd become obnoxious toward people who had only been trying to make conversation, who'd shown an interest in my book because Frances had wanted them to be interested, for my sake, and hers. Because Frances had wanted an enjoyable holiday, spent among family and friends. And who could blame her? Except me.

When I glanced up again, the girls and Arlen were staring at the waning fire, which shot out blue sparks as a log broke in two. On one side of Frances, Wen-Yi gazed abstractedly at the tips of his black loafers. Walter had closed his eyes on the other side of her and leaned his head back against the sofa cushions.

Only Frances was staring at me and I'll never forget the expression on her face that night, as if she'd just seen something cruel done to a child.

Then I thought I heard my father say, "I don't get it."

He was sitting more upright than he had all evening, his wheelchair pulled up near the sofa. His sparse white hair fluffed around his head, catching the lamplight behind him like a nimbus, leaving his face as dark as a mask.

"You don't get it?" I turned toward him in despair. "*What* don't you get? Why I'm writing this story?"

My father gazed steadily back at me.

"I'm not writing *this* story," I told him, making a great effort at patience. "I'm just giving you the story behind the story I *am* writing. In my story, nothing bad happens to these girls at all. They live in a big fancy house with servants and lots of pets. Their parents love them. They put on funny plays and meet famous people and have wonderful Christmases. That's *my* story."

The room filled again with silence, which to my ears sounded as discordant as the organ music had a little while before. Then Sarah said quietly from her place on the floor, "Why do you want to do this kind of thing?"

"What kind of thing?"

"Tell stories like that about people."

"I'm not telling stories." The back of my throat ached. "I'm telling *a* story. I'm writing a book for girls."

"I know——," began Sarah.

My voice was starting to rise. "I can only write the story one way. There's a formula we have to follow. I'm not Mark Twain, I'm not trying to be Mark Twain."

"But what's the *point*," insisted Sarah, "of what you're doing?"

"I thought points were for arguments," murmured Jane by the coffee table.

"Everything's got a point," Arlen said, a little too wisely.

The heels of my hands were pressed so hard against the wooden seat of my chair that my thumbs hurt. "Fine," I said, releasing my hands and focusing on the red haze of Arlen's track suit. "You want a point? Okay. Here it is. The *point* is that Mark Twain's daughters had every reason to expect better lives. They were good girls. They were good enough."

I'd turned to face my father again, speaking slowly and carefully, the way Frances spoke to him, as if he were deaf.

"Everything started out right for them, but their mother got sick and their father couldn't do anything about it. He tried, but he only made her worse. Then she died. He said he loved his daughters, he said he'd take care of them, but he didn't. He was too selfish and irresponsible. He was a genius but he was also an idiot—he was like everybody else, only more so. And so what happened to them was even sadder and more pathetic than what happens to most people."

The faces around me had started to blur.

"It's a *joke*," I said loudly, "what happened to Mark Twain's daughters. But no one wants to hear a bad joke, do they? No one wants an ugly sad story with a lousy ending. So you rewrite it. You redecorate. You make it a nice story. And then little girls will read it and feel that history is a nice place, full of nice families with nice sisters who loved each other. And even if their own lives aren't so nice, they'll believe everything will get nicer someday, because history always repeats itself. That's the *point*."

No one said anything. The candles wavered atop the organ, while another log broke up in the fire.

At last Walter stirred from his place on the sofa and gave an exasperated sigh.

"Okay then," he said, clapping his hands together, then turning them inside out and stretching out his arms, "that's it for me." As if the credits had finally started to roll after an overlong movie, through which he'd sat dutifully. He dropped his arms and leaned forward, putting his hands on his knees. "It's late. Don't you agree, Frances? It's getting late and our guests need to get on the road and the rest of us need to get to bed.

"Frances?" he repeated, standing up.

"Yes," she said, not looking at him.

Everyone but me and my father stood up, too, and rubbed their eyes and straightened their clothing. Almost immediately there followed the general self-conscious bustle that always accompanies guests' leave-taking, the business of finding coats and hats and remarking on the temperature outside, *Such an early winter, isn't it a shame, I heard we're in for another cold snap,* Jane wheeling my father into the hall so that he could say good-bye as well, and Mary Ellen not being able to thank Frances enough, and Frances saying she hoped Mary Ellen's uncle felt better soon, then Wen-Yi saying his own stilted good-byes, while Sarah and Arlen wished him good luck with string theory and his doctoral dissertation,

Don't get tied up in knots! before coming back wordlessly into the living room to collect dessert plates and teacups, careful not to look at each other, and through it all I sat alone by the fire, which was now only embers, and tried to remember exactly what it was that I had just said.

Jane announced that she was going upstairs to watch television in her room. Sarah and Arlen were still in the kitchen, drying and stacking dishes, wiping counters, putting the last of the Fareeds' pies into plastic containers. "Here I'll get that," they kept saying, seizing a dish towel or a plate, "I can do that." When I offered to help they smiled obliquely and said not to bother, they would take care of it. Finally I sat down at the table and began drying Frances's Blue Willow platters and serving dishes by hand, because Sarah and Arlen had not been thorough, and china, especially old china, should not be put away damp.

After Walter had wheeled my father off to get him ready for bed, Sarah told Frances that she should go to bed, too. "We'll take care of everything," she said. "We're almost done." If Sarah and Arlen were ignoring me, they were treating Frances as some sort of invalid, taking plates out of her hands, refusing to let her help wash the wineglasses.

"Go to bed, Mom," Sarah repeated. "You're worn out."

"Well, I am tired," she agreed reluctantly. "All right. Thank you, dear. You've been such a help." She leaned toward Sarah to give her a kiss.

"And why don't you sleep late tomorrow." Sarah stepped back, hugging a large oval aluminum tray in front of her. "There's no reason to get up. We can take care of our own breakfast. Stay in bed."

Frances froze and looked at Sarah and the aluminum tray. Then suddenly she did seem exhausted. "I guess I will then. That's very thoughtful of you, Sarah."

Without acknowledging me, she turned and left the kitchen. A moment later we heard her go slowly up the stairs. Sarah and Arlen went back to moving around the kitchen, rinsing a few last cups and setting the roasting pan to soak in the sink. I continued to dry those fine old dishes by hand with a soft cloth, as Frances herself would have done, losing myself for a few minutes in a calm blue intricacy of pagodas and bridges and curving willow trees.

"Can I make you some tea, Aunt Cynnie?" asked Sarah. I shook my head, then watched as she and Arlen prepared cups of chamomile tea for each other, giggling slyly over some reference to dorm life that I didn't understand. At last, yawning and stretching, they told me good night, said they hoped I'd sleep well, and went upstairs to watch television with Jane.

After they left I returned to the living room, intending to turn off all the lamps and blow out the candles before going up to bed. But it was so quiet in there, after the earlier tumult of guests and conversation, so restfully quiet, that after switching off the lamps I left the candles burning and settled onto the sofa. I poured myself a little of what was left in the sticky bottle of Calvados, still sitting on the coffee table amid Jane's unfinished jigsaw puzzle. Outside, the wind had picked up, racketing around the north side of the house, making the windowpanes rattle.

I'd been sitting there for perhaps a quarter of an hour when I heard Walter walking around downstairs, turning off lamps. He came into the living room and paused, noting the candles and my presence on the sofa. He came a few steps farther, then stopped by the fireplace and picked up the tongs to poke at the smoldering logs, at last coaxing a flame out of the embers. The sofa cushions sagged under his weight as he sat down beside me.

"Hi," he said.

When I didn't answer, he reached under his glasses to rub the bridge of his nose between his thumb and forefinger, closing his eyes for a moment. At last he smiled and leaned back, twisting his face toward mine.

"An okay Thanksgiving, I thought."

"Yes."

"It turned out all right."

"All things considered."

"Do we have to consider all things?" he asked quietly.

I reached out to brush away a fragment of piecrust that had fallen onto the sofa cushion between us. "I suppose not," I said. "The turkey was good," I added, "even though it was toxic."

That's when he took my hand between both of his.

It was so welcome to feel the warmth of Walter's hands around mine. I was so grateful that I almost wept. Grateful, too, for his kindness in sitting in the living room with me, though it was late and he must have been tired. I had done an unforgivable thing. I had tried to ruin Frances's Thanksgiving. And yet Walter seemed to understand that I was not myself in this house. Also that my mistakes were probably punishment enough and that what I needed most at the moment was not reproach but simply company.

For a while longer we sat together on Frances's sofa, neither of us speaking. Outside the wind roared. Once more the fire died down to embers. And as we huddled in that cold room, listening to the wind and watching the fire, I began, idly at first, to imagine Walter's laying the palm of his hand against my cheek.

The pads of his fingertips would be slightly chapped, the dry hands of a doctor, who washed his hands often. I imagined his fingers lightly stroking my cheek.

Hush, he would whisper.

Again and again I pictured this: his hand rising to cup my face, his voice gently urging me to hush.

Until finally, somewhere in the middle of this small fantasy, I realized that Walter was no longer watching the fire, but was instead looking at me, and had been looking at me for some time. When at last I glanced up and met his eyes, I was not entirely surprised to see that the expression on his face did not say *hush* at all. Instead it was an expression I knew well enough—too well, perhaps—a look of attention rapidly deepening into consideration, which is less focused than attention, but hungrier.

The candles on top of the organ had burned low, lighting the room with the murky glow of an old Dutch painting. Walter's breathing had become shallow. Confusion dulled his big face as he gazed back at me; I suppose I looked enough like Frances in that indefinite light, and enough not like Frances in my red dress, to allow him to obscure what was going on in his mind. My own mind had grown suddenly clear and sharp, even as my arms and legs had gone heavy, and my heart began to run fast with the thin peculiar triumph that comes to me in moments like these, an exultancy wavering between arousal and disgust. But of course I wanted him to want me. It would be warm and comforting, and also vindicating, to be desired by Walter, decent upstanding

Walter, to have him groan and pull me against his chest and run his hands through my hair, and say that he couldn't help himself. As his hands dampened around mine, I thought of his shirts hanging on the back of the study door. His black socks balled on the desk.

I'd been in this deliberately vague charged-up situation often enough to predict what would happen next: his stubbly cheek rasping against mine, the sour smell of alcohol on his breath as our mouths met, then his tongue probing, my neck craning back until it ached. That prediction was almost enough to make me stand up and say good night.

But Walter was still holding my left hand between both of his, looking at me intently. I glanced down at the back of his hand, which was broad and hairy; the nails were very clean. When I laid my right hand on top of his I could feel his bones under his skin. Gently, very gently, I began circling the base of his thumb with the pad of mine.

He made a small hissing noise between his teeth.

For a long moment the two of us sat there, staring at each other, until once more I began that gentle circling with my thumb. His palm moistened, arched. But as I leaned in toward him, Walter moaned and pulled his hands away.

"No," he said.

Around us the living-room furniture emerged from the shadows to loom over us. My face was so hot that it felt scalded—it must have looked scalded. My hands were freezing. Ravening maw, I repeated to myself silently, with scornful detachment. You are a ravening maw. How could you be such a ravening maw?

Eventually I heard myself say, "I guess we got a little carried away tonight."

"You've had a lot to drink," he said hoarsely.

From far off in the woods, a high-pitched howling began.

"I think it might be better if I left tomorrow instead of Sunday."

"You don't have to go, Cynthia."

"I think I should."

"Frances won't want you to."

"I've had enough of what Frances wants."

Two or three votive candles guttered on top of the organ, their saucers filling with wax. The howling continued.

"And if Frances *knew*—," I began with a little laugh.

"Knew what?" he said shortly.

"What you and I—"

"Forget it. It wasn't anything."

"Frances wouldn't forget it," I said.

He gave me a flat look. "Nothing just happened, Cynthia. Do you understand? You are drunk."

We sat surrounded by the dark shapes of Frances's beautiful things. Then Walter's beeper went off. He unhooked the beeper from his belt, glanced at it, then turned it facedown on the coffee table. Watching him, I recalled his apprehensive expression when his beeper had gone off in the car, and it came to me that I'd probably been fooled by Walter, too, dependable Walter, so solid and reliable in his blue Oxford shirt. That he might be as big a liar as Frances.

Those new trendy eyeglasses, the restlessness, the casual pressure of his hand on my arm, my shoulder, lingering a few moments longer than necessary. What had nearly happened just now on the sofa. He wouldn't want calls on his home or office phone; his beeper number would be the best choice.

"So who are you sleeping with?" I asked. "One of your patients?"

Walter stared at me. Then he sighed and passed his hand over his face.

"Come on," I said.

Evidently Walter had drunk too much that night as well. Or maybe he felt he owed me something, after rejecting me. Most likely he just had to confess to someone, the way guilty people always do.

Because finally, unwillingly, he looked at me over the top of his glasses and said: "It wasn't a patient. And it was only once. Frances and I have never had problems that way, if that's what you're thinking." He paused and glanced away, pushing his glasses back onto the bridge of his nose.

"But you cheated on her."

He flinched. "It was a misjudgment I made," he continued after a moment.

"That's one way of putting it."

"It wasn't anything," Walter said crossly. "It didn't mean anything to me."

"Just physical?"

He frowned. "Men and women are different."

"That's a cliché, Walter."

"So what," he said brutally.

Suddenly I felt so tired that I could hardly summon the energy to add, "And by the way, Frances *knows*."

"No, she doesn't."

"I heard you two arguing the other night."

"Oh, that." He gave a dismissive shrug. "What you heard," he said grimly, "is Frances being worried."

"She *suspects* you, though. And it turns out she's right."

"She's not right. There's nothing to be right about."

I considered this statement for a moment. "So you *don't* want to sleep with Mary Ellen?"

Walter made an irritable gesture with his hand. "God no. I don't know why Frances is so obsessed with that woman. Or why she insisted on inviting her tonight." Now his face was screwed up in angry perplexity. "Who the hell knows what she wanted to prove."

Then his face cleared. "Anyway, she knows I'd never leave her."

"Why not?"

He looked at me sternly. "Because I wouldn't. I'm married to Frances. People can act badly in a marriage and still want to stay married. That's pretty elementary, Cynthia. I'm not excusing what I did, but I didn't do it to hurt my marriage."

Such a sap, I thought. Walter is a sap. Even in cheating, he's a sap. Going out and sleeping with people who don't matter to him, pretending Frances would understand.

"I love Frances," he was saying.

"Of course you do," I replied. "That's why you lied to her."

"People lie to each other all the time, for all sorts of reasons, some of them good. For godssake, Cynthia," said Walter, losing his temper. "What do *you* know about it?"

"You'd be surprised at what I know. Especially what I know about Frances and lying."

"Such as?" said Walter tensely. He must have been thinking of Wen-Yi. Men like Walter can't imagine being betrayed by their wives except for a younger man.

"Did you know that my father was a card shark? A con artist?"

"What?" Walter looked bewildered.

"Nothing big. Before he met my mother and got into the insurance racket."

"I don't understand what you're getting at."

"He's half Jewish, though he pretends to be such a WASP. I bet you didn't know that, either."

"Cynthia," said Walter. "What are you telling me this stuff for?"

"Because you don't know anything," I said. "You don't even know what you think you know. Frances hasn't told you anything. She doesn't think our father killed our mother. She thinks *she* did. And she thinks our father set her up to do it."

"Why would she think that?" Walter looked horror-struck.

I stared back at him.

"You're exhausted," he told me. Shrewdness had come back into his eyes. "And you've had too much to drink."

"So have you."

A muscle jumped in his cheek. Even in such poor light, I could see that he was struggling to say the right thing, to climb out of the dangerous position he'd put himself in by sitting too close to me on the sofa, and breathing hard, then offering up his confession. Probably he'd never found himself in this sort of moral quicksand before, not even with his cheating, his one "misjudgment," which to his mind was probably no worse than forgetting to defrost the turkey. But what could he say that wouldn't sink him further? He must have been quite frightened.

"I'm sorry, Cynthia."

"Not as sorry as you should be. She doesn't care about you half as much as she cares about him."

Walter stood up so abruptly that he bumped against the coffee table, hard enough that several of Jane's jigsaw pieces fell onto the carpet. For a moment he stared down at them, unable to decide whether to pick them up or leave them there.

"Worry about yourself," he said unsteadily. "Frances will be fine. Frances *is* fine."

Behind his heavy glasses his face looked elderly and querulous, as if I'd glimpsed Walter ten or fifteen years from now, at a time when he himself was no longer well.

"Frances has always been fine," I said, gazing up at him.

But Walter wasn't listening to me. "And for your information she doesn't feel anything but sorry for your father. It's been twenty-five *years*. She wants to get on with things. Stop trying to drag her back into things that don't matter anymore."

"Me? Dragging *her* back?"

"So the hell with you and what you think you know."

How could we have gotten to this point? It was only a few days ago that Walter and I had sat in his car, discussing Frances like two comrades. A few minutes ago he was holding my hand by candle-light. I could not understand how I could be so unfairly accused of being stuck in the past, when clearly it was Frances who was stuck, when she was the one who had engineered our father's arrival in her house, who had schemed to get our grandmother's organ, who wouldn't turn up the heat or allow for decent lighting. I hadn't lied to anyone. I hadn't cheated. How could I be to blame?

Because it was convenient. Because it was believable. Even I half believed that I was to blame for everything that had gone wrong, from Frances's plans for a nice family Thanksgiving to Walter's "misjudgment."

Carefully I reminded myself that all I had done was to try to be of help, the lapses of this particular evening aside. I had come to Concord with every intention of being reasonable, of acting the way sisters were supposed to act when presented with the ungovernable fact of a father who was old and sick and most likely about to die. If my visit had resulted in falseness and confusion, it was not entirely my fault; in fact, it was possible that it was not my fault at all. It was also possible that it did not matter who was at fault.

"I've heard enough," Walter was saying. "I'm going to bed."

"Walter, listen. It was Frances who—"

"I've heard *enough.*" He was already halfway across the living room.

But just then Walter stopped dead. Not to reconsider anything we'd said, but because both of us had become aware of a strange sound.

At first it sounded like a distant crumpling, like tin foil being uncrinkled and smoothed out, a low caustic rustling. For a disoriented moment I thought it might be a dog or a coyote that had somehow slipped into the house through the back door, drawn by the smell of turkey carcass, nosing in the garbage. But the sound was coming from the dining room. Part hiss, part crackle, part long ghostly sigh.

Then suddenly it resolved into a single voice, as if a guest had been forgotten and was still sitting at the table waiting to be served.

"She's so out of it."

Another voice answered, less distinctly.

Then the first came again: "I mean it, she is so totally *out* of it."

More mutterings, followed by static. It was Sarah and Arlen, I realized. Though it took me another minute to figure out that they'd gone into Sarah's room, where earlier that evening the Fareeds had set up their portable crib and the baby monitor. In their hurry to depart the Fareeds must have forgotten to take the baby monitor with them, and Sarah and Arlen's voices were being transmitted from upstairs.

"She's *always* been out of it. But now she's like this—*freak*."
Sarah was perfectly audible now. "I mean, did you get a load of
that dress?"

"She's not a freak," came Arlen's light drawl. "She's depressed."

"Of course she's depressed. Who isn't depressed?"

"No, more than that. I talked to her."

"You did—"

"We had a long chat."

"Well, good for you." Sarah sounded angry.

I pictured Arlen and Jane sitting together in the living room
by the shelf of carved birds. It had probably made Sarah jealous,
that cozy little scene. Sarah had always been possessive about her
friends, never willing to include her sister or overlook Jane's ec-
centricities, even though Sarah had had all the advantages. But
there was nothing wrong with Jane that getting away from home,
and out from under Sarah, wouldn't cure.

"Cynthia," Walter said, not moving.

"It's just Sarah and Arlen," I told him, raising my hand.

Arlen's drawling voice had continued on, "Though if you ask
me, I'd say it's more than simple depression, I'd say she's in some
kind of arrested—"

A clarifying word or two was lost here in the static, then Arlen's
voice returned: "A *pre*tense at normalcy, but everything comes
back to—"

"You think everything's about people's mothers," interrupted
Sarah.

"Well, *because*—"

More static.

So it was Frances, I realized, sitting back against the sofa cushions. Not Jane. It was Frances they were discussing; Frances who
was depressed, whose life was arrested, who was out of it. Hadn't

Walter told me the same thing in the car? No longer able to drive, spending days in her room. How had I missed how deeply disturbed she was? I thought of Frances's story at the dinner table, about my father carving the Thanksgiving turkey. Arlen, the outside observer, had recognized that story for what it was, a pitiful attempt to polish the past. Frances must have gone over this incident again and again in her mind, trying to smooth every jagged edge, just as she'd done with our father and everything she recalled about him. But now here he was in her house, as unregenerate as ever, the fly in her amber. It all made sense. Arlen was very sharp. Nothing got by him.

"Let's turn it off," I said to Walter, who was still standing motionless in the middle of the room, staring at the dark doorway. He'd heard enough about Frances for one night. "Let's not listen to them. They don't know anything. They're kids. We don't need to hear what they think."

But the voices had begun to crackle once more in the dining room, small and thin and persistent. "She's *pathetic*."

"She's *fine*," I told him.

"Cynthia." Walter had turned finally and was staring now at me. "Just who do you think they're talking about?"

It was long past midnight, though exactly what time it was, I didn't know, having forgotten to put on my watch when I was getting dressed. Everyone else had gone to bed. Only I was still awake, wrapped in the shawl Wen-Yi had worn earlier, still sitting in the living room in the fading candlelight.

Outside the wind was still battering at the dark windows, tearing at the ivy and blowing down the chimney with a hollow sound. It hadn't been coyotes howling earlier, just the wind as that cold front blew in from Canada. I could feel the barometer dropping.

The fire had gone out long ago and Frances's furniture had settled deeply into the gloom. Only the white pillar candles still burned, the color of moonlight on top of the organ around the Spode vase. Burning lower and lower in their saucers, their wax walls thinning and curling inward, but still burning.

And then wax began to overflow the saucers.

I didn't notice at first. Dripping candle wax doesn't make a noise, like dripping water, and I had closed my eyes for a few minutes. But gradually an acrid smell drifted toward me from across the room. When I opened my eyes I saw a thin white stream run down the mahogany side of the organ cabinet. Then another, and another. Like little burst dams, the candles on top of the organ gave way, one by one, releasing spills of hot wax down the front of the cabinet now, then onto the carved fretwork, onto the scrolls and garlands, the stop knobs and finally onto the keyboard, seeping between the celluloid keys. Silently I waited to see what would happen next, amazed by all this quiet damage that I had done nothing to cause, while white wax continued to spill unctuously onto the organ.

Then a twig fell sideways from Frances's arrangement of dried grasses. Just a twig. The bottom half of the twig stayed lodged in the vase, but the tip of it fell into one of the candle flames, a tiny flame, which had burned so low it had turned blue.

It took only another few moments for the vase of dried grasses and cattails to catch fire, almost as if it had been put there for that purpose, an enormous wick set atop the enormous candle of my grandmother's organ. Soon a warm busy glow lit the room, a homely glow, not particularly menacing, even as the flames shot higher.

I wish I could deny that I sat and watched this small conflagration take place. Watched calmly, almost greedily, and with something more than fascination. But that would be a lie. Nestled on the sofa in my sister's lovely living room, wrapped in her lovely shawl, drunk on her lovely bottle of Calvados, and with gladness in my heart, I watched her only bona fide family heirloom catch fire and took the time to note that the living room did not have a smoke detector fastened onto the ceiling. Nor did the front hall, for that matter. Smoke detectors, like television sets, don't go well with antiques, and both had been banished from the lower regions of Frances's house.

I am only human, although I regret it.

Even so I couldn't have remained on that sofa for longer than a few minutes. Before the flames had a chance to catch at the curtains or the carpet, or even to scorch one of the lampshades, I had scrambled to my feet.

My first thought was to douse the fire with water—not having any water at hand, I seized the bottle of Calvados and unwisely emptied what was left in it onto the organ. This of course made the fire blaze higher. Next I tore off the shawl and tried to smother the flames with it—somewhat more effective, though I knocked over the vase, which broke into pieces and sent burning grasses scattering onto the Persian carpet. I slapped at the grasses with the shawl, until the shawl, too, caught fire. Then I ran to the kitchen, threw the shawl into the sink, which was full of soaking pans, found the fire extinguisher beside the refrigerator, and ran with it back to the living room to spray onto the organ.

After that it took only a few moments to put out the flames, which had not actually grown very big. Nor was the damage very serious, once I'd turned on a lamp to see by: a brown scorch mark had seared onto the ceiling, the Spode vase was broken into several pieces, a palm-sized hole was burnt into the carpet.

The organ itself was a smoking mess—beyond all hope of reclaiming—but the rest of the living room was spared. And at last my head cleared enough that I could look around and evaluate exactly what had happened, or rather what I had done, by not doing anything.

Four

Walter was the first one downstairs on Friday morning. When he saw the charred organ in the living room, the scorch marks on the ceiling, the broken vase, I thought for a moment he was going to call the police. Then I thought he was going to put me in the car and take me straight to the airport.

I hadn't gone to bed that night at all. I'd stayed up airing the living room and putting to right what I could. When Walter arrived downstairs, I was on my hands and knees in my velvet dress, picking bits of burnt grass out of the carpet.

"What is this?" he said faintly, stumbling as he stepped into the living room. He tightened the cord on his bathrobe. "What happened here?"

I explained that I had fallen asleep on the sofa and that when I awoke the room was in flames.

"Why didn't you call any of us?"

I didn't answer. Walter had just started to say something else, less faintly, when Frances came creeping downstairs in her long blue flannel nightgown.

Her hands flew to either side of her face. "Oh my God, Cynnie," she cried. "Are you all right?"

I'd expected tears and recriminations, once she'd seen her spoiled living room, but Frances had only sympathy for me and what I'd gone through.

"How *awful* for you," she kept saying, hardly glancing at the room.

I went off to wash my hands in the bathroom. The sight of my face in the mirror gave me a start. Red-eyed as a banshee, hair wild, my cheeks and forehead streaked with soot. No wonder Frances had looked so concerned. As I came out of the bathroom a few minutes later I heard her and Walter talking in the front hall.

"I can't *believe* you, Walter," Frances was saying, making no effort to keep her voice down. "What's wrong with you? She saved the house from burning to the ground."

"All I'm saying—," Walter began, but then Sarah and Arlen came downstairs, and everything had to be explained to them.

They were not as sympathetic as Frances.

"So it was the candles?" Sarah asked me, her eyes narrow, her serious young face still pink and puffy with sleep. "You passed out and the candles overflowed, and then one of them caught the organ on fire? And you didn't bother to tell anyone?"

Arlen leaned against a doorjamb, watching me as he stroked his downy little black moustache.

Frances spent the rest of the morning making calls to house painters and restoration specialists, while I sat with her in the kitchen. I should have gone to bed, but I was afraid that I wouldn't be able to sleep. I was also afraid of leaving Frances alone to listen to what the others might tell her.

After her first shock when viewing the damage to her living room, Frances declared that it wasn't much, after all. She could have the room professionally steam-cleaned in a day and the ceiling repainted. The organ looked unsalvageable to me, but Frances claimed that she'd seen a lot worse. A man she knew in Reading specialized in reconditioning antique musical instruments, even ones that had been through floods and fires. I could not understand how she could be taking the injuries to her living room so calmly—Frances, who was normally unhinged by dirty plates left in the sink. The carpet, too, she concluded, could be neatly repaired, the coffee table repositioned to cover the damaged spot, though it would be expensive to match such old wool. But when I offered to pay for everything Frances wouldn't hear of it.

"I can't stand to think what would have happened if you hadn't woken up. No, it's *my* fault," she said, "for not making sure all those candles were put out."

Jane, too, seemed to think I was some sort of a hero. "And the whole time the rest of us were *asleep*." She looked at me with admiration.

As for my father, when he was wheeled into the kitchen for breakfast and treated by Frances to the story of my brave night, he didn't make any comment at all, just kept staring at me, a little blankly, the way you do with someone you can't quite place, but whom you know you've seen before.

THAT WAS FRIDAY. Sarah and Arlen left on Saturday morning, a little before nine. Originally they had planned to stay in Concord until Sunday, but on Friday afternoon they announced that they needed to get back to New York for a rally they'd forgotten they had promised some friends they'd attend. I didn't believe them, and I could tell Frances didn't, either, but she made only a token protest ("You just *got* here"), barely seconded by Walter. Sarah would be back in three weeks for Christmas. And I wasn't the only one who'd suffered under the scrutiny of Sarah and Arlen.

Walter drove them to the train station Saturday morning, and then went on to the hospital for his scheduled rounds. Otherwise he might have gone to Hartford with us. He did not seem keen on our trip to see the Mark Twain House and on Friday evening had tried several times to dissuade Frances from going, first suggesting that I go by myself, then, when Frances declared that she wanted to go with me, pointing out that my father could not be left alone for the entire day.

"He's coming with us," announced Frances.

I'd lost all interest in visiting Hartford myself and said as much to Frances. I explained that I could use photographs of the Mark Twain House to get the furniture right and what I remembered of Hartford to fill in the flora and fauna and the street names. I even mentioned an historical novelist I know who never bothers with period detail in his novels but simply begins the first chapter with "London 1865," or "Vienna 1703," and the reader imagines the rest.

It was Frances who insisted.

"You flew all the way out here for this," she told me in the kitchen. "I'm going to make sure you get what you came for."

"The traffic on 84 is going to be terrible." Walter was resting both hands on the back of a chair. "It's Thanksgiving weekend. All those people going back to New York."

Frances made a careless gesture with her hands.

"And they're calling for more snow."

"Walter, stop it. I'm sure we'll be fine."

"What about Jane?" His voice hardened. "Go if you want, but there's no way I'm letting you take Jane."

I thought it was all over then. Walter had finally made himself clear. But, pale and quiet in her black wool sweater and faded denim pants, Frances only stared back at him. "Fine," she said at last, setting her jaw. "If you're that worried about the weather, Walter, Jane can go into Cambridge with you. I'm sure she'd love to spend the day poking around Harvard Square."

He turned from Frances to look at me. I cannot describe the expression on his face because I could not stand to look at him. "If you're driving, Cynthia," he said, in a low, even voice, "I'm warning you, you'd better be careful."

Though Friday had been overcast, and Walter kept predicting more bad weather, Saturday proved to be a clear bright day, one of those late fall mornings when the sky is the impossible blue of a child's balloon, expanding behind scribbles of bare tree branches.

It was just after eleven. I was once again driving Frances's van. She sat beside me in the passenger seat, in her high-collared black cashmere coat, my father in the backseat. Concord appeared deserted, the streets of the village almost empty of cars, the stores still closed. Clapboard houses shone in the cold sunlight, snug and insular behind their well-tended hedges.

"Isn't this exciting, Dad?" said Frances. "Going to Hartford? I'll bet you haven't been there in years."

I looked into the rearview mirror. He was sitting behind Frances staring out the window at the passing trees and houses.

He did not look well this morning. His face was gray and one of his eyelids was drooping; bluish hollows dented his cheeks. A few minutes later he fell asleep, his head angled toward his shoulder. As we got onto the highway, Frances began to say something about checking the oil before we left, but then stopped herself. Soon enough, we'd passed Worcester and within half an hour I was slowing down for the Sturbridge tolls, and then we were on I-84, heading southwest.

It had been twenty years at least since I'd driven from Boston to Hartford, yet everything looked more or less the same. Rocky outcroppings, hills, woods, some light industry. A highway service island appeared on my left, where Frances and I had once stopped for gas in a borrowed car when we were both in college, then spent half an hour trying to figure out why we couldn't get the car started again, only to realize that Frances had left it in gear. We'd shrieked with laughter for miles.

The sky had clouded over and the traffic, which had been light as we left Massachusetts, began to get heavier. Frances leaned back against her headrest, gazing out through the windshield at the highway. In the winter sunlight her skin looked worn, almost brittle, the color of old porcelain. Dad was still asleep, snoring lightly through his nose. Frances turned her head to glance back at him.

Then in a small, determined voice she said, "I have something to tell you."

At first I thought she was going to bring up the fire in the living room and tell me that she knew what I'd done, by letting it get out of hand. But instead she said: "It's about what I said at dinner the other night, about there having been misunderstandings."

"Oh, that," I said, relieved.

She peered at me alertly. "It's about what happened. All the old stuff. It wasn't the way you think."

"What are you talking about?"

"When I went to see Dad on the Cape." She furrowed her eyebrows. "I didn't tell you but I went a bunch of times, not just once or twice. We spent a lot of time together and had a chance to really talk. It was pretty amazing. I mean for the first time he told me about his mother, about going to her grave every year on December 16. He told me about that day when she died. It was so traumatic for him, Cynnie. It's colored his whole life. He was just a little boy."

"So?" I said thinly.

Frances took a deep breath. "So, we really had a chance to go over everything. We'd never done that before, told each other what we remembered."

I kept my eyes on the road and said nothing.

"I've been waiting for the right time to tell you. But after the last few days—well, there's never going to be an exact right time, so I want to go ahead now. Because we put it all together, Dad and I."

"You put all what together?"

Frances looked at me with compassion. "What happened, Cynnie. To *our* mother. And why everything happened that happened afterward."

"So that's what this whole Thanksgiving has been about?" My voice was very calm.

"I needed to bring you and Dad together, while there's still time."

When I didn't say anything, she reached out and touched my sleeve. "Dad explained it all to me, what I hadn't known, and I explained to him what he hadn't known. Now we both understand."

Cars kept switching into my lane to avoid the ones coming off the entrance ramps. Twice I had to brake suddenly. I glanced into the rearview mirror, but my father appeared to be fast asleep.

Frances was still talking. "You were just a little kid then. I didn't want anyone thinking it was you."

"*What?*"

She looked at me patiently. "Please listen. I'm trying to explain. Remember how strangely I acted afterward about Mrs. Jordan? How rotten I acted about Ilse? I was trying to look *guilty*. I didn't really think that you'd done anything, but her dying was so sudden, and you were always so angry. Don't you remember, how angry you were back then? And that awful story you told about the soup being poisoned, when I *knew* she hadn't eaten any. I was the one who took it up to her. It just seemed so—weird. So suspicious, I guess. So I had to pretend, to make it seem like if it was anyone, it was me."

"I have no idea what you're talking about."

"Of course Dad believed me," Frances continued, lowering her voice still further. "I wanted him to, but I guess part of me also couldn't stand that he would, that he could think that about me." She paused to take another breath. Then with a little laugh she said, "All these years, I thought I was covering up for you, and he thought he was covering for me."

What followed then was a very peculiar experience, perhaps the most peculiar of my life. As Frances went on to relate her version of this story, a version she and my father had pieced together between them, I heard what she was saying, but not in the normal way of hearing. Her words came to me more as images projected on a screen. Images that were both familiar, God knows, though I'd spent years trying to forget them, but also as strange as if I'd never seen them before:

A girl heading upstairs, carrying a tray into the room where a woman lies in bed. Steam from a vaporizer hissing on the floor, the night table cluttered with medicine bottles and vials of pills. The girl sees the glass knocked over onto the floor, the tissues pulled out of the box and scattered. It offends her, this disorder, and confirms her feeling of being unfairly burdened, having to contend with such a mess. She does not stoop to pick up the glass or the box of tissues, does not even see the empty vial of pills, lying on its side. The woman in the bed stares as the girl puts down the tray, then refuses the spoonful of soup the girl reluctantly offers. But the woman is often not hungry; her refusal to eat tonight is not unusual. After a few minutes the girl takes up the tray and without closing the door behind her, goes back downstairs.

A younger girl climbs the stairs to the same room. Stops at the doorway to glance in, then steps inside, coming closer and closer to the woman on the bed. What does she do? She straightens up the room. Why does she feel she must straighten up the room, pick up the fallen glass, fill that water jug?

What is she cleaning up after?

Then it's a man, sometime later, who passes the open doorway of that same room. Something also causes him to stop and look in. Is it the glimpse of that empty medicine vial on the night table that makes him pause? The vial is neatly lined up beside a regiment of other bottles—not tipped over, as it had been an hour or so before, as if dropped by a clumsy hand. And missing its cap. The man was in the woman's room earlier that evening, putting his head round the door to say hello, before remembering that he had his pipe in his mouth. The room has been tidied since then: plumped pillows, a filled water jug with an empty water glass beside it. Every surface wiped clean. He takes time to note all this.

Then he sees the woman on the bed.

After a little while, after he has sat for a time on the edge of the bed, and before he has called the ambulance, which will arrive much too late to be of use, this is what else he thinks about:

A crabbed message on a school notebook. Strong athletic arms and legs, growing thinner and thinner. Failing grades, lost friends. Her cold avoidance of this room.

And gradually, over the next few days, he calculates all of it, the whole dreadful equation. He had pushed Frances to it. In all his years in the insurance business, indemnifying people against the terrible things that could happen to them, he'd never had to pay for one like this: *How long are you going to keep me waiting?* he'd demanded that night, when she balked at carrying the soup upstairs to our mother's room. *Frances can do it,* he'd said, when I offered to carry the soup up instead. So Frances had done it. Emptied the pills from that vial into her hand, then into the broth, watched them dissolve. Because she loved him, because she needed him, because she was afraid he was being driven away by the suffocating vapors of illness and grief. That was the story he put together from all those details, a story that, like most stories people tell themselves about other people, was mostly about him.

Keep going, he'd told her. Don't let anything stand in your way. *No matter what.*

But he'd been talking about her homework.

In the end, what frightened him most was not what Frances had done but what other people would do if they became convinced she was guilty. (Who knew what a young girl would say under questioning?) They would come for her. Put her somewhere. In

a hospital. Jail even. For whole nights, he had lain awake thinking. He'd lost his mother and his wife; he wasn't going to lose his
daughter, too.

But how to keep others from suspecting? Especially sullen
Cynthia, who seemed to notice everything, and what she didn't
notice, she imagined. *There's something wrong with Frances. Frances
is the one who's the problem.*

Find a distraction, a diversion. Make a bargain with fate. A
bargain that he probably never intended to honor—since fate always wins in the end, cheating once you've got what you wanted
seems justified. Anyone in the insurance business understands this
kind of reasoning. In time all would be resolved—that's what he
thought. *Time heals all wounds,* etc.

Send us off, drive us away, only long enough to invite us back
again, or at least get Frances back. That was his plan. Almost
three decades later, during those long secret intimate lunches
on the Cape, in dark little clam shacks decorated with fishing
nets and lobster buoys, he had laid out for Frances the whole sad
scheme, how every apparently selfish thing he'd done had all been
an effort to save her.

But Frances knew she had not killed our mother. Of course not.
And she never believed that he had, either, for the simple reason
that she thought I had done it.

Use your head, I'd said that wintry night, when Frances came up
to my bedroom and sat on the end of my bed, kneading the cov-
erlet between her thin fingers, eyes hopeful, eager to believe my
father's insinuations about why Mrs. Jordan had been sent away
that morning in her black straw Sunday hat. Mrs. Jordan would
have solved everything.

And as far as I knew, Mrs. Jordan *had* solved everything, by
taking the cap off that vial of pills and leaving the open vial on

the bedside table, within reach of even the most maladroit hand, if that hand was truly determined. But Frances never knew about the cap in the bathroom wastebasket. She never knew that my mother had reached out and been accurate and deft enough to seize my wrist that night and squeeze it hard. Because I had never told her.

That's what he wants you to think, I'd said instead. *I know what he's hiding. Don't bother asking him. He'll just start talking about your special bond.*

"You always minded it so much," Frances said now, turning to me in the van, fixing me with her sympathetic blue eyes. "The closeness between Dad and me."

"You're crazy," I said.

"Listen to me, Cynnie. It was a long time ago. I've tried to be as careful as I could in helping you realize what happened. I'm sorry if I'm being clumsy now. But we're running out of time. I'm just bringing it all up to lay it to rest."

Waking a sleeping baby to put it to bed.

"Pretty tidy, don't you think?" I tightened my grip on the steering wheel, feeling light-headed. "Both you and Dad, exemplars of selflessness."

"What I'm trying to say—"

"It's a bunch of bull, the whole thing, and you know it."

"Cynthia." Frances put a hand to her face.

Exits were coming quickly now, one after another as we neared Hartford. Signs flickered by, announcing all the old towns: Wethersfield, Newington, Waterbury. The highway dipped as we went downhill. Hills, trees curved upward on either side of me. It was like driving inside of an enormous bowl.

Frances was talking again. "I'm only telling you all this because tomorrow you're going back to California and I don't know when we'll see each other again. I don't know if you'll see *him* again. It's so important after all we've lost not to lose any more chances."

"Chances for *what*?"

"To get on with life. That old stuff is over. It doesn't matter. Let it go. Dad just wants us all to be happy."

"I *have* been getting on with life. In case you haven't noticed."

Her voice was very sad. "That's not my impression."

I checked the rearview mirror to see if my father was still asleep, then I said, "You were the one who hated her."

"No." Frances stared straight ahead. "I hated her being sick."

Two oil trucks thundered by, making the van shudder.

"Frances," I said, my head starting to throb, "don't you see what he's really after? Can't you see why he's fed you all this crap? He knew his marriage was going south, probably quite a while ago. He's an old opportunist. He always has been. Talk about chances. *He* knows how to grab a last chance when he sees one."

Though wouldn't it be wonderful, I found myself thinking in sudden exhaustion—the dazed, trembling exhaustion that always precedes one of my headaches—wouldn't it be wonderful if it were true? That all my father's selfishness had really been an act of heroic protection. Why not give in to it? One story's as good as another. And as this thought came to me, I realized at the same moment that it didn't matter. None of it mattered. We would never know exactly what happened to our mother and knowing wouldn't change anything, anyway. Because what both Frances and I understood perfectly well, what neither of us could forget or forgive or admit to each other, is that while our mother was alive we'd wished she would die so that we could stop worrying about it.

"Did Ilse find out about all this?" I demanded, as another mystery was suddenly solved. "Did she get to hear this tale of noble sacrifice?"

Frances made an ambiguous noise.

"Let me ask you another question," I said hoarsely. "How come Dad never told anyone else this story?"

"He still thought he was protecting me." Frances turned toward me again, her eyes shiny with unshed tears. "He didn't want Walter to find out, or the girls. He thought it could still ruin my life. But when Helen died, he realized there wasn't much time left. For us—"

"It wasn't me," I said.

"I *know*," she said, and now the tears began to fall freely down her cheeks. "Oh Cynnie. But you were so angry back then, and she'd been sick for such a long time. You were really young and not really a part of things, somehow, not the way you should have been, and it was all so confusing. It just seemed like it could have been—"

"How long," I said, "did you think that?"

Frances shook her head gently. "All I want you to know is that it's not important. We still have each other. Nothing's changed."

My palms were damp and my fingertips ached with cold. One at a time, I lifted my hands off the steering wheel to run them against my pants' leg.

"Are you all right?" said Frances suddenly.

There was an old weigh station, fortunately, on the side of the highway. I pulled the van safely off the road, bumping over a low curb and bouncing across a rough apron of grass and dirty snow, broken glass popping under the tires, finally coming to a stop beside a rusted trash barrel. A thick metal chain gated off the abandoned scales directly ahead of us. I turned off the ignition, then leaned forward to rest my forehead against the steering wheel, drawing deep shaky breaths while Frances reached around to unroll my window a few inches.

"Forgot to eat breakfast this morning," I muttered finally. The taste of the coffee I'd drunk rose in my throat.

Frances turned in her seat to ask my father if he was all right and he gave a few reassuring grunts to indicate that he was unharmed by our unexpected detour. Cars hurtled past us on the left, the rush of displaced air buffeting the side of the van. The breeze from the open window blew icily against the back of my neck, filling the van with exhaust fumes.

"I think we should sit here for a few minutes." Frances laid her hand on my back as I closed my eyes, my forehead still pressed against the steering wheel. "Let's just take a few minutes and rest here."

"Don't touch me," I said.

She took her hand away. But soon enough there was her kind, inexorable voice again. "I packed some things this morning for the drive, I'm sure I have something in here you could eat."

"I don't want anything."

She began rummaging in a canvas bag at her feet, then held up a bag of dried apricots and a jar of cocktail peanuts. "Your hands are shaking," she said, looking at me closely as I sat back in my seat.

"I'm just cold."

"You need to get your blood sugar up."

Frances poured me a cup of tea from the stainless steel thermos she'd also thought to pack. Then once she'd made sure I'd had a few sips of tea, she told me to get out of the van. "Switch places with me. I'll drive."

When I stared at her, she held up her new bifocals. "I brought them along, just in case." When I continued to look at her, she said, "Cynthia, this is my van. I drive it all the time."

We changed seats and Frances put on her glasses, then started the van.

"Just keep taking deep breaths," she said, glancing at me. Then she leaned over the steering wheel, concentrating on the traffic before pulling back onto the highway.

FRANCES LOOKED TENSE but she drove carefully and competently. It seemed only a few minutes before downtown Hartford's familiar gray skyline rose up before us. Gritty, bland, forlorn Hartford, which Twain once described as a pastoral dream of commerce, a sober, affluent town, balancing "capacious ornamental grounds" with business and factories.

"Travelers," said my father, quite clearly, as we took our exit. After a moment I realized that he was referring to the insurance company.

"Aetna," he added. "Life and Casualty."

"What's he saying?" asked Frances.

"Nothing," I told her.

After another block or two, we turned onto Farmington Avenue. The Mark Twain House comes up sooner than you'd expect in that glum stretch of apartment buildings, which seemed unchanged since when I was a child. Broken cement steps, buckled sidewalks, overgrown lawns.

When my father was a boy, grassy lots sprawled in place of the liquor stores and cheap apartment buildings. Once there had been flowering trees, handsome houses, acres of green lawn. Farmington Avenue had been one of the most beautiful streets in Hartford when Twain built his house here.

Just at that moment Frances cried, "And there it is!"

She slowed down as we approached Twain's brick mansion, sitting behind a scatter of leafless trees. I thought I remembered it facing the street, but it was set back from the road, overlooking what had once been a ravine but was now a parking lot. Against the drab November landscape of Farmington Avenue, the house glowed reddish orange, like an enormous jack-o'-lantern. Bands of brick shone in a complex pattern of polychromed scarlet and black. All the woodwork and railings had been painted a rich brown. In my memory, the house was an old haunted mansion, dark and decrepit, with boarded up windows and rickety balconies.

"See," said Frances, gesturing toward her window. "Completely restored."

Farmington Avenue was the main thoroughfare into West Hartford and I'd often passed Twain's house when I was a girl, though I went inside it only once, with the rest of the fourth grade of West Hartford Country Day. We were allowed no farther than the entrance hall, where the tiled floor was littered with what looked like pencil shavings. A handsome carved mahogany staircase reared up to the second floor, but some of the steps were broken and spindles were missing from the banisters. Plaster had fallen from the walls, and yellow tape stretched across doorways as if we had walked in on a crime scene.

I was remembering this as Frances pulled into a space in the almost empty parking lot. "Well, here we are," she said, a little shrilly, sliding her hands off the steering wheel. "Everybody out."

But in a reprise of the day we visited Greenswood Manor, my father at first refused to leave the van. Without warning he'd turned sullen and mean, as if he'd gotten a jolt of something besides surprise when we ran off the highway. He wouldn't look at Frances when she asked what was wrong and batted at her hands when she tried to unclip his seat belt for him.

"Dad," she said finally. "Just what are you going to *do* out here by yourself?"

He stopped batting at Frances's hands and she persuaded him to swing his legs over the runningboard so that she and I could help him down into the parking lot and then seat him in his wheelchair. Frances said not to bother trying to get his overcoat on him, since we would be going directly inside. She placed his old fedora on his head then draped his overcoat around his shoulders.

Above us towered the house on its hill, reachable only by a steep set of stairs, which had not been recently shoveled, and an almost equally steep handicapped ramp. But by pushing together, Frances and I got the wheelchair up the hill. Small brown-painted signs, the sort you find in national parks, directed us to the gift shop at the back of the house, where tickets could be purchased for both the Mark Twain House and the Harriet Beecher Stowe House next door.

However, once we arrived at the door marked MUSEUM SHOP we were met by a laminated rectangular white notice declaring that both houses would be closed for the next two weeks "for security reasons." The notice thanked the public for its patience and cooperation. It was signed THE MARK TWAIN MEMORIAL.

Our breath rose in clouds in the cold sunlight as we stood squinting at each other.

"I thought you checked the Web site," I said to Frances.

"I did, but that was a couple weeks ago. There wasn't any mention then of the house being closed."

"Isn't that strange."

She gazed calmly back at me. "You could have called ahead, Cynnie. I just assumed it would be open."

My father sat looking at us from his wheelchair, his fedora cocked rakishly on his head. His expression was similar to the one he'd worn on Thanksgiving morning, when we discovered that the turkey was still frozen.

It was Frances who suggested that we might as well look around. Cupping our gloved hands around our eyes, we pressed against the windows of the dark gift shop to peer in at shelves of books and displays of corncob pipes, straw hats, mugs, china figurines of Huck Finn and Tom Sawyer, calendars featuring Mark Twain in his famous white suit, posters of Mark Twain puffing on his pipe. Even a china toothbrush holder, decorated with a picure of Mark Twain with a cigar in his mouth.

"He would have loved this," I heard myself say.

"You mean he would have hated it." Frances stepped back from the window.

"No, he would have loved it but pretended to hate it."

With Frances pushing Dad's wheelchair, we walked around the side of the house to look at it from the lawn, a sharp wind scattering brown leaves across the snowy path. Not a security guard in sight. We could have broken a window and climbed in if we'd wanted to. Clouds like old ragg wool socks rolled overhead. Though I was pretending otherwise, I was glad the house was closed. I'd spent the better part of a year trying to imagine what had gone on inside those brick walls, and yet now that I was here I found myself reluctant, even afraid to step inside, as if the dimensions I'd invented for those girls might vanish when I was faced with actual ceilings and doorways.

"You're shaking," observed Frances.

"I'm just cold."

It *was* cold standing out on the lawn, so we followed the path to a carriage house set a little distance away, pausing to look across at Harriet Beecher Stowe's trim cottage, with its regular lines and kitchen garden. Writing about sensible Harriet and her even more sensible sister Catharine would be a relief, I decided, though I was sure that neither of them would remain sensible for long, once I started looking into their history.

"Quite a place he built for himself." Frances was again looking at Mark Twain's house. The sun had come out from behind the clouds, making the roof slates glitter. "Did he live here most of his life?"

"No. It's where his daughters grew up, though. None of them wanted to live here again after Susy died. When he was an old man, he built another house called Stormfield."

"What a gloomy name. Is that where he entertained the Angel-fish?"

I stared at the house, pretending not to hear the question.

In the course of my research, I'd sometimes flattered myself that Mark Twain would have liked me, if we'd ever met, that I might have been chosen to be an Angelfish during those final years of his life, when everyone he loved seemed to have left him. Young, smart, high-strung, pretty enough, I would have listened to his stories, played cards with him after lunch, dressed up in scarves and performed a harem dance in the parlor. I would have welcomed it all, even the spasmodic grip of an elderly hand on my arm, the malodorous breath, the yellow teeth. And not for the sake of being able to say someday, "Oh yes, I knew Mark Twain." But for the attention itself. The nervous intoxicating bask of it.

For Frances's benefit, I pointed out several windows at the top floor of the house, where I thought Twain's study must have been, then to what were probably the windows of the girls' schoolroom below. I described the historical plays the sisters had staged, with Susy and Clara playing rival queens, ordering each other's heads chopped off, while Little Jean played the bailiff, signing death warrants.

"You really do know everything about them," said Frances politely. She bent down to adjust the collar on Dad's tweed jacket, then pulled his overcoat more securely around his shoulders.

"But here's what I'd like to know," she continued, in the same polite tone as she straightened up, "if Twain was such a bad father to his daughters, why don't we know about it?"

"Because," I said sharply, "Clara protected him. After he died she made sure only praiseworthy information got out about him."

"Well," said Frances, smiling patiently at me, "how do you know that it wasn't all true? That what Clara wanted people to know about him wasn't the same as how he really was? Maybe because she loved him she wanted good things said about him."

It seemed I wasn't any better than Walter in avoiding Frances's ambushes, except that I had finally learned how to surrender once I'd been waylaid. For instance, I happened to know that for twenty-seven years after her father died, Clara had left his gravestone blank. I also knew that Clara hadn't told her daughter, Nina, that Mark Twain was her grandfather until Nina was a teenager. But I was tired of sharing facts like these with Frances, who would only find a way to twist them so that they meant the opposite of what I thought they meant. Probably I would never understand what had happened to Mark Twain's daughters any better than she did, but at least I was willing to admit it.

"If we leave right now," I said, consulting my watch, "we could be back in Concord by four."

"But Cynnie." Frances blinked at me. "We have to at least have lunch."

I don't believe it was ever a conscious part of Frances's plan, to visit our old house in West Hartford that day. Like me, she probably believed she intended to drive straight back to Concord after lunch, to be home before dark. Even Frances had her limits when it came to revisiting the past. But as we were finishing our sandwiches at a Subway shop on Farmington Avenue, Frances said that she wanted to see if the old neighborhood looked the same.

"Maybe some other time." I got up to throw away our napkins and paper plates and put our soda cans into a green plastic recycling bin.

"There probably won't *be* another time." Frances gazed up at me. "Come on, we're all the way here. It's only another mile or so." Frances turned to our father. "What do you think, Dad?"

He shrugged. He had hardly touched his roast beef sandwich. His head was sunk between his shoulders and a corner of his mouth hung open.

"Dad seems tired," I said. "He doesn't look well. I think we should be getting home."

"Cynnie. We're *here*. We'll stay in the car," she said. "We'll just drive by. It won't take more than a few minutes."

I said that I didn't feel very well. My headache was worse and I'd felt queasy all through lunch. Frances took out her bifocals and put them on again. She announced that she would drive, she knew the way. I could sit in the passenger seat and close my eyes.

"You don't even have to look," she added.

"Of course I'm going to look," I snapped.

But as soon as we started driving Frances got lost, turning up first one side street after another, each time thinking that the street was an old shortcut she used to take years ago on her bicycle. As we crisscrossed Farmington Avenue, shabby apartment buildings fell away; the trees got taller and the houses bigger. Bungalows mixed with brick colonials, set amid parklike expanses of lawn. By now it was almost three o'clock. The sun was getting low, shining right in our eyes, making it difficult to see.

"Here," Frances kept saying. "I know it's right here."

Half an hour passed before we were heading down the road that led to Stone Ridge Farms.

Frances pointed out various landmarks. *There's the Harpers' old house. That's where the Marlatts lived. My goodness, they've added another story.* Not much to see. Stone Ridge Farms had become just another subdivision. Houses, yards, driveways. I recognized a flounce of cattails along the road, where there had always been a marshy stretch. Otherwise, the woods were gone. The fields were gone.

When we reached Woodvale Road, Frances slowed down, then after a minute or two pulled over and stopped the van altogether. We were at the curve where the potato field had once stretched for acres, wide and rutted, off to the left. Now a girdle of asphalt ran past a series of oversized stucco Tudors with brass doorknockers and Palladian windows.

"Will you look at that," she said in a wondering voice.

"All right. I've seen it. Let's go."

My father said nothing. He had fallen asleep.

"Just a little farther." Frances was driving again, but she sounded as if she'd been holding her breath. "We haven't even reached the house yet."

The afternoon sun was directly in our eyes now as Frances slowed down, then once more stopped the van. I had to raise my hand against the glare.

"What are you *doing*?" I asked. "You're in the middle of the road."

"There it is," she said.

The house looked more or less the same as I remembered, only smaller, which is so much the rule in these situations that even its smallness wasn't a surprise. Gray-painted shingles, black shutters, a holly wreath on the front door. The rhododendrons were still there, though they had been pruned. Neatly shoveled brick steps. In the yard, a half-melted snowman wearing a red scarf.

What had I expected? Crumbling masonry, missing shingles, splintered front door hanging off its hinges. Open garbage cans, a chained barking dog. Children in torn pajamas, weeping on the steps. Actually, I think I'd simply expected the house not to be there at all. Deleted, along with my presence in it. A skipped space in the row of houses. But there it was, shingles intact behind the rhododendrons, windows unbroken, one of those wire cages on top of the chimney to keep the raccoons out. Though I did not look at Frances, I understood that she felt the same way, though for different reasons. Perhaps in the whole of our lives, we had never felt so alike as at that very moment, as we stared at our old house and were disappointed by the plain sight of it, and also relieved. And disappointed to be relieved. After all the ghost stories about the past we'd told ourselves over the years, we had neglected to imagine anything so terrifyingly commonplace as a gray-shingled house with a lawn, where we had lived until it was time to move on and where nothing had been done to us that was much worse or much better than what we had gone on to do to ourselves.

And yet it was at that same moment, as we crept past the respectable home of our childhood, that out of nowhere an enormous black car came hurtling at us from the opposite direction.

As anyone who has ever been in even a minor car accident knows, there's a lucid, arrhythmic moment before the collision happens. Time lengthens. Colors brighten, right angles sharpen. There's also a sense of quiet, as in music, when the tempo changes and arrives at the grace note. So this is it, you think. What it's all been leading up to. You would like to make better use of that grace note, that glass instant, when all should be made clear. But of course, you don't.

A voice was calling and calling, calling from somewhere outside my window, a voice that had gone thin and cracking.

You idiot, shouted the voice.

Perhaps, I thought, this is what it feels like to be dead. An insulting flatness.

From the far corners of my vision, I saw Frances shifting around in the driver's seat. Her air bag had not inflated.

"I'm so sorry," she kept repeating.

"Idiot!" shrieked the voice outside my window.

Slowly that voice came into focus. Straight blonde hair cut to her chin, a mouth smeared with red lipstick. A hard, unpleasant face. But something was wrong with my neck and I could not move my head to turn away from her.

"I have *children* in my car," she screamed.

"I'm so sorry," Frances was insisting.

"NECK INJURY," SAID the ambulance driver to his partner. "How about the old guy?"

"I checked him out. Just a bruise on his forehead. They weren't going very fast."

"Friggin' air bags."

"Friggin' SUVs," said the driver, glancing across the road.

The driver was young and red-haired, with pink bunchy cheeks. His partner was older, with a dark, withered-looking face and thick black eyebrows above gentle furtive brown eyes. He smelled of breath mints. A drinking problem, I decided, having ample time to examine him as he leaned over my seat to examine me, recognizing that delicate, almost formal withdrawal in his face, which I've also seen on the faces of homeless men who sit all day in the park across from my apartment. Though his hands, as he fixed a foam collar around my neck, were perfectly steady. As were Frances's, I realized, as she tried to offer me a thermos cap of water.

"She can't have any water yet, ma'am," he told her. "Not till she gets checked out at the hospital."

"Why?" said Frances. "What are they going to do?"

"A CT scan. Chest X-ray. She's got a possible concussion. Maybe a broken rib."

"I'd like to call my husband." Frances began to climb out of the van.

"You were driving, ma'am?"

THE AMBULANCE DRIVER and his partner were trying to shift me by degrees onto a hard narrow board laid across the front seat.

"Try to breathe slowly," said the ambulance driver.

"Keep as still as you can," urged his partner.

"We can't get you out of here unless you stay still."

"Calm down, Cynnie," whispered Frances from somewhere behind them. She sounded frightened. "Stop laughing and calm down, okay?"

As a child, I often got in trouble for laughing at inappropriate moments, in French class, for instance, or during graduation ceremonies, or while a visitor was saying grace at the dinner table. Frances, who never had this problem, once told me her secret: if you want to stop laughing, imagine something sad in detail. This strategy did not always work for me and in fact sometimes had the reverse effect. But sometimes it did work. The ambulance driver and his partner were both frowning now, one with frustration, the other with what seemed to be genuine concern, telling me to keep still.

And so because it was the first sad thing that came to me, I pictured December 16, the day my father's mother died. Killed, perhaps by accident, perhaps not, by stepping in front of a streetcar at the intersection of Main Street and Asylum Avenue.

It would have been cold that day as well, just a week or so before Christmas. The streets would have been gray and crowded, already getting dark at four o'clock. Her little boy lagged behind her, whining about the cold, complaining that his feet were wet, asking for toys she could not afford. Still she walked on, ignoring his cries, seeming not even to hear them. One last shop to visit. One more shop. This was how she got through the tiring duties of her life, by repeating to herself that she had to do them until they were done. One more shop. She began to cross the trolley tracks. Then suddenly, for no reason that onlookers could later explain, she stopped. Hesitated in the middle of the tracks that snowy late afternoon, in a big black coat, her arms full of packages, the child clutching at her sleeve. Wet trolley tracks stretched to either side of her, vanishing in opposite directions. Voices called out to her. The clanging of the streetcar became deafening, then even louder.

Loud enough to wake the dead. But it was not upon her yet; she had one more endless moment to hesitate. And as she stood there she repeated to herself that she was tired. Her back hurt; she had a cough; she was sick of shopping. Her life had been unhappy and was unlikely to improve. That could very well have been her last thought, a trite self-pitying reflection.

But I don't believe it. She was a mother, after all, no matter how worn out and uninvolved. As the screech of brakes filled her ears and a smoky wind blew her black coat about her ankles, she reached out to seize the little boy's wrist, hard enough to leave a mark, hard enough to thrust him back, and out of the way.

Don't watch, she said.

"THERE YOU GO," said the partner with relief.

Someone took my hand. I felt a sharp pressure above my wrist. The ambulance driver was busy with some equipment, a pole with a clear plastic bag attached. "I just gave you something to relax," he told me. He seemed to be speaking to my father as well, whose wheelchair had been pushed close to where I was now lying on a rolling metal cot. Above us the sky was beginning to darken.

"I'm fine," I tried to say.

"It's all right," a voice said. "Just an accident."

My father's face was level with mine, not six inches away. It was the same face he'd always had, a long triangular elegant face, only much older. After a moment or two I expected him to turn away, perhaps to look around for Frances. But he kept his eyes on mine.

"They said I can go," I told Frances, when I found her sitting in a row of hard-looking plastic chairs near the emergency room door, my father asleep in his wheelchair beside her. Evening had come on. The waiting room windows were dark. A potted palm tree stood under the fluorescent lights a few feet away from the reception desk, its green fronds casting long slender shadows on the floor that stirred whenever anyone passed by.

"Oh my God." Frances stood up and reached out to touch my neck brace.

I moved away from her hand. "The doctor said I'll have to wear this thing for a while. Otherwise I guess I'll be fine."

To avoid looking at Frances, I looked at my father, who had a mottled purple bruise on his forehead.

"Is he okay?" I asked Frances. "Did someone examine him?"

Frances explained that an emergency room doctor had taken his blood pressure, then given him an EKG and found that his heart rate was normal, then ruled out the need for an MRI. As she was finishing this report, a stout nurse with gray bangs appeared and repeated all the same things. My father opened his eyes to listen to her.

"We were concerned about that," the nurse pointed to the bruise on his forehead, "especially since he's had a stroke. If it were up to me, I'd keep him here overnight for observation, but she"—the nurse looked at Frances—"won't agree to it."

"But is he all right?" I asked.

"Dr. Kirsanov says he's okay," the nurse went on, squaring her shoulders. "She's our attending that talked with your sister here. That bruise looks worse than it is, but he should go to his own doctor tomorrow and have a full physical. He's an old man." The nurse frowned at Frances. "It's not doing him any favors, you know, putting him through all this."

"It was an *accident*," said Frances.

WALTER LOOKED HARRIED and upset when he arrived in the emergency room waiting area in his Burberry coat but almost comically relieved to see the three of us more or less ambulatory. In the car, Frances sat up front with him and I sat in the back with my father. My father fell asleep right away, while I listened to Frances's murmuring voice explain to Walter what had happened ("Who was driving?" he'd asked, almost immediately). Otherwise it was a quiet trip home. Snow was falling again, not very hard, more of a cold white mist.

Most of the house was dark when we arrived sometime after nine o'clock. Walter unlocked the back door to the kitchen, then returned to the car to help my father into his wheelchair. In the dark kitchen a tiny green light shone from the dishwasher, indicating that it had completed its cycle. I switched on a lamp by the door. The house was warm after the chilly outdoor air, yet once we took off our coats I felt a draft and also noticed the acrid smell of smoke, left over from two nights before. One of the kitchen windows was open an inch or two, letting in cold air mixed with a little snow. Frances must have opened it before we left that morning, to air the room out, then forgotten to close it again.

"Home sweet home," sighed Frances, coming in behind me.

She offered to make something for a late supper, but my father indicated that he wanted to go to bed. Jane came into the kitchen to greet us and ask questions about what had happened. She peered with concern at my neck brace and hoped my neck didn't hurt too much; but once she had satisfied herself that we were all right she said that she was tired and went upstairs to her room. While Walter was getting Dad settled for the night, Frances went into the dining room and came back carrying Jane's Thanksgiving centerpiece, which she set on the kitchen table. Then she poured herself a glass of red wine from a half-empty bottle on the counter. She offered a glass to me. I said that I'd like water instead.

"I've been meaning to ask," she said, getting up to fill a glass for me at the sink. "Why were you laughing this afternoon? What was that all about?"

"Nothing."

"No really. What was so funny?"

"Just something I remembered."

"You do know I'm sorry"—she set the water in front of me—"for everything that's happened."

"No, you're not," I said. "You just realize you should be."

Frances sat down again across from me and took a sip of her wine, then leaned her elbow on the table. "One would think," she said, gazing at me tiredly, "that after a day like today, you'd at least want a glass of wine."

"One would think," I agreed.

"Oh well, you probably shouldn't, anyway. After those tranquilizers."

"Probably not. By the way," I said, pointing to a sprig of bittersweet in the centerpiece, "that stuff is poisonous."

"But it's pretty," said Frances.

For a silent moment we looked at each other. Then Frances sighed and got up again. She opened the refrigerator and took out a pot of turkey soup she'd made the day before to heat on the stove. When Walter came back to the kitchen, he placed a few calls to his hospital to arrange for my father to have a physical examination in the morning. He wanted an orthopedic surgeon, a friend of his, to take a look at me and at Frances as well. Just to be on the safe side.

"You're not leaving tomorrow," he announced to me gruffly. "We'll have to call the airline." He accepted the glass of wine Frances had poured for him.

"Poor Walter," said Frances, sitting down with him, wisps of reddish hair curling around her face. "What a lot of trouble we've been."

"To trouble." Walter raised his glass, though he didn't look at me.

They sat together at the kitchen table and drank while I sat and watched them. Walter put his hand on Frances's shoulder as he got up to retrieve a second bottle of wine from the basement. She smiled up at him, a slow contrite smile, then reached out to pull his empty chair closer to hers. With his rescue of her from Hartford, their gravitational system had been restored. Frances relied on Walter, he needed her to rely on him. Elementary.

Frances stood up again to check to see if the soup was hot, saying that Walter must be starving. She found a loaf of French bread in the pantry and a wedge of Parmesan in the refrigerator. In a few minutes she had made a salad of spinach leaves, walnuts, and sliced apple. The warm salty fragrance of turkey soup lit the air and I realized how hungry I was. Frances grated cheese to sprinkle on split quarters of the bread, which she placed on a cookie sheet to slide under the broiler to toast. Hardy, nourishing fare, the perfect supper after a long day. It was wonderful to watch Frances concoct something good and meaningful out of almost nothing. She had a real talent for such things.

"And poor Cynnie," she said, opening a cabinet and lifting down glazed earthenware bowls for the soup. She set them on the counter beside the stove, glancing at me over her shoulder. "You look kind of like a priest in that collar."

"Well, don't expect any absolution from me."

Frances laid out red cloth napkins and woven Mexican straw place mats, then went to fetch silverware from a drawer under the cabinets. "I wish you knew yourself better," she said quietly. "I really do. If I had one wish, it would be that."

"Waste of a good wish," I said.

But Frances, as usual, wasn't listening. "If you could only see what's been in the way, all this time, the misunderstanding between us and Dad—"

"I don't want to hear about him anymore."

"It's just that—"

"It was no misunderstanding," I said as sharply and clearly as I could manage, "that I grew up feeling like no one cared whether I existed or not. Don't argue with me," I insisted, as Frances started to interrupt. "It doesn't even matter *why* I felt that way or whether I was *right* to feel that way, only that I did feel that way.

"And don't try to tell me that you understand," I went on, my voice getting louder. "Because you don't. You don't know. You will never, even if you sat down and wrote a whole book about it, have any idea how I felt."

Frances stayed silent, laying out our places.

"And you know what else?" I said, losing my temper altogether in the headlong, violent, brokenhearted way I had as a child. "When you get right down to it, Frances? Do you know who hates him more than anyone, hates him so much that she'd like to erase him from the face of the earth? It's you. That's who really hates him."

Frances caught her breath. "You have no idea what you sound like."

"You're the one who's never forgiven him for what happened," I said coldly. "You're the one who tried to off him this afternoon, right in front of our old house."

"Oh my God, Cynthia." Frances was shaking her head as she went back to setting the table. "Oh my God. If you could only hear yourself."

"I hear myself well enough." But now my conviction was beginning to flag, my blaze of self-righteousness burning down to sullenness. "You can pretend all you want that it was something different, but our childhood was a stupid mess. Our father was a cheater and our mother died, and by the end we all wanted her to."

"That is not what it was like." Frances looked up at me with dignity, a spoon in one hand. "That's not what it was like for me."

"Then lucky for you."

Even before the words were out of my mouth, I knew they were true. Her childhood, spent in the same house, with the same parents, had been luckier than mine. It was as basic and as complicated as that. And not because of any real difference in what we'd been given—though Frances *had* been given more, by my father, by birth order, by genetic happenstance. But what we'd received hadn't, in the end, created the disparity between us: it was simply that Frances had always been able to make more out of what came her way. That was her nature.

"Lucky for you," I repeated.

"I'm sorry you're still so angry," she said, stepping back from the table as if to admire her arrangement.

"Yeah, well you can stop feeling sorry for me, because I'm going home tomorrow."

"Oh come on, Cynnie. Don't be like that."

"You lied to me. You knew there wasn't room for him at that nursing home. You were pretending the whole time."

"I did not lie," said Frances evenly. "I just took a chance."

"A chance?"

"If there *had* been room for him that day we would have left him there, but since there wasn't we took him home."

"But you knew there probably *wouldn't* be room."

"You never know with those places." Frances began wiping down the stove with a sponge. "And anyway, people lie to each other all the time. Sometimes for the other person's own good."

"I can't listen to you anymore," I said. "I will lose my mind."

"I'm just trying to explain." Frances had dropped the sponge and was moving around to my chair.

"Leave me alone."

She leaned over me, her eyes full of concern. "No, I won't leave you alone, Cynnie. You're my sister. I want you to be happy. My family's happiness is the most important thing in the world to me."

And as I stared back at her I saw that it was true. Frances did want us all to be happy. She would do anything to make us happy. There was no unclearness in this regard, for Frances. I also saw that nothing had gone wrong for her today, in spite of Mark Twain's house being closed, in spite of the accident and my injuries. In fact, those difficulties had only strengthened her hand; if I were truly paranoid, I'd almost think she had planned them. My account of our past was officially shut, hers flung wide open—soon to be the accepted story. She had gotten everything she wanted. We were even going to have a nice meal to end the day. Tomorrow various doctors would pronounce us all healthy and well, and we would return home for another thoughtful dinner served on suitable place mats with cloth napkins. My father would never have to go to Greenswood Manor. In a few days, Frances would call the medical supply store in Watertown and ask them to deliver a hospital bed, while she went to work rearranging one of the downstairs rooms for him. By next week, she would have hired a nurse, a big soft-spoken middle-aged Carribbean woman with an Englishy name, Edwina or Millicent, who would perform all the onerous, embarassing duties that go with tending elderly patients, leaving Frances free to knit him bulky sweaters in soft yarns, bake custards for his lunch, sew a crazy quilt for his bed.

He could live out the end of his days with her, surrounded by ease and graciousness, and she would finally have what she'd been searching for, all these years, at estate sales and antiques fairs.

"I'm not hungry," I said, standing up. "I'm going to bed."

"Oh, don't be like that," said Frances once more, this time putting a hand firmly on my shoulder. "I know you're hungry. Sit down."

By the time I got into bed that night Jane was already asleep in her bunk, her light snores interrupted by occasional puppyish whimpers. I thought her snoring and my neck brace would keep me awake, but Walter had given me two Percocets after dinner and I fell asleep almost immediately.

I must have slept deeply for several hours. Then suddenly I wasn't asleep anymore. The room was dark except for Jane's blue nightlight, plugged into a socket near her desk. As I lay in bed looking at the nightlight I was reminded of those companionable little blue lights in the sleeper compartments of passenger trains, which seem to be provided to reassure you, if you wake in the dark, that wherever you're going will be a calm and reasonable place. One winter when I was very young my whole family took an overnight train to Chicago so that my mother could consult a specialist there. It must have been in the days when her disease might still have been possibly nothing, something all in her head, because I remember hearing later that the specialist was a psychiatrist. But all I recall of that trip is traveling on the train at night, lying in the bunk I shared with Frances, looking up at that little blue light and rocking with the motion of the train, listening to Frances's steady breathing as we rushed past snow-covered towns and cities and farms and forests, the whole dark territory of the world outside our window.

Jane had stopped snoring. I should have closed my eyes and gone back to sleep, but I was very thirsty and my head hurt. Also, the foam collar around my neck was uncomfortable. So I got up slowly and painfully, being careful not to wake Jane, and felt my way out of her room and then downstairs to the kitchen to get a glass of water.

The kitchen was dark save for the illuminated clock on the stove. Outside, the snow had stopped and above the black juniper trees hung a new pale moon. I poured myself a glass of water at the sink and swallowed two more tablets from the vial Walter had set out for me on the kitchen table. It was after four, by the clock on the stove. Despite those tablets, I doubted I would get back to sleep that night, so I decided to make a cup of tea.

While waiting for the kettle to boil, I thought I'd just look in on my father. It must have been a difficult day for him, as well, all that time riding in the van, the visit to his old home and then the accident, the long hours spent in the hospital waiting room. I had an idea that he also might want something, a glass of water or a cold washcloth for his head, but be unable to get out of bed.

When I stepped into the passageway outside the kitchen that led to Frances's bedroom, where he was sleeping, I saw that the door was open and that a light was on in the adjoining bathroom, lending an anemic white glow to the room. Sure enough, whatever contraption Walter had rigged up was gone; if my father had needed to get up and go about his business, there would have been nothing to support him. But he was lying in bed asleep, breathing loudly, one hand resting on his stomach. He looked quite small, lying there in that tall white bed. Afloat in Frances's big empty room, with its long dark windows and that wide gleaming floor. Like a boy asleep on a raft, a wash of night sky over his head.

I drew nearer to the bed and looked at him in the pallid light from the bathroom. His lips were parted and his cheeks sunken, his profile sternly defined against the white pillowcase. On his forehead was the dark medallion of his bruise. *My father,* I thought. I hoped he would open his eyes so that I could tell him I had come to see if he needed anything.

It was only then that I realized his breathing sounded wrong: It was too harsh, too shallow, too rasping and labored. Each breath began with a hollow intake and ended with a hard, drawn-out sigh. Rough breathing filled the room, and it seemed to come at me from different directions, as if more than one person were breathing.

I felt frightened and in sudden confusion turned to go back to the kitchen, but something prevented me from leaving. Old loyalties, the oldest kind of loyalties, mixed with old longings that even now I don't care to name, mixed with an old familiar dread. And probably some of the same curiosity that underlies my interest in debunkings.

Not sure what else to do, I put my hand on his.

My father grew restless. His hand clenched. His chest rose and fell with each breath, like a bellows. He began to twitch and grimace in his sleep, although he did not seem to be in pain so much as gripped by annoyance. A tremor shook him. His lips drew back from his teeth, giving him the appearance of bitter impatience. It was an expression I recalled well from my childhood, the expression on his face whenever we were stuck in traffic. *Enough,* that expression said. *I've had enough of this.* Filled with misgivings, I continued to watch his face, torn between a wish to console him for the affliction of being, once again, stuck somewhere he did not want to be, and a strange detachment. *My father,* I thought again, but this time indifferently, as if questioning whether it was true.

By then the room had become extremely cold and my teeth began to chatter. I tried to understand what I should do. His breathing was deafening. I must call someone. I must call Frances and Walter. I imagined myself going upstairs to Frances, calling her name softly until she opened her eyes, allowing her the chance I had denied to her, all those years before. *Come and say good-bye.* Or perhaps I would use the word *farewell,* which was more formal and poetic, a touch Frances might appreciate.

I must call Frances, I decided, trying to shake off my concern about what words to use, angered that even in a moment of extremity I had no choice but to go on being foolishly myself. But then I began to worry that my father might die while I was upstairs waking Frances, who was a heavy sleeper, and I could not stand to think of him slipping away from me like that, all alone. So I hesitated, knowing that either way I was losing an opportunity and unable to decide which one to lose.

What do you want? I asked silently. *Tell me what you want.*

As I stood holding my father's hand, listening to his harsh, insistent breathing and asking for his guidance, which I did not expect to receive, his love of maps suddenly came back to me. And his skill at identifying trees, and his love of birds, which he could identify even by their calls. And the encouraging way he used to carol songs as we marched in the chill morning air through the woods. In his own way he had tried his best with us, with me and Frances and Helen, the best that was in him. He had shown us how to walk in the woods. He had pointed out the accidents that could befall people and insisted that we learn to spell, thereby improving our chances of going through life unimpaired and correctly understood. Whatever he had done for us, or not done, must have seemed justifiable to him at the time. My mother, too, had done what she could in the midst of her illness, by asking little of us, except that we not watch her too closely. They, like most people, had done their best. You love whom you love, you fail whom you fail, and almost always we fail the ones we meant to love. Not intentionally, that's just how it happens. We get sick or distracted or frightened and don't listen, or listen to the wrong things. Time passes, we lose track of our mistakes, neglect to make amends. And then, no matter how much we might like to try again, we're done. Whatever inspiring song we hoped to sing for the world is over, sometimes to general regret, more frequently to small notice, and even, if we were old or sick, to relief. It's not easy to sit through the performance of another person's life; so often it is music without music, as Mark Twain once said, referring to something else in one of his maxims. Though we have to try to hear it. It's unbearable to think we can't at least try.

I watched my father's face, which seemed filled now with a fierce and somber privacy, dark and graven against the pillowcase. Eighty-two years of thoughts and imperatives were gathered within his body, and I knew so few of them. Yet even at this stark moment, I could not concentrate on my father. My head hurt. I kept thinking about how cold I was and about his clenched hand, which felt so fixed and unyielding under mine, as if it were an ashtray or a big seashell.

O my father, forsake me not.

I had not planned to think of these words—I am sure I had never thought them before in my life—but as soon as they came to me, they began to run through my head.

O my father, forsake me not.

The antique sound of them comforted me and I repeated them silently, over and over, until I was telling them like beads, until they became a gentle nonsense, like an old lullaby.

O my father, forsake me not.

My father jerked his head impatiently.

I *must* call Frances, I told myself.

But then I pictured, perhaps unfairly, what would inevitably follow if I went upstairs and roused Frances. The hysterical scene she would feel required to stage, with weeping and proclamations and frenzied prayers, while Walter called for an ambulance, which would probably arrive in time. Then the tubes, the injections, the mask over my father's old face. The rush to the emergency room. Lights in his eyes. The rattle of curtains pulled, metal carts drawn up. Unfamiliar, unremarking faces peering down at him. Followed by heroic measures—so grueling and undignified for the object of heroism, splayed like a fish on the table. All so that he could live long enough to celebrate Christmas in Frances's house, captive in his wheelchair in a corner of her living room, stuffed with custards and swathed in quilts, King Lear under the mistletoe, photographed for posterity and displayed proudly to visitors, the crowning heirloom in her collection.

No matter what he'd done, he didn't deserve a fate like that.

I pressed his hand twice, to remind him I was there. Then I went into the bathroom to switch off the small distracting light that Frances had left burning. A folded blue woolen blanket lay at the end of the bed; I unfolded it and wrapped it around myself and then, because I was so cold, and because there was nowhere else to sit in that empty room, and because it seemed somehow the right thing to do, given the loneliness of the hour, I climbed onto the bed. In a moment I will go to Frances, I thought. I will wake Frances. But after a little while, I lay down beside my father.

When I awoke the room was colder, as rooms always are just before morning. I don't know how much time had passed, perhaps only a few minutes. Outside the stars had faded and somewhere deep in the house a heating pipe began to clank. I lay shivering under my blanket watching the sky lighten outside the window. Gray tree branches were becoming visible and an old curving stone wall reappeared at the edge of the lawn. The snowy rhododendron leaves at the window had turned faintly pink.

It was at that awful, tender, insubstantial hour, so full of promise for the innocent, so desolate for the guilty, that all my courage failed me. Even now it was not too late. I could still run to Frances, still turn everything over to her. But as daylight seeped into the room I remembered my father's advice to us, which was to keep going, no matter what, and finally that implacable advice, in all its obvious complexity, became clear to me.

Once more I reached over and took his hand. His breathing had grown harsher, each ragged breath ending in a reluctant hiss as if he could not believe he would be required to go through all that again. It didn't seem that he would have to wait much longer, but I would keep him company regardless. For the lonely moments of life, one wants company. And he was my father, after all.

It has been mostly for Jane's benefit that I have set down this record of what happened over Thanksgiving, so that sometime in the future, when Frances has ceased to believe that anything untoward happened at all, my version of those few days in November will stand as an argument for the unreliability of memory. I do worry about Jane and those silvery scratches on her arm, and I'd like her to know that even stories you believe to be exclusively yours can have various sides, and perhaps more than one ending, apart from the inevitable one.

For instance, right now Frances would tell you that I watched coldly at my father's bedside and did nothing. Walter would imply that my decision not to call an ambulance for a dying man ranks just below murder. Jane, who as a student of algebra understands variables, would probably conjecture that somehow or another, my father's death was a misjudgment, even a misunderstanding. But soon enough all their memories of that night will change and what they will tell you may be something altogether different.

I SHOULD ALSO MENTION that the bookstore owner and his wife just had twin girls. I have been contemplating whether to send them an inscribed copy of one of my books, maybe *Mark Twain's Daughters,* recently published, praised by School Library Journal as "the moving story of a charming, difficult man and his fascinating daughters" and called "more complexly imagined than is commonly found in historical fiction for girls." On the title page I would write: *To the joys of reading.* Carita thinks I'm being maudlin, but my intentions are sincere, and I do believe in promoting the joys of reading.

In fact, I've spent the last three weeks touring around the country to promote this latest book. I even stopped briefly in Hartford, though I have not been home, by which I mean Frances's house, since my father died, over a year ago now. Nor do I think I'll be invited to visit any time soon. Carita has been a reassuring friend during this period, listening to my side of things, pointing out that people always behave toward their families in ways that would be considered criminal with anyone else. She and Paula and I were guests at Don's newly renovated house in Berkeley this year for Thanksgiving; he prepared a turkey stuffed with oysters, which was slightly underdone.

But I'm fairly confident that one of these days Frances will tell Walter that she understands what I did that night, or did not do, and why. She will explain how traumatized I was by my childhood, very much as my father was traumatized by his, both of us losing our mothers so young. She will say that she wants to let bygones be bygones, that we have a special bond. Time is precious and she doesn't want any regrets. And there is that responsibility older sisters feel toward their younger sisters.

Walter will resist at first. He will mention the disturbing scene at Thanksgiving, the fire in the living room, the ghastly morning when I was discovered asleep on my father's bed. He will suggest instability. Or, not being an alarmist, he may employ the term *dysfunctional*, which Frances will rightly reject, pointing to the recent publication of my fourth book. If he has to, Walter will admit to Frances that I tried to seduce him on one of her Knole sofas.

But Frances will find a way to excuse or explain all of it, and what she can't excuse or explain, at least to Walter's satisfaction, she will dismiss.

"Blood is blood," she will say.

ACKNOWLEDGMENTS

A number of books were useful to me as I was writing this novel, in particular Justin Kaplan's biography, *Mr. Clemens and Mark Twain*, and *The Autobiography of Mark Twain*, edited by Charles Neider, who also edited *Papa: An Intimate Biography of Mark Twain*, Susy Clemens's biography of her father. In addition, I read and found informative *Mark Twain in the Company of Women*, by Laura E. Skandera-Trombley; *My Father, Mark Twain*, by Clara Clemens; *Susy and Mark Twain: Family Dialogues*, arranged and edited by Edith Colgate Salsbury; *Twain's World, Essays on Hartford's Cultural Heritage*, published by the *Hartford Courant*; and *The Quotable Mark Twain*, edited by R. Kent Rasmussen. I'm grateful to the Mark Twain Memorial in Hartford, Connecticut, where I learned a great deal from several enjoyable tours I took of Mark Twain's house over the last few years.

I am indebted as well to E. J. Graff, Suzanne Matson, and Laura Zimmerman, who read early drafts and offered invaluable suggestions, and also to Madeline Drexler, Jeffrey Harrison, Marcie Hershman, Eileen Pollack, Phil Press, Marjorie Sandor, and Renee Shea for their encouragement and advice while I was working on this book, and to Allison Mendenhall, who long ago described defrosting a turkey. Thanks to Dr. Carrie Bernstein and Dr. Mark Ellenbogen for answering my questions and to Ann Stokes for providing me with a quiet place to work for a crucial week of revision. As always, I am deeply grateful to my agent, Colleen Mohyde, and to my editor, Shannon Ravenel, who I pray will never retire. Finally, I cannot thank Eve Berne and Ken Kimmell enough for their good-humored support and optimism on my behalf.

But most of all I would like to thank my dear friend Maxine Rodburg, who read more drafts of this novel than should be humanly endurable, or at least medically advisable, and is the most generous, patient, and insightful of critics.

The Ghost at the Table

A Short Note from the Author

Readers' Group Questions and Topics for Discussion

What I Don't Know about Mark Twain

A Short Note from the Author

ooooo

When I was about ten, I discovered in my father's study a shelf of handsome, red, limp-leather volumes, their covers embossed with a man's bewhiskered, scowling profile. It was a full set of Mark Twain's books, given to my father as a boy not long after his mother died. He'd read them over and over, he told me, adding that Mark Twain had just about saved his life during those sad years. My father's motherless boyhood was almost unthinkable to me—how could I survive without my own mother?—but I was impressed that his life had been saved by a writer, so I read the books as I found them, starting with *Roughing It* and ending with *Joan of Arc*. At times, I hardly understood what I was reading, but I carried on anyway, wanting to oblige my father and mesmerized by the voice of Mark Twain, that intimate, keen, wisecracking, impatient, thunderous, all-knowing voice. It sounded to me then like the voice of God.

Twenty years later on a cold November afternoon, I arrived in the driveway of Mark Twain's house in Hartford, where a tour was already underway. A young guide was telling a small crowd that visitors often believe that Mark Twain designed his house to look like a steamboat. I stepped back to look up at the house—which is large and rambling and built of bricks, and yet seems somehow buoyant, with a prowlike veranda and cheerful little balconies and three smokestack chimneys—and sure enough, it *did* look like a steamboat. But then the tour guide added that Twain did not intend for his house to look like a steamboat and that a host of other misconceptions were really wishful thinking on the part of his admirers.

She went on to tell us that Mark Twain had fathered three daughters, the oldest of whom was called Susy. This was also my childhood name, spelled slightly differently. Susy and her sisters used to put on plays in their schoolroom, in which they wore their mother's gowns and impersonated English queens and ordered each other's beheadings. I recalled similar dramatics with my own two younger sisters—we were likewise drawn to bloodthirsty themes. Our tour guide described how Twain had entertained his little girls by the living room fire, making up thrilling stories about the bric-a-brac on the living room mantle. My father, too, had been an inventive storyteller. He used to sit us next to him on the piano bench and tell wild, funny stories about ogres and witches based on the notes he played, ending always with a reverberant glissando.

A dangerous but absorbing confusion began forming in my mind as I wandered through Mark Twain's house, peering at his wallpaper and admiring his carved Venetian four-poster bed. The more I discovered about Mark Twain's daughters, the more I felt I already knew. Their father had been hot-tempered and humorous; so had mine. They had lived in a big beautiful house, which was later lost to them; so had I. It hardly mattered that the differences between our families were far more numerous than the similarities; that there were similarities at all between my family and Mark Twain's seemed heady enough.

Ten years after visiting his house, I began a novel about Mark Twain's daughters. It would be a historical novel, I decided, set in Hartford during the Gilded Age. I could already visualize the Merchant Ivory movie that would follow—three decorative little Victorian girls in white pinafores bowling hoops on a green lawn while their fierce-looking father smoked his corncob pipe in the background. But after three years of trying, I found that I could not do it.

I sat down and listed various theories to account for my failure: Mark Twain would have resented such an intrusion into his family life. I had done too much research and become musclebound with facts. I identified too much with the daughters. No plot that I could devise did justice to the girls' complexity, plus my motives for writing about them were murky and contaminated by self-regard. All true.

Yet it was at this painful moment that the book I was eventually to write came into being. What really interested me, I finally understood, were the ways in which we claim to understand other people's lives based on our own. Misconceptions and wishful thinking are as much a part of what we know about other people as any "truthful" details about them. As the narrator of my book says about her father, whose version of her childhood does not agree with her own: "That was the story he put together from all those details, a story that, like most stories people tell themselves about other people, was mostly about him."

This character, who writes historical novels for girls and happens to be writing about Mark Twain's daughters, has finally figured it all out. Then again, the minute you think you've got the last word on someone—well, that's exactly when he gets away from you, isn't it?

Readers' Group Questions and Topics for Discussion

1. In the first few pages, Cynthia freely admits that she and Frances have a strained relationship, though she also says that "of all the people in the world I probably love Frances best" (page 1). Now, however, after many years of refusing Frances's invitations to come visit during the holidays, Cynthia decides to fly back east for Thanksgiving. What do you think changes her mind? Why is it so important to Frances to have Cynthia come to her house for the holiday?

2. In addition to Frances's family, Arlen, Wen-Yi, the Fareeds, and Frances's assistant, Mary Ellen, come to Frances's house for Thanksgiving. With such a guest list, Jane goes so far as to call it "Thanksgiving at the UN" (page 30). How have all these outsiders to the family come to the table, and what impact do they have on shaping the events of the evening?

3. At the Thanksgiving table, Frances's daughter Sarah proposes that they take turns describing what they are most proud of having done for someone else (pages 207–11). Compare the answers of each sister. Why does Cynthia find Frances's answer so difficult to hear?

4. *The Ghost at the Table* opens with a quotation from *The Autobiography of Mark Twain*, "a person's memory has no more sense than his conscience." How does this statement pertain to each sister? To what degree does it explain Cynthia's and Frances's different recollections of the past?

5. Both Cynthia and Frances have very different views of their childhood. More specifically, they have opposing accounts of what happened to their mother. Whose version is more cred-

ible, and why? Discuss the possibility that *both* sisters' recollections are accurate.

6. Frances is an interior decorator; Cynthia writes inspiring history books for girls about domestic life. Why do you think they've chosen those professions? How do their jobs provide a comment on who they are or aren't?

7. What role do you think Mrs. Jordan plays in the story?

8. At one point, Cynthia remembers her sister Helen asking their mother what the mother looked like when she was a girl. Instead of listening to her mother's answer, Cynthia is struck "by an appalling, fascinating thought: What if you looked into the future and didn't recognize yourself? What if you saw someone else looking back at you instead?" (page 131–32). Do you think Cynthia the child would recognize Cynthia the adult? Would your childhood self be able to identify the adult you've become?

9. In Cynthia's mind, Frances's daughters, Sarah and Jane, roughly correspond with Frances and herself when they were younger. Is Cynthia simply projecting? In what ways does the past continue to influence the characters' perceptions of the present?

10. Soon after her mother's death, Cynthia implies that her father played a hand in it. She then goes on to tell Frances that Frances unknowingly helped him (pages 155–57). A few days later, though, she retracts the accusation. Do you think she was being honest or dishonest in either case?

11. The day after Thanksgiving, Frances insists that she and Cynthia visit Mark Twain's house in Hartford, with their fa-

ther in tow. When they discover that the Mark Twain House is closed, they proceed to visit the house they grew up in. What do they find at these houses? What are they hoping to find?

12. Who, or what, does the ghost of the title refer to, and why?

13. Who are Sarah and Arlen really discussing when Cynthia overhears them on the baby monitor (page 240)? How do your feelings about Cynthia begin to shift at this point?

14. When Cynthia wakes up after falling asleep alone in the living room, she sees a pillar candle overflowing with wax. As the organ catches fire, she sits silently watching (page 242). Why, at first, does she do nothing to stop it?

15. Although Cynthia and Frances's father is unable to speak, he makes his presence known in the house. Discuss each sister's behavior toward him and his reaction to both.

16. What motivates Cynthia to check in on her father when everyone is asleep (pages 287–91)? Do you think she should have called Frances when she discovered he was having trouble breathing? Why didn't she? In the end, how would you describe what happens between Cynthia and her father?

17. Cynthia says, "It has been mostly for Jane's benefit that I have set down this record of what happened over Thanksgiving" so that "my version of those few days in November will stand as an argument for the unreliability of memory" (page 293). How do you think Jane would respond to this record? Although this is Cynthia's story, did you find yourself identifying with one sister over the other? Who in the story did you have the most empathy for, and why?

JERRY BAUER

SUZANNE BERNE'S first novel, *A Crime in the Neighborhood*, won Great Britain's Orange Prize and was a finalist for both the *Los Angeles Times* and the Edgar Allen Poe first fiction awards. Her work has appeared in the *New York Times*, *Allure*, and the *Washington Post*, among other publications. Both *A Crime in the Neighborhood* and her second novel, *A Perfect Arrangement*, were named *New York Times* Notable Books.

Other Algonquin Readers Round Table Novels

Saving the World, a novel by Julia Alvarez

While Alma Huebner is researching a new novel, she discovers the true story of Isabel Sendales y Gómez, who embarked on a courageous sea voyage to rescue the New World from smallpox. The author of *How the García Girls Lost Their Accents* and *In the Time of the Butterflies*, Alvarez captures the worlds of two women living two centuries apart but with surprisingly parallel fates.

"Fresh and unusual, and thought-provokingly sensitive." —*The Boston Globe*

"Engrossing, expertly paced." —*People*

AN ALGONQUIN READERS ROUND TABLE EDITION WITH READING GROUP GUIDE AND OTHER SPECIAL FEATURES • FICTION • ISBN-13: 978-1-56512-558-2

Water for Elephants, a novel by Sara Gruen

As a young man, Jacob Jankowski is tossed by fate onto a rickety train, home to the Benzini Brothers Most Spectacular Show on Earth. Amid a world of freaks, grifters, and misfits, Jacob becomes involved with Marlena, the beautiful young equestrian star; her husband, a charismatic but twisted animal trainer; and Rosie, an untrainable elephant who is the great gray hope for this third-rate show. Now in his nineties, Jacob at long last reveals the story of their unlikely yet powerful bonds, ones that nearly shatter them all.

"[An] arresting new novel. . . . With a showman's expert timing, [Gruen] saves a terrific revelation for the final pages, transforming a glimpse of Americana into an enchanting escapist fairy tale." —*The New York Times Book Review*

"Gritty, sensual and charged with dark secrets involving love, murder and a majestic, mute heroine." —*Parade*

AN ALGONQUIN READERS ROUND TABLE EDITION WITH READING GROUP GUIDE AND OTHER SPECIAL FEATURES • FICTION • ISBN-13: 978-1-56512-560-5

On Agate Hill, a novel by Lee Smith

A dusty box in the wreckage of a once prosperous plantation on Agate Hill in North Carolina contains the remnants of an extraordinary life: diaries, letters, poems, songs, newspaper clippings, court records, marbles, rocks, dolls, and bones. It's through these treasured mementos that the irrepressible Molly Petree comes alive. Spanning half a century, *On Agate Hill* follows

Molly's journey through love, betrayal, motherhood, a murder trial—and back home to Agate Hill under circumstances she never could have imagined.

"Smith is such a beautiful writer, tough and full of grace, that soon you are lost in the half-light of Molly's haunted landscape, listening to the voices of the ghosts, wishing they'd let you stay longer." —*The Atlanta Journal-Constitution*

"The willful Molly is no hot-house flower, and her determination to live her own life—for better or worse—is the driving force of this powerful novel." —*USA Today*

AN ALGONQUIN READERS ROUND TABLE EDITION WITH READING GROUP GUIDE AND OTHER SPECIAL FEATURES • FICTION • ISBN-13: 978-1-56512-577-3

Responsible Men, a novel by Edward Schwarzschild

When a divorced man from a family of mostly upstanding salesmen decides to change his less-than-honorable ways, things do not go exactly as planned. This is the story of three generations of men struggling to be good sons and good fathers in a world of big dreams and bigger temptations.

"Marvelous. . . . It's impossible to avoid falling for Max." —*Entertainment Weekly*

"A compassionately and deftly told story."
—William Kennedy, Pulitzer Prize–winning author of *Ironweed* and *Roscoe*

AN ALGONQUIN READERS ROUND TABLE EDITION WITH READING GROUP GUIDE AND OTHER SPECIAL FEATURES • FICTION • ISBN-13: 978-1-56512-543-8

Brave Enemies, a novel by Robert Morgan

Set during the Revolutionary War, *Brave Enemies* is the story of two people brought together by chance and the ravages of war. Alone and lost in the woods, sixteen-year-old Josie Summers accepts a young preacher's invitation to assist in his itinerant ministry. When he's kidnapped by British soldiers, Josie, disguised as a man, joins the militia in a desperate attempt to find him.

"Readers of Morgan's *Brave Enemies* . . . are unlikely ever to take their eyes off the page—or even take a breath." —*The Christian Science Monitor*

"Impressive. . . . Morgan deftly conveys the complex world views of people in the past." —*The Charlotte Observer*

AN ALGONQUIN READERS ROUND TABLE EDITION WITH READING GROUP GUIDE AND OTHER SPECIAL FEATURES • FICTION • ISBN-13: 978-1-56512-578-0